TRINITY

Kristin Dearborn

First Edition

Published by:
DarkFuse Publications
P.O. Box 338
North Webster, IN 46555
www.darkfuse.com

Copy Editors: Steve Souza & Bob Mele

Grandma, Grandpa, Nana, and Gramps.
You all have always believed in me as a writer
and were never afraid to show it.
Thank you, and I miss you, Gramps!

Acknowledgements

No artist works in a vacuum, and the list of folks who have contributed to this book, via edits, read-throughs, and just support as I slammed my head against the keyboard is a big one.

Special thanks to Tim Waggoner and Scott A. Johnson, without whom this book would be very different (and far inferior). Proud to be a SHU mean girl forever. Thanks to Seton Hill crit partners, Jared, Paul, Christina and Dave. To Dr. Arnzen. To the BWG, who remember this book when it was Alien!: Douglas, Dan, Beth, Althea, Heather C-M, and Jenn. Thanks to Heather T, who's spent maybe more time than anyone poring over my work and is never afraid to tell it how it is (but always with love!). And to the people who supported me away from the keyboard simply by being themselves: Monica, Aunt Sue, Mom, Karen, Brian, Jeff, Chris, Glen, Steve B and Steve M. And last, to Maggie, who always had a wagging tail and knew when I needed to go for a walk.

None of this would exist without these guys, and it wouldn't exist either without the wonderful editors at Darkfuse who took a chance on an unknown author and made this book a reality. And it wouldn't exist without you, readers. I hope you enjoy.

She is awake in the night, her body drenched in sweat. The perspiration pools between her breasts as she brings a hand to her swollen stomach. It's all she has left.

Every night, she leaves the bathroom light on, because she can't face the dark. In the light that creeps through the cracked door, everything looks too white. She strains her ears, listening. There is an ice machine in the hall; it clunks to life. Outside, a car turns into the lot of the cheap motel, its headlights dragging across the wall, turning dim white bright.

She can't run forever. She's just one woman.

They are infinite.

Maybe it's all right. Maybe she can close her eyes, go back to sleep. Before that, she checks the pistol on the nightstand. Loaded. Good. She listens a while, satisfied that it was just the ice machine down the hall that woke her. She closes her eyes. Thinks to the baby, *It's going to be all right…we'll find a way.* But she wonders if she can keep that promise.

As she is drifting off to sleep she hears something else in the hall. Sitting bolt-upright in the dim bathroom light, she waits…watches.

So white…so impossibly *white…*

A hand at the doorknob. Testing it…turning it…finding it locked.

She draws into herself, sitting up, knees tucked up as far as her pregnant stomach will allow. Holding the pistol as steady as she can, she aims it at the door.

Even if I shoot this one, there will be others.

She waits. The lock proves to be a minor challenge. The door opens, meeting resistance with the chain. Blinding white light pours in. She lifts the hand with the gun to shield her eyes, the other remains on her stomach. Despite crippling terror, she will protect the baby until she dies.

Against the blinding white, fingers creep inside, groping, feeling for the latch.

They are not human.

She could shoot…but knows it will be fruitless. So she lies on the bed, cradles the gun and her unborn baby… and waits…

1

Felix was late. Sun bleached the long dusty road as Valentine Slade squinted to see down its emptiness. He dropped onto his ass in the dust, his few meager belongings by his side. A bench, metal and baking, sat by the chain link gates to the New Mexico State Penitentiary, but Val preferred to sit here in the warm dirt while he waited. Without a watch, it was difficult to tell how late Felix was.

He looked to the cloudless sky, up at the sun, and decided to wait a while longer. Too much blue, too bright out there. He'd been inside for too long. The sun felt good on his skin, and he smiled at the mundane worry of a sunburn. Let it burn. After six years, let it burn.

A truck blew past, kicking up dust that stung his skin. It was too hot to get angry. Maybe they'd give him a drink of water if he went back inside. That would be a little like admitting defeat, though. He wished for a cigarette, to have something to do with his hands. But he'd quit smoking years ago.

From behind him he heard an engine. A shiny red Monte Carlo slowed down at his side, one of the new ones.

Val sighed. He hadn't heard much from Felix in the year since he'd left through this very same gate, but it would surprise him to hear the car's purchase was legit.

Felix slammed the brakes, kicking up a dust plume in its wake. He pounced from the driver's seat in a single fluid motion and wrapped his arms around Val in a huge bear hug. Pearl Jam and air conditioning poured from the Monte Carlo's open door.

"Easy there, tiger," said Val.

Felix pulled away and beamed at him. Same old Felix. Thick black hair, Latin good looks, eyes so pretty you'd swear they belonged in a woman's face.

"You're out. How are you?"

Val rolled the question around in his head. There were a million ways he could answer. Thirsty, terrified, in awe of all this sky…

"I think I'm all right." He picked up the paper bag holding his shit. "Ready to head home."

"Well let's go! Hop in."

Val got in on the passenger side, setting his bag between his feet. The music seemed too loud, the air too cold. "Can we do windows for a bit? I've had about all the canned air I can handle for one lifetime."

"Want to stop for a beer or something on the way home?"

"Not today. We will. Later this week. I want to get home, get myself settled." He paused. "See Kate."

Felix turned the car around and peeled out, spraying loose gravel on the brown New Mexico State Penitentiary sign.

Val stared at the yellow dashes in the road, which started to blur together as Felix accelerated. He should have called someone from home, someone who wouldn't bring him back to the time on the inside. This was behind him now. But Felix was Felix…after all their time together he was more a part of Val than just a part of Val's time in prison. He glanced behind him, at the pink adobe and barbed wire growing smaller and smaller. In the silence, beside him, Felix sat, staring straight ahead. For a moment he made Val think of an automaton, something that mimics humanity but falls short. Then he turned, grinned, and asked Val why he hadn't had Kate pick him up.

It was a complicated question.

"I wanted to get a chance to see your ugly mug."

Felix cocked an eyebrow. He wanted a real answer.

"I want to get my groove back before I see her."

"I know what you mean. It's crazy, getting out. The pen spreads her legs and pops you out…you're naked out here."

Melodramatic though it was, Felix's analogy was apt. Val did feel naked but told himself to cheer up. He was out. More important, he was going to get to see his girl.

* * *

By the time they pulled down the dirt driveway to Val's mother's mobile home, Val was tired of Felix's chattering. He loved the guy, but everything seemed so overwhelming. The gaping brown desert hemmed him in more than the prison walls did. He wanted some time alone.

"Thanks," Val said, picking up his stuff—a few changes of clothes and some law books—from the car's floor where it rested.

"Sorry," Felix said, letting the engine idle. "I know how it is. Let me know when you want to go for a beer." He smirked. "Have a good time with Kate."

Val left it there. Kate had come to see him once every month while he was inside.

"It's crazy you two are so strong, even after..." Felix let his voice trail off, he usually knew when to stop talking. "Well, watch out for her brother. If you need my help, give me a call."

"You're in town for a while?" Val asked. An anti-social part of himself wanted the answer to be no. He knew, though, once he cheered the fuck up, he and Felix would tear the town apart.

"Yeah, I found some road work here, up on Lobo Street. I'm around."

"I'll look you up soon. We'll go drink." Val forced a smile. He bet it looked as plastic as it felt, and Felix's sad nod confirmed this. He lifted a hand in a wave, said "take care" and drove off, kicking up a plume of dust behind the Monte Carlo.

Alone in the driveway, Val looked at his house. Peeling paint, dark windows, no mother inside to deal with.

When Val's mother went to the hospice almost a year ago, they'd said she would survive a month or two, tops. Still she clung to life with a mysterious stomach cancer which followed its own agenda.

The sound of Felix's car faded away to nothing. Using the key tucked into the eaves of the little porch overhang Val let himself in. For the first time in years there was no one to be macho for, no one to stop him from crying. He couldn't deflect his sorrow and his fear with a joke. It constricted in his chest and he clapped a hand over his mouth to keep in a sob.

There was nothing to do but cry.

And Val did, sinking to the dusty, peeling linoleum, crippled by self-pity, fixating on how far he could have gone.

Instead, he was back here.

The tears blew over like a storm, leaving Val a drained, snotty mess on the floor. A hum resounded in his head, a low droning, on the near edge of his consciousness. He walked to his bedroom and raised a hand to tear down old posters: *Black Flag, Fear and Loathing in Las Vegas, Reservoir Dogs,* then resisted. He sat on the edge of his bed. Everything was as he'd left it before college. It reeked of high school here. He brought his hand to his forehead, trying to block out the hum.

It couldn't be called a headache because the throbbing didn't actually hurt. The hum filled his head like a giant machine, vibrating his silver fillings. It rose in a crescendo, not in intensity, but in his awareness of it. The hum was like something refracting off broken glass, gritty and bright. It built and he wondered if his brain would simply explode.

The sensation was constant at least, and after it became apparent it wasn't going away, Val made a thorough search of the small trailer.

Maybe the air conditioner was malfunctioning.

He even dragged himself through the crawl space underneath, dirt and dry pine needles sticking to his sweaty skin. Nothing. Not even the sounds of *Bad Religion* or the *Descendants* could cut through it and as dark fell he turned the music off, leaving the house stark in its silence. He trudged outside into the night.

He sat on the hood of his truck, a hulking old Ford F-100. Once glossy black, now it looked like an angry dinosaur.

The hood and windshield radiated heat along Val's back, and he looked up at the sky, watching the last traces of orange and pink bleeding away into purple darkness. The stars glittered overhead, their strength building as night grew. So much sky.

He didn't get up when Kate arrived in her shitty yellow Daytona. Maybe the car was nice in 1988 when it rolled off the assembly line in Detroit, or back when her brother Rich bought it for himself, but even six years ago when Kate inherited it, Val thought it was like a dog that needed to be shot and put out of its misery.

He chose to watch her as she walked by in the failing light, jeans and a wife-beater, unruly mane of tangled hair pulled back into a bushy ponytail. Kate was always self-conscious about her smallish tits—she claimed she looked like a pre-pubescent boy. But she did not, and never had looked like a pre-pubescent boy. He called her name just before she got to the wooden steps. She jumped, dropped the six-pack she carried, and let out a small yelp. She turned to him, backlit from the yellow glow of the kitchen window.

"Sorry," he said, unable to keep himself from smiling.

She bent to pick up the beer, her ponytail spilling over her shoulder. He wanted to touch it, and he felt bad for scaring her.

"I can buy beer now." She held it up like a prize.

Val nodded, drinking her in. There was no thick plexiglass between them, no phone which felt filthy and germ-drenched even though they wiped it between prisoners with disposable bleach wipes. After all the phone calls, the letters, the glassed-in visits, everything was real again. Seeing her was enough to distract him from the hum, though as soon as he noticed he wasn't thinking about it, it came back with a vengeance. She set the six-pack on the hood and looked at him.

Val couldn't decide whether to tell her he missed her or tell her he loved her, so instead he decided on "Do you hear something? A hum?"

"Yeah," she said. His hopes soared. Then what the hell was it?

"Not a hum, though," she said. "A car."

Yes, there was a car approaching, one with a throaty engine sound. Val turned to Kate, who—judging by her expression—came to the same conclusion.

Her hands balled into fists.

"Aw, fuck," Val said. The vehicle rounded the bend in the short dirt driveway; the halogen truck light bar on Rich's Wrangler washed the driveway in blinding whiteness. At least he wasn't driving his patrol car. Val raised his hand to shield his eyes. He could feel his pupils shrink and felt the omnipresent hum around him like a muffling pillow.

Val hopped off the hood, heard the squawk of an emergency brake. Rich stepped out of the Jeep, mirrored on the other side by TJ Drinkwater. He left the engine running. It mixed and blended with the hum in Val's head.

"Sister," Rich called.

"Get off my land, Fulton."

Rich reached into the Jeep and pulled out his Mossberg shotgun. It looked long and lethal in the low light.

To her credit, Kate didn't ask Rich any dumb questions like "how did you know you would find me here?" "Go home, Rich," she said instead.

TJ stepped up behind Rich. Val remembered a time when he was the one standing at Rich's shoulder.

"Got yourself a new flunky?"

"Shut up. Let me handle this." Kate cast a withering glare over her shoulder, and while it wasn't the time or the place, Val thought she was fucking hot when she was pissed at him.

Val suspected it wouldn't be quite that easy. After Val went to jail, Kate told him TJ had been asking her out, confessing his love for her, all that jazz. That in itself was enough for Val to want to punch him so hard he'd be shitting teeth for a week...but the new Val, ex-con Val, refused to head down that road. So he smiled a big mean jackal smile and kept his mouth shut.

"I want you to come home, Kate. Florence worries about you."

Kate laughed. "Florence's too drunk to know if I'm there or not."

"She's not doing too well. She been asking about you. All I can tell her is I don't know."

"Put her in detox," Kate said. "Rich, leave. Go home."

"You think it's easy? I have to deal with this while you're whorin' around with this child molester."

"You have a hearing problem?" Val said. "She asked you to get the fuck out of here."

"No one asked you," Rich answered.

"Rich, can't we do this another time? I'm real tired, really looking forward to fucking your sister tonight—"

"Val!" Kate snapped. She knew Rich couldn't stand down a taunt. It didn't take him long to heave his bulk across the distance between them. Val could smell Rich's fetid landfill breath, see his pores.

"Come on, you don't need to deal with this," TJ said, from behind Rich.

Rich whirled. "You're not here to talk." He turned back to Val. "Take it back, you sonofabitch."

"Are we in seventh—" *grade?* Val meant to say, but it came out a muffled, garbled mess as Rich, in one fluid movement, raised the shotgun and jammed the muzzle in Val's mouth. The cold metal of the gun mashed his lip into his teeth, splitting it. The gun knocked against his teeth and rammed the back of his throat and he gagged, smelling gun oil, tasting blood and spent powder, and thinking of prison. Other cons don't much care for child molesters, not even likeable ones like Val. He took a half step back, and his head clunked into the side of the truck, and for the first time he began to question his safety. He gagged again, his stomach roiling and his eyes watering in bright light. His mouth filled with thin saliva and goose bumps rose on his arms in the hot night.

"Rich, cut this shit out!" Kate shouted, not touching him for fear his finger might slip. From the corner of his watering eye, Val saw TJ put a pudgy hand on Kate's shoulder. She shrugged him off without looking at him.

Val made some vowel sounds.

Kate said, "Rich. I'll go see Florence with you."

Before pulling out the barrel, which clacked against Val's teeth just as it had on the way in, Rich added a final jab that sent Val into a coughing fit. Val slid his tongue around his mouth to make sure all his teeth were still intact.

Between the light and the hum, everything seemed distant. Val tried to blink the sensation away, but it hung with him like a cloud. "You can't—"

"We'll go tomorrow," Kate said. "Now leave."

"It's always tomorrow with you, kid sister. Someday it's gonna catch up to you." Val swallowed down all that spit and drew himself up to his full height in front of Rich. His mother would be proud of his good posture. Rich was wider but Val was taller, by just a little bit. It was a point of contention when they were younger, boys standing back to back measuring height.

"Time to go," Val said. "Buh-bye now." He couldn't think through the hum. Fuck, if only he could focus.

"Please," TJ whined. His doe-eyed admiration of Kate made Val want to stave his face in. His goddamn hand was back on her shoulder.

"Watch your back, Slade. I'll make you wish you were back on the inside. You'll wish the Aryan Brotherhood used you the way you use my baby sister."

Kate made a disgusted noise.

Val, knowing some Aryan brothers quite well, could not fathom a reality where that statement would be true. "At least I never raped her," he said. Val caught the way TJ turned to Rich and recognized he'd spilled some secrets. Kate took TJ's moment of surprise to pull away and move back to Val's side.

"I told you to keep your mouth shut, Val," Kate said to him, her voice quiet.

Val did a lot of fighting before prison, even more on the inside, and he blocked Rich's punch with ease. Rich was fast for a big guy, but if you knew what to look for, the windup signs were clear. Val was faster, and in the opening he'd created deflecting the punch, he cracked his fist into Rich's chin. He bit back a wince, keeping his face wooden. Those knuckles would be swollen tomorrow.

"Get out of here, Rich," Val said. "Maria wants you home in one piece."

Rich raised the gun and Val knew he'd taken it too far this time. He wasn't sure what he'd taken too far, but their encounters in the past involved more chest puffing and macho bravado, more pool cues over the head, less gun-in-face.

Behind him, Kate froze and stopped talking.

"You're going to die, Slade." A statement of fact, pure and simple. Rich tended to get what he wanted, and it made Val a little nervous to hear this, particularly staring down that long black tube. He disengaged the safety on the gun. "Right here, tonight."

Before Val could move or open his mouth, it was over.

Instead of a thundering boom, a sterile click sounded in the night. Val almost didn't hear it over the hum. His knees threatened to buckle, and he brought his hand to his temple. He was rather pleased he hadn't soiled himself.

Rich cursed, and in checking to make sure the weapon was loaded, (it was—Val could see the red of the shells exactly where they were supposed to be, through the tangible viscosity of the hum) Val had time to yank the Mossberg out of Rich's hands. *Breaking parole!* A faraway voice shrieked in his brain. "Get out, Rich." Val said, holding the gun at his side, pointed at the dirt.

"I don't know why you do this to me," Rich said to Kate, his face bright red. "He's trash, Kate, can't you see?"

"Get out of my sight," Kate said. Rich reached for Kate, one parting hurrah, and Val shifted his grip on the Mossberg, landing the stock on Rich's shoulder. He relished the meaty thump it made, and the *oof* of Rich's exhale. Kate pulled out of his grasp. Rich stumbled and caught himself on the truck's bumper.

"You're done, Rich." His voice sounded as if it came from a million miles away. "TJ, get him the fuck out of here."

Val didn't let TJ do much more than open his chubby mouth before he brandished the shotgun at him like a club. "Go, before someone gets hurt."

"I am hurt, you fucker," Rich said.

"It's only going to get worse."

"Remember that," Rich said; the malice in his tone tempered by his leaning on TJ's shoulder.

"Out! Away! Go!" Val shouted.

"Doesn't your own blood mean more to you than this?" Rich asked Kate, casting a meaty hand at Val.

She looked up at him, her face white, bangs in her eyes. "Get out of my sight,"

Instead of looking at Kate, Rich fixed his piggy little hate-filled eyes on Val. "Watch it, friend."

Val gave a mock salute, biting down a torrent of wounded sentimental bullshit brought on by the use of the word *friend* as Rich and TJ backed away. He didn't want to be Rich's friend ever again. Rich got in the jeep, TJ scurrying to follow, and left in an elaborate show of flying dirt and revving engine, taking the floodlights with him.

Devoid of adrenaline, Val felt weak. He sagged against the front bumper of the truck and let the Mossberg drop the few inches to the ground. His fingers found his temples and massaged them, hoping the hum might stop. He spat into the dirt, unable to rid himself of bad tastes.

"You sure you don't hear a hum?"

"How can you even ask that? Were you paying attention back there?"

"Extremely close attention. He's your brother."

"How are you so calm about this? He tried to shoot you. He did shoot you!"

"Only one of us needs to be in a panic at a time, I think. Since I was the one staring down the barrel of the gun you'd think it would be me, but—"

She slapped him, clacking his teeth together. "Shut up,

Val." Kate shook her head, her arms wrapped around her chest.

"I don't like your brother," Val said, his hand at his chin, biting back a smile.

"I know." She paused. "I don't like him either. It's why I left. I don't see why you couldn't meet me in Santa Fe. Why we had to come back here."

"We'll go to Santa Fe. I need to see my mother for a few days. We'll go, give it time."

"I've given it time!"

"Just...easy." Unsure of what to say to her, he stared at the sky.

She didn't have to come and meet him here. She could've stayed in Santa Fe. Eventually he would have made his way up there.

Val pulled a beer from the six pack and studied it for a moment.

"Drinkwater's a fucking putz," Val finally said, opening the beer, taking a swig and swishing it around in his mouth.

She shrugged. "He's got his moments."

Val closed his eyes and felt the warm dark of the night pressing all around him. The temperature was dropping; it was comfortable outside now. If they stayed out here too much longer, it would start to get cold.

"Val," she said, her words a breathy whisper in the dark.

He opened his eyes.

"I'm sorry."

He knew that. She didn't even need to say it. This all went along with his earlier, mopey feeling—it wasn't supposed to be like this. He was out of jail. His lady should have leapt on him; they should be living it up right now. Instead Rich forced him to fellate a shotgun and now all he could think about was the fact that this fucking hum in his head wouldn't leave him the hell alone.

In a palpable gust of self-pity, Val said, "What do you want with a child molester, anyway?" and took a long swallow of beer.

"That's not fair—"

"I pled guilty. You were there."

"Come on, Val. You know you never molested anyone."

"That's not what the state of New Mexico says. Not what your foster mother says, and certainly not what most of my *pals* on cell block four thought."

"Fuck them then," Kate said.

Val abstained from a sarcastic remark, though there were plenty to choose from. He could feel her gaze on him, but he chose to keep his eyes on the darkness beyond the soft light of the window.

"You're out. You're here. Come on."

He knew if he looked at her he'd cave. She put her hot hand on his shoulder, he could feel the warmth through the thin button-down shirt he wore, and for a moment he wanted to cry. Again.

"Look," she said, grabbing his chin and forcing him to look at her. "We both know you never raped me."

He shrugged, tried to turn away.

"Come on, Val, say it."

"You want me to say I know I never raped you?" he asked.

The corner of her mouth twitched, almost a smile and he knew he was done.

"I guess that's kind of stupid, isn't it?" she asked, the twitch growing into a smile, the smile that would chip away at Val's carefully constructed façade of stern surliness. She arched her eyebrows and he noticed they were the slightest bit red and puffy; she'd waxed them today, just for him.

The silence swelled between them. Val had heard of comfortable silences, but he'd never experienced one. He inhaled with the full intention of speaking this time, or maybe bursting into song, anything to fill the night. He wanted to affirm that being here with her was worth sucking off a shotgun, worth setting her family against her… but she took the initiative and placed her lips against his, closing her brown eyes. He watched her for a moment before closing his own eyes. For the first time, here on the warm hood of the F-100, here with her, he felt like he was home. Reaching out, finally permitting himself to bury his fingers in her hair, he felt at peace.

Except for that damned hum firing behind his eyes, and wondering why Rich's Mossberg failed at such an opportune time.

2

Felix parked his Monte Carlo around back of his apartment complex. After the day he'd had, he was ready for a beer. How easy to slip into the human way of doing things. His body was tired, the aching muscles registered as a dim unpleasantness. He would rest, feet up, watching television. He walked up the outside steps, feeling the peeling flecks of paint on the sun-warmed railing, ready to take all of this out of his head for a night. Be a human. The wooden porch creaked in all the right places—

His door was ajar.

Felix distinctly remembered locking it before leaving to pick Val up that afternoon. Remembered it because he dropped his keys.

He reached into his pocket and pulled out a pistol... but not a pistol. It was gray, smooth and looked like plastic. He held it like a gun, his finger on a button instead of a trigger.

He kicked the door in with one booted foot, denting the cheap wood. He made a pass of the room with the pistol, and saw nothing in the dim light. Maybe Travis was in, looking at the sink. It had been dripping for months. Perhaps when Travis left, he forgot to latch the door?

Nope.

A rhythmic *drip, drip, drip,* still played from the kitchenette.

The apartment felt empty in the afternoon heat, still and quiet, but Felix stood a moment longer, scanning the furnished room, noting the couch, the chair, the TV, everything in perfect order, just as he'd left it. Okay then.

He slipped the pistol back into his jacket pocket.

Okay.

He closed the door behind him and made a move for the fridge, going for one of those beers, when he heard his name. Not in English, not in Tylwyth.

He turned on his heel, looking for whoever spoke.

A little gray form sat in a chair.

It made a sound, his name, a name centuries older than the body he inhabited.

He reached for his gun. Found his arm frozen. Found everything frozen except his voice. When this was all over this wouldn't be a problem anymore.

"What are you doing here?" Felix didn't speak in English either.

You got him out, said the little shadow. *Now leave him be.*

Felix made a snorting sound, as close as he could come to a laugh with his face frozen. "Why do you think we'd go after him? We've had him locked up for half a decade."

We brought one of the Lharomuph with us.

Oh, shit. He started planning, reaching; trying to figure what they could do against that evil. "Here?"

It's going to be watching him. Unless you call your... things...off.

"You brought it to Earth? Who knows what it'll do. Jesus, man." Jesus, Felix noted, was a human expression. The gray being smiled at him; its black eyes glittered in the afternoon light.

I know exactly what it will do. It will do as it's told. It will watch him. Kill any of you to protect him.

"It doesn't know anything about this planet. It doesn't know what's a threat. It'll kill anything that gets near him." Felix swallowed, one of the few things he could still do. He'd known they would be all over this, but he thought he had more time. Val hadn't been out for three hours yet, and here was this freak, sitting in his living room like it owned the place.

Be reasonable. The little creature's voice was a soothing monotone.

"None of this concerns you." Felix tried to move, to adjust his screaming muscles.

Vivisecting innocent beings? He is –

"You've done your share of experimentation," Felix said. He would give anything to scratch his forehead.

Science and warfare are two different breeds.

"Are they?"

The little gray face peered up at him. It didn't answer.

Worry started to take him. He should have checked in as soon as he saw the door ajar. But he was thinking like a human, from too much time here. He thought someone was after his TV, or looking for cash. He didn't think the *Sangaumans*, particularly not one of their medical officers, could find him in this apartment. He was never here. And that was his mistake. Now he was captured and helpless. Unacceptable.

"Are you going to kill me?" It was better than the alternative.

The gray shape shook its head, light from the curtained windows catching on big, black almond eyes.

"Are you going to take me?"

It shook its head again. It stood up, its full height just under four feet. *No.* It walked closer to him, and he could see the texture of its smooth, rubbery skin. *I'm warning you. Leave him be, and everything will be fine.*

He would have shaken his head, but he couldn't move. "You know that isn't my order to give."

You've moved up since I saw you last. I think you're capable of a lot more than you let on.

"Haven't moved up that much, buddy."

The little gray mouth twitched into a smug smile. *Maybe*. It walked around behind him and he couldn't move his neck to look at it. Its footsteps were soft. He strained to hear them. *You leave me no choice, then?*

"You'll compromise us all."

I'm bonding it to him at dusk unless you tell me otherwise.

"That thing will kill anyone who gets near him."

Anyone of yours.

"It'll be on their news."

It shrugged its shoulders and Felix wanted nothing more than to choke it. He even went so far as to try and move his arms, but the air bound them like steel.

"You're going to regret this," Felix said, well aware of how foolish he sounded.

Someone is. I'm not sure if it will be me or not.

The door clicked behind him and Felix remained immobile. Was the little shit just leaving him like this? Was it walking around outside? Where people could see it?

His muscles relaxed like a loosening bowel, and he dropped halfway to the floor before recovering his balance. He ran to the door and threw it open; the little alien was already gone. There wasn't anyone in the parking lot that would have seen him. Did he plan this, or did he take a chance? Of course he planned it. You couldn't be here, in this strange land, without planning. You'd wind up captured.

He shook out his arms, muscles cramping from the strain of being immobilized. Sitting on the couch, Felix pulled his cell phone out of his pocket. Goodbye, quiet night at home.

3

"You didn't hear nothing," Rich shouted.

TJ blinked at him, so Rich repeated himself, louder this time.

Rich lived in a nice neighborhood, a new housing development, and TJ knew too much more of this yelling would involve the police. Granted, Rich would talk them down and they'd leave, but the embarrassment would make him even more pissed off than he already was.

"I didn't hear nothing," TJ said, hoping to pacify him. The lights behind the kitchen window clicked on behind nice curtains, and TJ could see Maria there, peering into the night. TJ raised a hand to wave, but Rich interpreted this as TJ's not paying attention.

"Slade is a lying motherfucker."

"He is. Absolutely." TJ could do nothing but agree. He was good at it, it served him well.

"And nothing he said is true." Rich punctuated this with a sausage finger jabbed at TJ's chest.

"Nothing," TJ echoed.

TJ's agreement seemed to only anger Rich more. He eyed his Suzuki, parked on Rich's driveway, and wondered if he could go soon.

"I mean nothing he said is true."

This conversation started as they left Val's trailer, at first Rich roared about his hatred for Val, TJ piping in when it seemed necessary. Rich pulled out some road sodas, they drank, nothing outside the ordinary, but Rich turned his anger towards TJ now. This didn't usually happen, and getting away was the only respite.

"I gotta run, man," TJ said, staring at the neat asphalt of the driveway.

Rich held him by the collar of his Fox jacket before he could raise his eyes. Bloodshot and brown-eyed, Rich glared at him from inches away. TJ wondered, in a quiet little place in the back of his mind, how Rich could do this and still be a cop.

"I don't think you understand me."

"I do, I do," TJ said, a whine creeping into his voice. He shot his eyes to the left. Maria still watched from the window. TJ couldn't imagine being married to someone so angry. She'd calmed him down, though. He was better than he used to be. You gotta keep looking on the bright side.

"Just go," Rich said, releasing him and shoving him so he almost lost his balance.

"G'night, Rich. I'll see ya tomorrow."

Rich made an angry bear sound and turned away, entering his cookie cutter house and giving the door a window-rattling slam. Maria's face disappeared, and TJ fumbled his bike key out of his pocket.

Kate.

Maybe things weren't so great with her, but he could hope. TJ turned his bike out of town, towards Kate and Val. Val was skinny, and mean, and always thought he was smarter and more clever than everyone else. He wasn't funny. He wouldn't be funny when TJ broke his nose. Kate needed the right kind of rescuing, that's all.

The ride relaxed him. Between the light traffic on these dirt roads and the starlight from above, TJ gained confidence. The roar of the bike's motor soothed him, grinding out all the other sounds into a steady white noise. The trees around him had new leaves; they flapped in the wind like a thousand little flags. He wasn't the kind of guy to get sentimental, but this was one pretty night and—

Something tan moved in the trees beside him.

A deer? He smiled. Didn't see them too often. Whatever it was slid out of his line of vision before he had a chance to get a fix on it. He remembered jacking deer with his dad as a kid, he missed that. You had to be real quiet, watch them at the lick then be ready to go when the lights went on.

He hit a pothole, jarring his arms, and it got him thinking about the task at hand.

How could she love Val? She just thought she did. Now that he was out, TJ suspected Val Slade wouldn't be sticking around for too long. TJ was the kind of guy who sticks around. Yessir. He'd get her away from Val and get her away from her brother, didn't sound like she needed either one of them. He tried to ignore what Val said, what Rich made him say he didn't hear. Was TJ the only guy in town who hadn't raped Kate?

The cone of light the Suzuki threw out lit the bright green of the leaves, the only color in the grayscale of night.

It didn't light up the man in the road until it was too late. TJ made a little whispery gasp of surprise as he mashed on the brakes, hand and foot, and jerked the bike to one side. The back tire lost its purchase on the road and TJ went down, the gravel chewing into his skin, pushing up his jacket and shredding his jeans. The bike stalled; the ticking of its engine the only sound.

TJ's pulse pounded in his ears as he took a mental inventory of himself. Road rash, yep, but nothing broken. He was fine, the bike was probably fine...but what had—

The man stepped into the light.

He wore a light leather jacket and jeans, his hair and eyes were dark. The light, coming from below, played strange shadows on his face. His eyes were luminous pools.

"You all right?" TJ asked, getting to his knees, plucking a little bloody stone out of his side. He wanted to ask what the fuck the guy was doing out here, but his momma raised him better than that.

The man pulled a glass bottle out of his pocket. It looked like a mayonnaise jar. When lit from underneath, TJ saw something in it. Did the guy have a jar of tequila? That would explain a lot, as it was the only drink he could think of that would have a worm in it. TJ stood, wobbling. He'd thunked his head on the road, but not hard. He rubbed at it as he took a step towards his bike to pick it up. The gas cap didn't stay on too well, and he wanted to get it up before the spilled gas got on the paint, but the man took a step towards him.

No, TJ thought, in answer to his own question. This man was not okay. Without even meaning to, he took a step back.

Uneasiness washed over him, dulling the pain in his hip and side. The man was so silent, so precise, yet something about the way he peered past TJ into the night unnerved him, made him turn too, looking for whatever the man thought was out there. The night felt warm, but now that he was off the bike, he caught a chill, a goose walking over his grave.

No way he'd let some drunk city fellow scare him off from his own bike. He took another step forward, and the man did too. Now they were nose to nose. TJ opened his mouth to speak, but the man reached out, faster than TJ could prepare for, and grabbed his chin. Two of the man's fingers were in his mouth and he could taste them, salty like skin, but there was also a formaldehyde under-taste to them. He stumbled back and started to fall, but the guy held him by the chin and TJ dropped down to his knees. He swung at the guy, hitting the cloth of his jacket, but the angle was wrong, and he swatted like a girl. He swung again; he wanted the man's fucking hand out of his fucking mouth. He gagged and tears sprang up in his eyes.

The lid was off the jar, and the man poured it at TJ's face, mostly hitting his open mouth, but also gushing into his nose, down his chin, up into his eyes. It tasted like nail polish remover, like acetone. He screamed, but it came out as a gurgle.

It wasn't tequila, but there was a worm, and it was in his mouth now. The man had moved around behind him, gotten both of his arms, held them back there and kept his head pulled back because now the hand on his chin was gone.

The thing in his mouth was longer than his tongue, about half as wide, and it was alive, because it was moving, plunging towards the back of his throat, blocking up the airway, Jesus Christ he couldn't breathe! It was soft and hard all at the same time, expanding and contracting, not down his throat but up into his sinuses. He gagged, his airways were suddenly clear and he sucked in the sweet spring air, but he could feel it up behind his nose, like a pisser of an allergy attack, but one that moved and squirmed and settled itself in like it was getting comfortable.

Tears streamed from TJ's eyes as he dropped onto his shredded butt, and when he pleaded with the man to get it out, his voice sounded high and nasal.

The man let him go, stepped back and wiped his hands on his jeans. The city boy patted TJ's head, like he was a dog or something, and then took off. TJ turned, slow and stupid, in the direction the man ran to. His head feeling like it weighed a million pounds. Was there something out there? The light from the bike made it seem so dark everywhere else.

TJ sat, focusing on breathing. It was okay, he was okay.

And then darkness.

4

With a pulsing drone, Val woke from a white dream with the empty click of Rich's shotgun echoing in his ears. It took a moment for him to gather his bearings. All he could remember from the dream was the color white, vague looming beings backlit by a light so bright they were reduced to long vertical shapes. His pulse raced, blood pounding in his ears. *White*. He sat up in the darkness and took a mental inventory. This wasn't his cell, the air was much too fresh here, filled with quiet night sounds like birds and wind whistling through rocky outcroppings and rustling the scrub brush. The hum he'd carried with him all evening was stronger here, like sitting too close to the speakers at a rock show...but without the actual volume. All low-end, and nothing else. After the white of the dream, the night's darkness was absolute, and it took Val another moment to realize he wasn't indoors anywhere, but out on a grassy plain in the shadow of a pinyon pine. He closed his eyes, half hoping he'd wake up in his own bed, letting his eyes adjust to the night. When he opened them again it didn't seem quite so black, but the half moon was obscured behind scrolling tendrils of dark clouds.

It was like being inside a subwoofer, padded and muffled. Almost loud, but not.

He sat for a moment, trying to acclimate himself to the vibrations that buffeted him. When he looked down he saw dark blood on his hand, and saw a long scratch. He stood up—the pressure of the hum made it hard to move—and noticed he was only wearing his boxers, what he'd gone to sleep in. They were white, and he'd touched them at some point with his bloody hand, leaving a streaky palm print. Val shivered in the dark. The desert got cold at night. So, now to figure out where the hell he was and how he'd gotten here. Ignore the hum, just ignore the hum. It permeated him, rattled his fillings like chewing on tinfoil. He'd sleepwalked before, but only in his jail cell, and hadn't gotten far in an eight by eight room. It was one of those things he assumed he would be done with now he was free.

It had been a long while since he'd been out here in this brush, but it came back to him. He was off his mother's property, this had been a goat farm when he was in high school, but he didn't see any goats here now. SR-719 was somewhere over a little rocky outcropping to Val's left, and he could follow it home from there. He stretched in the dark, his joints popping in all the right places, and he made his way towards the dirt road. His hand hurt, now that he'd noticed the cut, though it didn't look too deep. He started to hum to himself, but it blended with the reverberating sound, so he whistled instead. He didn't like the un-empowered feeling that came from sleepwalking, but he was outdoors, there was no one watching him. He was a free man.

Walking past the dark truck and the nasty yellow Daytona, he noticed the windows of the mobile home were lit up. God, he hated that thing. He hoped Kate wasn't out looking for him, since that would mean he'd have to go looking for her, and there wasn't a lot around here that made for a landmark. There were snakes and abandoned mines. He glanced at his hand as he pushed open the trailer door. It would look much better with all the blood rinsed off. A long scratch, really.

Kate sat at the Formica counter. She glowered at him over a cup of tea. It pained him to think how old any tea found in this house might be.

"Where have you—" her expression softened as she saw the blood. "What happened to your hand?"

He shrugged, went to the sink and ran it under cold water. "Just a scratch."

"Where were you?"

She came to his side and touched his neck, tracking the long black tribal design that wove from behind his right ear down his arm to his right elbow. He shivered at her touch, remembering and enjoying it, and noticed the hum was softer, back to the level where it had been.

"I was walking, I guess. The hum was so intense when I woke up. It's quieter now. Though loud and quiet aren't really the right words to describe it."

"Sleepwalking?" she asked. He nodded and shrugged again, drying his hand with a towel. Kate stood before him, wearing only a diminutive pair of black panties and a tank top. He'd learned earlier in the night that her eyebrows weren't all she'd had waxed.

"Put some pants on if you want me to have a serious conversation."

The hum washed over him, less, but still there. Couldn't it go away? He rubbed at his temples, tried to focus on the way the little black strings on Kate's underwear sat on her hips. If she turned around, he'd see his name there, in flowery cursive script.

"Sleep now?" he asked.

"Are you going to stay put? Do I need to chain you

up?"

"You could, I guess. Don't you think it's a little soon for that kind of humor?"

She looked at him, startled for a second. "I meant it in more of a sexy way..." she said, before realizing he was joking and pantomiming throwing her mug at him. "Fuck you."

"As you wish," he said with a bow, and followed her back to bed.

5

With each step the jar in Felix's pocket slapped his hip. Of course it had failed. It seemed like a good idea at the time, using the guy who was already pissed at Val, but he was too close. The creature had been hungry, freshly bonded, and out for blood. Felix hadn't even waited around to see if it had taken properly. It didn't matter. It was a waste of a Beta, yes, but soon that wouldn't matter. He'd gotten where he was by thinking things through, not making rash decisions. It was just…he was so close.

Felix forced the familiar thoughts of what could be out of his mind and went back to the task at hand. He strolled the dark dirt roads of the Lincoln National Forest South Entrance Campground. He needed something for surveillance, preferably a human. A dog might not be a bad idea, it might be able to outrun the monster. But a human could cover greater distances and blend in better.

With the monster around, Felix wasn't about to send one of the Alpha soldiers in. A Beta would do for this mission, probably would wind up as cannon fodder. Monster fodder was more like it, though once that thing got through with people they wished it had been a cannon.

Felix lingered near the outhouse, not relishing the stink of excrement. Humans were disgusting. So much waste. Breath, shit, sweat, piss, tears…they leaked *something* from every possible spot at every opportunity. In the quiet warm night Felix heard the zipper of a tent. They were headed for the outhouse for sure. He needed to use it, too, but it could wait. When he had his own body, this wouldn't be an issue. Stars blanketed the sky. Felix had long ago given up looking for home.

He stayed in the shadows, letting the human use the outhouse. Better to let it void first. He caught his first glimpse of the human as it stepped out of the outhouse and let the wooden door slam shut behind it. It was a male, a large one. It turned away from Felix, swinging its flashlight, lighting up crazy swatches of the spring desert.

Felix sprinted and tackled the human from behind. "Hey!" it exclaimed, before it fell, catching itself with its hands. The dirt road scraped its hands, and Felix could smell the blood. He kept himself on the human's back, pinning its arms beneath it.

"What the fuck're you doing?"

It thrashed under him. It was good, knew how to move its body. But Felix was better. He threw the bottle at the ground by the thrashing human's face. His Beta would find its way.

"What's that?" The thrashing intensified, Felix knew the Beta was making its way towards the human's mouth. If it couldn't get in that way, it could use the nose. Humans were easy because they couldn't close their noses. Not if their hands were bound. Felix covered the human with his body, stilling some of the writhing. "What the hell?" It was sweating profusely, sending of waves of stink and fear.

The human's words degraded into inarticulate sounds, squealing and grunting. Felix hazarded a glance at it, and saw the Beta filling one of its nostrils, the thin skin stretching and plumping, then dropping back to nothing.

Felix let go of the human's hands and stepped back. He knew, from experience, it would only be focused on getting the Beta out of its head. As predicted, it pawed at its face. It didn't break the skin, but left red welts. Felix watched, feeling the earth under his shoes, wishing the legs and arms were his own. *Soon*.

When the human stopped thrashing, Felix knew the Beta had taken hold.

"How are you feeling?" he asked; voice devoid of interest. The monster took his last Beta, it would take this one, and the next one, but it would also provide a beacon to Val's whereabouts. In some ways, it was a good thing.

"I feel…I have a headache," said the Beta.

Felix nodded. "Yup. Val Slade's your man, keep an eye on him. If you can do it without him seeing you, great, if he sees you once or twice, fine. Don't let him know he's being followed."

The Beta looked confused. It was still inhabiting its new host body, still fusing synapses, making connections with the nerves.

"You got me?" Felix asked.

It nodded but was confused and sluggish.

The Betas didn't blend as well as the Alphas. They could never pass; never fully integrate into the host's society. That was fine, they didn't need to. They were lucky.

"Val Slade."

"I understand. License plate number AU407, address 14149 SR-179, Lott, New Mexico, 87203. No known telephone—"

"Yup, you got it—"

"—number or email address."

"That's him. Good luck," Felix said, walking back to his car. When he'd first come to earth he thought their cars were ridiculous. He didn't like them, thought burning gasoline was a stupid way to get around, stinking and inefficient. But it grew on him. Mostly amused him, as he learned how the humans were so passionate about their cars. Funny.

The engine roared to life. Felix looked in the rearview mirror. The Beta stood in the middle of the dirt road, looking confused. This one, Felix predicted, wouldn't last long.

EXCERPT #1

from *Trinity* by Judd Grenouille ©1988

No one believed Adrienne Goldstein (not her real name) when she said someone had taken her baby. When I met her, she was in a group rehab session for a crack addiction, and one of the girls in her therapy group recommended her name to me. Adrienne has a very special story to tell, a story addled with heartache, drug addiction, and unbidden contact from the skies.

In my first book *Close Contact: First Hand Reports of Third Kind Encounters* I gave a general survey of alien abductions, but Adrienne's story is a special one, a story of three intergalactic species, terminally entwining themselves with the fate of the known universe.

Adrienne's story starts like a lot of stories that someone in my line of work hears. Another girl in Adrienne's class had experienced being taken and recognized that Adrienne's dreams may not be only dreams. She encouraged her to get in touch with me and she did, albeit reluctantly. Many people who have never experienced Contact think that abductees do it for the fame or notoriety. I assure you, this is not the case. Abductees suffer the same psychological symptoms of rape victims. There is a stigma attached to both that transmutates victims into perpetrators, where there should be sympathy, there is only blame. Adrienne was all apologies, she worried she was wasting my time.

So I asked her about her dreams.

"It's nothing," she said. "Really, it isn't." She perched on the edge of her seat as if I was going to tell her to leave. She wore a simple yellow dress that hung on her thin frame. The drug use had been hard on her body, I could see that. I didn't know much about her then, but I knew she had a son that lived with her sister on the east coast.

"Please," I said, well aware of the tone I ought to be taking with someone like her, and favoring her with a smile. "Relax."

She gave me a smile back, and leaned back a bit in her chair. Her hands still worked at one another, picking at the skin around the fingernails.

"They took my baby," she told me, after a deep breath.

"You dreamed they took your baby?"

She studied me for a moment, with light blue eyes. Looking into Adrienne Goldstein's face was like looking into a husky-dog's.

"You've talked to other people who've been through this, right?"

I nodded. It's more common than you would think.

"I was pregnant in 1979. I took the pee test and the blood test, all of it. Then," she looked around. "Then I got my period. I shoulda been three months pregnant, but I got my period, normal, like any other month. I went to my doctor and he said I should forget about it. A friend of mine, they fixed her when she had her baby 'cause she didn't have a lot of money, and I think he wanted to do that to me."

False pregnancies are common, yes, but so are stories

like Adrienne's. I told her so, and her face lit up with a new light. It's amazing the reaction when people discover they're not alone.

"I don't know who the father was, either," Adrienne said. "I had another strange experience right around the time the baby was conceived."

I nodded. "Think back further." Abductions very frequently run in a family. I wanted to ask about that, but was afraid of leading her on.

She chewed at her lip.

"I had some dreams. When I was a kid." She looked around. "And I got this scar. On my leg." She uncrossed her legs and pulled back her dress to show two little dimpled scars. "I don't know where they came from. I gotta go," she said. "Do you think we can meet again?"

"I'd like that very much, if you'd like to talk to me."

She said she would, and left, back to the rehab facility where she was staying.

When she contacted me next, it was six months later, after I'd written her off as someone with a terribly interesting story I'd never get to hear.

* * *

One evening, Adrienne called me long distance. I keep my offices in New York, and she lives in New Mexico. It took me a moment to place her name.

"It's happened again. And I think they're after my boy, my Cal."

I wracked my brain. The boy, as I recalled, was living in New England with relatives. We talked a while longer, and I decided I would make another trip to New Mexico, this time to the small town of Lott, where Adrienne lived.

I pulled into her driveway late in the afternoon. Her trailer was small and not particularly neat. She lived in it alone, one of the rooms set aside for the boy to stay in, if he ever were to come home. With some pride, she told me she'd been clean since the last time we talked. I congratulated her.

"I'd like to hypnotize you," I said.

Her expression darkened. Hypnosis isn't like the movies make it out to be. It's perfectly safe, a way to dig deeper into a person's subconscious. It cannot correct for incorrect memories, nor can a person be made to do something they wouldn't be willing to do under ordinary circumstances. It's commonly used for phobias, for weight loss, all manner of things that people need a little help in doing. It also lets you remember. That first session, we established that Adrienne's abductions had been ongoing since she was nine years old. She and her father lived in a trailer a lot like the one she now owns, on the far side of town in a trailer park. She told me what fun it used to be to play with the other kids. "The rest of the town called us white trash, but when you're seven or so, you don't know yet that you're supposed to be ashamed of it. You're tickled you got all these kids to pal around with. You have pity on those kids with the nice houses, all away from everything." When she was nine, Adrienne stopped playing in her neighborhood, without warning. That was about the time, she told me, that the scars appeared on her leg.

* * *

"I don't know what woke me up," said Adrienne during our next session, her eyes looking less clear this afternoon than they had before. She told me she was clean, but I also noticed an abundance of alcohol bottles, and a sweet tell-tale scent on her breath. I wasn't surprised. Abductees, before they can really admit what has happened, use a variety of coping skills, not all of them productive or healthy. She licked her lips and continued. "I woke up and I couldn't fall back asleep. Dave—a guy I had over—was out like a light next to me. I kind of thrashed around in the hopes that he might wake up and we could do something, but he was out. I was thirsty, so I got up and went to the kitchen, and instead of getting a glass of water, I stared out the window over the sink."

Adrienne pointed, and I looked out the window. It overlooked the driveway, a shed, and some desert.

"The moon was full that night, and it was bright as noon, but all silvery, you know? Is that too much detail? You want more? Less?" She kept looking at the cassette tape recorder I'd set up on her table.

I assured her it was fine, and encouraged her to continue.

"I went outside in my bare feet, wearing a pair of boxer shorts and a tank top. It was hot that day, but at night it was nice and cool. That was before we had AC, so inside was still hot from the sun.

"I don't know why, but I got in my car and turned it on. I didn't even realize I'd taken my car keys. I drove really slowly. I was still a little buzzed from partying with Dave, and pulled off at the Olympus Mine. It shut down, like, ten years ago. They keep it gated off 'cause it's dangerous, so I parked next to the gate, and walked in, my feet were a mess the next morning, let me tell you.

"And that's all I remember."

She paused, staring at me.

"I woke up in bed; car was in the driveway, in the exact spot where I'd parked it. The only reason I knew it wasn't a dream is that my feet were filthy when I woke up. Dave really flipped.

"I found out Dave and I was pregnant the next day. That was the baby I lost, not Cal"

"Adrienne," I said, keeping my voice as low and calm as I could. "I'd like to hypnotize you again. Perhaps we can discover what else happened that night." I had some private doubts as to whether or not the hypnosis would work if she was drunk.

"I don't think so," she said, immediately drawing in on herself. She crossed her arms over her chest and withdrew, like a threatened sea anemone.

We talked about other things for a while, I asked her about Cal, and she told me he was starting kindergarten in Rhode Island; that he had a cousin very close to his own age and they had a wonderful time playing together. As she spoke of her son she became more animated.

Finally, she withdrew again, re-crossed her arms on her chest, and said "Okay. You can do it."

What I present to you here is an actual transcript of our conversation.

JG: The moon is full, and you have stepped out of your car. What happens next?

AG: I walk. It isn't far, and the dirt road hasn't grown over much.

JG: And then?

AG: Then I see the opening of the mine.

JG: What does it look like?

AG: Like a cave...like a big, black gaping mouth. I wonder if bats will fly out at me.

(fidgets, frowns.)

JG: What next?

AG: Light. Everywhere. White, brighter than the moon by a million times.

JG: Is the light coming from one place? Do you see a ship?

AG: A ship? No, it's...there's light, my whole world is light and I can't move. I can't move...why can't I move?

JG: Relax (I make my voice soothing here, trying to calm her. Sometimes they can forget that they're safe and sound at home. I reminded her of this, and after a moment, her breathing returned to normal. When she spoke there was only a slight tremor in her voice.)

AG: I started floating. Up. At least I think it was up.

I couldn't even move my eyes, and all I could see was white. And then there were men around me.

JG: Men? What kind of men? What color was their skin?

AG: They looked so normal except their eyes. There wasn't any love in their eyes. No affection, no compassion. They were flat and dead.

JG: The eyes, were they big and black? Almond shaped?

AG: No…they were normal looking. At first.

(This doesn't fit with the standard abduction scenario. Abductees from all around the globe universally agree on what the visitors look like, and nine times out of ten they don't look like humans. But sometimes I get reports that the visitors look like people. More on that later.)

AG: I'm on an examining table. I'm naked. My clothes are gone, and I was freaking out before, but now I don't care. I'm as placid and dead as the men around me. I feel like I'm at the doctor's, there's this one guy at the community health center who seems like he really doesn't like being there, everything is clinical and impersonal. That's what all these guys are like. Then the table breaks apart under my legs and takes them with it…like the table becomes a Y shape, and now my legs are spread. Something inside me. (She squirms in her seat again.)

JG: (I am starting to wonder if she isn't misremembering a rape, or a crime committed by earth denizens.) Are you aroused?

AG: No. (The corners of her mouth draw down into a frown. She isn't faking. The people—usually women—who are faking will say yes, they're aroused. Adrienne looks agitated with me, I take it to mean she's telling the truth.)

JG: Then what happened?

AG: Like the doctor's. They pulled it out and went about their business. Just ignored me. The table moved and my legs went back together. I tried to sit up but I couldn't. Then I was in bed, with Dave.

* * *

The next day, Adrienne had terrible cramps, could feel something in her stomach, and on a whim, bought a pregnancy test. It came back positive. Dave refused to take a paternity test and left her, and she never found out whose baby it was. A month later, Adrienne was taken again. This time she describes the gray Visitors that most abductees experience. A clinical benevolence, red, orange and blue flashing lights, a saucer. This experience is much more in tune with the average abduction scenario. She described it as an average OB-GYN visit, they poked her and prodded her in all the same spots. They seemed more curious about her than the humanoid aliens did, once resting a cool gray hand on her forehead.

"It was so cold up there. I was shivering. And it touched me. Really gently, stroked my forehead. It was nice, and I was still cold but I wasn't afraid of it no more."

The next day she had an actual doctor's appointment, and her physician, who would not be reached for comment, told her everything was progressing normally.

"I wasn't even drinking much then. I knew it was bad for the baby, so I was really trying to cut down. Then a few months later, right at three months, I woke up and I knew she was gone."

I interrupted her then—"She?" I asked.

Adrienne nodded.

"How do you know?"

"I mean, I don't, really. But I…I know it was a girl."

I asked her if I might hypnotize her again, and once more she looked reluctant. Finally she agreed, after getting up and pouring herself a glass of water.

JG: You've gone to bed. Then what happened?

AG: I woke up, and everything was white. I thought it was the next morning, but it wasn't it was night, and once again I couldn't move. There was a sound like a machine, and they were carrying me out, then we went up into something.

JG: Something?

AG: The ship, I think.

(Adrienne described a visit similar to the first one. These were the humanoid creatures, not the friendly Visitors from last time. She sensed none of the compassion they had shown for her. They poked and prodded, but then she felt something happening inside her…)

AG: It was like they were blowing me up like a balloon. It hurts so bad…my organs are puffing up and separating, it's all stretching. (She writhes in her chair, a tear snakes from the corner of her eye, rolling down her cheek. She's breathing hard, like Lamaze breathing.) It's…ugh… and…then they have the baby and she's so small, and all the air whooshes out of me, and I don't think I was meant to see her. (She pauses for a long time here. I was about to ask her what happened next, when she spoke again.) And that was it. I don't want to do this no more.

*   *   *

I didn't speak to Adrienne again for eight months.

6

Sleep didn't come back to Kate. She thought of her brother, her foster mother, this feud between Rich and Val. If she went to him, talked to him, a rational, grown-up conversation, without any macho posturing...then maybe she could get him to leave them alone. Rich wasn't a morning person, but as she lay in bed, watching the hands on the glowing analog clock face, she thought maybe a crack of dawn visit would breathe some sense into him.

She tried to move without disturbing Val. Gingerly pulling her arm out from under him, she flexed her hand. It tingled, all pins and needles. Short night. After his nocturnal wanderings it had taken him a long time to fall asleep.

In what little gray light snuck around the drawn shade, she pulled on her panties and jeans then searched for her top.

She and Val slept in his old bedroom, and Kate wondered if he would move into the master bedroom. She doubted it. She hoped they wouldn't be here long enough to need to.

She slipped out into the rosy pre-dawn light, closing the flimsy door behind her. A deer bolted from grazing in the yard as the door slammed, and Kate watched it go as she started her car. As she pulled out of the driveway, she looked over her shoulder at the trailer and the truck before heading toward Lott, towards her brother's house.

Kate didn't get far.

A half mile from the trailer she saw a mangled deer in the road.

As her headlights washed over the crumpled mess, it began to dawn on her what she was seeing.

The headlights also shone off something shiny in the ditch on the side of the road. A Suzuki dual-sport bike.

"Fuck," she whispered. She threw the car into park and opened the door, stepping onto the gravel, looking left and right, even up, to make sure she was alone. Maybe this wasn't happening. Maybe she'd wake up soon.

She knew from the checkered dirt bike jacket exactly who this was, but she rolled him over to be sure, maybe there was still a pulse, maybe she'd gotten here in time… and half of TJ's face was missing. Missing to the degree she could see sliced skull edges, and something horrible and gray and soft, already seething with flies that took off at the disruption, buzzing and irritated until they could settle in again. He'd lain on his stomach and the blood had pooled in what was left of his face, the skin looked waxy and purplish. She let go of his shoulder and backed away.

All that blood and sliced-open flesh and the smell and the buzzing of the flies made her head swim and her stomach bucked. She leaned on her open car door and brought up what was left of last night's dinner. Bile with a slight taste of beer made her heave again. He didn't lose his face in a bike accident. There were claw marks on him...or sword cuts. Maybe they looked like bear claw marks? She didn't even know if there were bears in New

Mexico. Black bears, but nothing that...large. A mountain lion? Still not big enough. This looked like a grizzly. A big one. Not that she knew anything about what a grizzly bear attack looked like, but she had seen those shows on Fox, where animals attack people and it's caught on film. Her empty stomach churned again...this wasn't television though, this was TJ. She breathed through her mouth until the next wave of nausea passed.

Hoping, and starting to cry, she went back and dutifully felt for a pulse. *If there's no pulse I can do CPR*, she thought, knowing no amount of CPR could fix what had been done. *He doesn't have a mouth anymore...how could I do CPR like that?* As soon as she touched TJ's skin, cold and plastic feeling, she gave up. She thought of his clumsy advances, and pushed thoughts of him from her mind.

The hitching wheeze of her engine contrasted with peaceful bird calls. Breathing in through her mouth, she could smell something; sort of half rotten meat, half feces, but with a strange nauseating sweetness to it. She *knew* this guy. This guy who was last seen (to the best of her knowledge) leaving her boyfriend's home after a violent dispute. The same boyfriend who not only was an ex-con, but had vanished in the middle of the night and come home with blood on his shorts. Had she fucked Val immediately before *and* after he'd hacked TJ to pieces with a machete?

No. She hadn't. Because Val wasn't stupid. After high school and before jail he'd started his undergrad on the pre-law track. If he were to kill TJ, he would have showed some degree of cunning or subtlety. Though...he'd kind of had a lot to drink last night. And the business with the hum was troubling. And he didn't have any kind of alibi. If he hadn't conspicuously vanished during what seemed to be the precise time TJ was being sliced apart, she would have known he didn't do it. But...this seemed like a damned big coincidence and Kate didn't believe in coincidences.

She pulled out her cell phone. Held it in her hand until it became warm, staring at the mess before her. Call the police? Call Val?

Calling the police wasn't an option. She couldn't lose Val again. But...where had he gone in the night? She looked up at the sky. A few clouds floated there against the blue, pink with the edge of sunlight.

She keyed in 911. Placed her thumb over the green send button, hovered there a moment, and noticed dirt under her fingernail, then scrolled down to Val's mom's number. She hoped it hadn't changed.

The ringing sounded a thousand miles away in her ear. Val answered; his voice thick with sleep.

"I need your help," she said.

"Where are you?" He paused a moment. "What the fuck time is it?"

"After five. TJ's dead."

"What?" He sounded clearer now. "How do you know?"

"I'm standing next to his body. He's in the road, 719 towards town. Someone killed him." Val said nothing, so Kate kept going. "You were one of the last people to see him. You just got out of jail. You know how Rich will spin this."

"What are you saying?"

"Get out here."

"Truck has a flat tire."

"You can walk." God, why was he being difficult?

"Okay."

He hung up. She put the phone in her pocket, and took a moment to breathe fresh air that didn't smell like decay before going back to TJ.

Exhaling through her mouth, she looked at the crumpled mess before her. This road didn't see much traffic, clearly he'd been dead for a few hours, the blood around his throat and face was a tacky dark brown in the building light. The sun peeked over the top of the pines, tossing long striped shadows across his mangled torso. His left arm was gone. Shit. Did the killer take it with him? Maybe a sword could do this kind of damage, wielded in a sequential way to make it look like claws? Did the killer like trophies? Or was it a bear after all?

Kate looked at her watch, 5:40 am.

The mine. The old Olympus Mine. Less than a half-mile from where she stood right this second. No one would ever find the body or the bike. She and Val had explored there some years ago, back when they were kids (everything with Val had happened some years ago, she reflected), and she recalled a fairly wide road in with a drop-off down into an impenetrable blackness. Once Val got here—she hoped he would run, get here fast, every second TJ lay in the road was time a car could come—they could take TJ to the mine. No one would find him there.

She popped the trunk open. Looked at TJ. Looked at the small trunk, with its dirty gray carpeting. If his blood got on the carpet, which it would, and the police linked it back to her, she and Val both would be in a world of hurt. She kept a dirty Indian blanket in her trunk. That should work. Doubled up, the blanket covered the gray carpeting of the car's trunk. Or should she wrap his body? That seemed more respectful.

This wasn't the time to cry. She blinked back tears. The pink had almost melted off the clouds overhead, they no longer looked like floating cotton candy. Shouldn't it be raining for this kind of thing? Thunder and lightning?

Sucking in a wavering breath and stifling a sob, she slid her hands under his armpits and hefted. Fuck. He'd needed to lose weight, and now that it was dead weight—even missing most of his left arm—she began to doubt her ability to do this. She had to wait for Val. She couldn't get him from the ground to the trunk of the car, he was too heavy. His blood stained her hands, and she wiped them on his jeans, the muscles underneath feeling so… inanimate.

She stepped away from him, to where she could breathe again. She listened to the bugs and the birds, the happy morning choir all around her.

And something heavy moved among the trees.

Her breath, almost a sob, caught in her throat as she whipped her head towards the noise. She wanted to call out Val's name but she couldn't make the sound come. What if the killer was back? Did it-he-want to claim TJ's other arm? Should she hide? She realized she was simply standing still, holding the blanket in her hands. The car wasn't too far, surely she could make it there before—

Val stepped out of the trees, wearing the same black T-shirt from the night before and his jeans.

"You scared the hell out of me."

"Who else did you think it would be?"

"Someone killed him. They could still be out here."

Val walked over to the body and pulled a pair of leather gloves out of his pocket. She saw something flicker in his eyes, the downturned corner of his mouth. She didn't think about gloves at all, but it made sense. The expression on his face passed, and he stretched like a cat. In the quiet morning she could hear his back crack.

"What do you propose?" he asked. His tone, his face… both were so cold.

"What?"

"You called me out here to do something, presumably with this body, what do you propose?"

"The mine."

His silence goaded at her. It made her angry to watch him contemplate the body. "They'll think you did it! Where did you get the blood on you last night? Where were you?"

"Back your car around so we don't have to lift him so

far. He wasn't a little guy."

Walking to the driver's side door she found herself mad at Val. Hadn't she called him because she knew he would get shit done? He was getting shit done, but she also wanted kind words. A hug. Something. *Poor Kate, you must be so scared.* That kind of attitude wouldn't come from Val, and she knew it.

Val directed her back and told her when to stop.

"Should we wrap him in the blanket?"

"If we wrap him in the blanket I can't get a grip on him. Line the trunk with it, I'll get him in."

She did as she was told while Val got his hands under TJ's armpits. She thought dead bodies were supposed to be stiff, but TJ's stump waggled pathetically, and he bent obligingly at the waist.

"Get his feet, please," Val said.

"Sorry," she said, stepping in and reaching for his boots. The leather didn't have blood on it, and she reached for it.

"Wait," Val said. "Don't touch him with your bare hands. They can pull prints off anything. Do you have gloves in the car?"

"No."

He threw a pair of yellow dishwashing gloves at her. "Enjoy."

She pulled them on, not enjoying the plastic feel up her arms, but she supposed this was smart. Too much to think about.

At some point, poor TJ had shit himself. She hoped, as she sort of hooked his ankles over the lip of the trunk and paused to pant in the building heat of the morning, it had been a post-mortem shitting. Though she would not deeply mourn his death, she didn't want to think of him being so afraid of something that he couldn't control his bowels.

She kicked dirt over the bloody spots in the gravel of

the road. A look at the sky suggested it wouldn't be raining any time soon. She kicked harder, trying to spread it as much as possible, looked at the heap that was TJ in the trunk, reached out and folded a corner of the blanket over his ruined face, then slammed the hatch shut.

"It looks like he was riding to your place," she said, looking at the bike.

"Mmmhmm," Val said. "Your knight in shining armor."

Or so it seemed. What did she know? "Goddamn it, TJ," she muttered under her breath, still somewhere between crying and not.

"I'll follow you on the bike," Val said.

Swallowing tears, she asked if he needed help picking it up.

"I think I got it." She waited to see if he did, and he used his knees to do it, turning his back to the bike and getting it up on its wheels easily. She started the car, and Val followed her. The car bounced down the rutted road, long unused, grown over in places with scrub brush, past a large NO TRESPASSING sign as per the orders of the New Mexico Energy, Minerals and Natural Resources Department, wishing she had Val's pickup instead of her own little car.

She skidded to a stop in front of an old metal gate which reiterated this was private property, a few pieces of steel across the road on a locked hinge. Val braked hard behind her, the dirt bike wobbling. They could walk around it, of course, the bike could get around, no problem, but carrying TJ's body? She got out and studied the lock. It was a simple padlock, looking quite rusted. She debated slamming through with the car, but the car was very yellow, and the gate was gray, and it seemed like that paint swap would make everything easier for the Otero County Sheriff's Department. If they got this far, she didn't want to give them any help.

Val came up behind her, off the bike now, with a rock in both gloved hands. She could see the muscles standing out in his arms from carrying it, and it only took him two hits to break off the lock. He tossed the rock off to the side.

Already in the heat, she was slick with sweat. Val walked the gate open, and she went back to the car. He followed on the bike. The opening to the mine faced west and in the morning light it looked like a gaping black mouth in the side of a hill. For at least a few hundred yards the road was wide enough to get a dump truck in. She anticipated no problem turning the car around and getting out. She took a moment to ponder the possibilities if she were to get it stuck. It was easier not to think about it until it became an actual problem. Her headlights illuminated the cavernous room. She stopped the car near the edge of a drop off. Pulling a large flashlight from the backseat, she shone the light down. Val turned the bike off, the only sound was the idling car. Bats fluttered near the roof, irritated by their interruption.

Kate opened the trunk. If they pulled him out by the feet, would the remainder of the blood in him come pouring out of his savaged head and arm, into the trunk? Was there any blood left? Val, looking peaked in the little light from the trunk, reached for the arm pits.

"Is this a good idea?" she asked.

"Not the right time to ask. We're long past the point of no return." Val flopped TJ's chest and arm over the lip of the trunk, she could tell Val was getting tired, and he heaved and dropped the body onto the dirt by the edge of the drop off. Kate picked up the flashlight again, and looked into her trunk. She pulled up the blanket.

There was some kind of dark stain there that she was fairly sure hadn't been there before. Using the heel of her hand to wipe the sweat out of her eyes, she closed the trunk. Its echoes ricocheted around the cavern. Val rolled the body the last few feet toward the edge then gave a final shove. She followed him down with the flashlight, but he dropped out of sight and she never heard a thud. Done.

Sweat beading on his forehead, Val started the bike again, filling the mine with deafening noise. Kate covered her ears with her hands. He walked the bike to the edge, then used its own propulsion to send it over the edge. It took a long time to land, but when it did there was a bright flash, a pop and silence somewhere far away.

"Let's get out of here," Kate said.

Val, in a shadow, said nothing.

She turned the light on him. He pressed his hands to his temples, his head down. "You really don't hear that? Feel it?"

"Feel what? Are you all right?"

"Yeah. No, I don't know, it's that humming. It's like I'm underwater, the pressure."

"Let's get out of here."

He took his hands away from his face and in the dim light of the flashlight she could see blood coming from his nose.

"You've got a nosebleed."

He looked at his hands, slow and stupid. He looked up at her, and she saw dark streaks on his face. Dirt? No, dark tears. She blasted him in the face with her flashlight, and he recoiled, smearing the blood on his cheeks, reaching out with bloody hands to stop the light. The streaks on his face: tears of blood.

"Val—" she said…a whisper.

Val brought his bloody hands to his temples and didn't answer. His nosebleed showed no signs of slowing. And his eyes...what did that even mean with the eyes? At least there was less blood coming from there.

"Tilt your head back," she said. "Get in the car!" Now the front of his shirt was soaked. Could someone die from a nosebleed?

"It's like my head's in a vice," he said. He mumbled,

and his walk was unsteady.

They weren't alone in the mine. The knowledge crawled over her, making her skin tingle, and she looked around into the dark, not daring to shine the flashlight. She didn't have any real reason to think there was something else with them. No warning jangle of the reptile part of her brain, no feeling of being watched.

"Come on, let's get you home," she said to Val, her voice quiet. She went to him, positive someone (no, not someone, some*thing*) was watching them. He leaned on her. Well, here was her hug she was looking for. When he took his hands from his temples she saw he'd left dark blood smudges there as well. She had to have something, an old T-shirt, in the car, something to catch the blood.

She told herself it was the bats as she led him to the passenger's side. She opened the door, found a sweatshirt, not an old one, but one she rather liked, and handed it to him. She walked back around the car, making sure the trunk was shut. Something vibrated. Something down in the hole. Bats. It had to be the bats. There were a lot of them, when their wings flapped it must sound like this. The taillights illuminated everything red back here, and she heard something in the darkness, something heavier than a bat. She sprinted the few feet to the driver's side and slammed the door behind her. She accelerated too hard at first, spraying gravel.

She took a breath through her mouth (breathing through her nose she smelled the sharp copper of Val's blood, which looked malignant and black in the green light from the dashboard) and tried to clear her head. She did better this time, keeping even pressure on the gas, but as soon as they broke into the blinding sun Kate started to cry. Val put a bloody hand on her shoulder, and that made her cry even harder.

7

Val quit bleeding as soon as Kate hit State Highway 12, about the same time the hum went away. He didn't notice it had stopped at first—it seemed so quiet in his head, blissfully empty. For a moment he sat, enjoying it, then Kate asked him if he was all right, panic in her voice. He pulled the sweatshirt she'd given him from his face. It was soaked with dark, red blood. She insisted he go to the ER anyway, and he agreed. He didn't think the doctor needed to know about the hum, or how the pressure down in the mine felt like it was destroying him, far worse than anything he'd felt the night before, his eyes, his ears, his skin feeling too tight all over. He was pretty sure pressure caused the bleeding, but Kate seemed unaffected. It didn't make sense. How could one person feel something like that, something that didn't even affect someone standing right next to them?

A hospital seemed too much like jail, and he didn't want to go back there.

The clinic even looked like a jail, another long, flat brown building on the outer edge of town. While Kate parked, Val pondered fight or flight. He followed her in, dragging his feet, keeping his eyes on the floor. He checked in, mumbling his name, then dropped to a chair, crossing his arms over his chest.

Val wondered how he was supposed to pay for this, his first medical expense in six years, but decided he'd figure it out later. It would be nice to know what was wrong.

He could feel the dried blood around his nose and eyes as he stood to go to the bathroom.

"Where are you going?" Kate asked, holding his arm.

"The john, I'll be right back."

She looked suspicious, and he kissed her forehead before he left. He wanted to go home. He wiped some of the blood off his face, the little bits by his ears. He could hear okay, so he guessed nothing had ruptured...he shivered at the thought. The whites of his eyes were pretty red. In the corner of his left he'd popped some blood vessels, leaving a dark red spot. Gross. It made the light blue of his eyes seem even lighter and more unusual. He raked his hands through his hair and left the bathroom without trying to make it lay down flat.

There was barely time to skim a three-month-old issue of *People* before a nurse came out to get him. The nurse took his blood pressure, which she said was normal.

"Bullshit," Val said. "Try it again."

She looked at him as if he'd grown a second head.

"Do it again. I don't have normal blood pressure. It's through the roof."

Kate put a hand on his shoulder to still him, and he wanted nothing more in that moment than to shove it away. He felt like an idiot. His body seemed to want to make a fool of him.

The nurse sucked her breath in through her teeth, pulled out the blood pressure cuff and repeated the procedure. "It seems all right," she said. Frowning, she showed him the dial and spouted some meaningless numbers at him.

With a little light-up tool she looked in his ears, nose and throat. Then she peered at his eyes and he could feel his pupils shrinking in the light. This was fucking jail all over again. How was his blood pressure not high? The nurse stood up and began to lead him towards the scale to get his height and weight. A vacutube dropped from the desk nearby. The sound of shattering glass made Kate jump and shriek. Val felt himself relax, though, a deep exhalation of tension.

She must have hit it with her hip...but he didn't think she had.

"You should be heavier for your height," she said, not looking at him, marking something on his chart before she called in an orderly to sweep the glass into a dustpan. In the slanted sunlight that shone through the small, high, prison-like window, the glass glittered and sparkled against industrial pink plastic.

"Thanks," he said. He felt better but not great. With some of the anxiety about the bleeding gone, flushed out by the joy of watching Kate recoil from the broken glass, he thought about TJ. The nurse told them the doctor would be in to see him soon, and left them. Kate looked pissed and worried. He looked down at the shallow slices on his arms. TJ carried a knife. If he'd done something to TJ, he would've gotten deeper cuts than this. And plus the layout of the bike and the body...he couldn't have done it.

When Kate said something he had to ask her to repeat it.

She looked wounded, all big brown eyes.

"Sorry. I was thinking."

"I thought we could get breakfast after this. I didn't mean to scare you."

"I've got a lot on my mind." He knew this would be an opportune time to reach out to her, to hold her, to say he was sorry, not because he actually was sorry, but because that was what she needed to hear. But instead he looked at the few glittery chips of glass left on the tiled floor. He could almost hear her waiting for him to say something, but he kept his mouth shut.

The doctor who bustled in was Mexican, Dr. Villanueva, and Val wondered if she'd been educated in America or Mexico. He supposed it didn't matter. She looked at his ears and eyes, at his chart, and put him on a saline drip because he was dehydrated. It took three stabs to find his vein, but he didn't hold it against her, they were always a bitch to find.

"Your chart says you were released yesterday from the New Mexico State Penitentiary?"

Why phrase it as a question if it's written right there on the chart, Val wondered. He nodded.

"How are you doing?" she asked in a soft accent that would have been soothing if it wasn't steeped in condescension.

"I've been out for about fourteen hours and I'm in the ER 'cause most of the holes in my head are bleeding. How does it sound like I'm doing?"

"You have a lot of anger." The soothing voice didn't help any.

"Is your PhD in the obvious? Tell me something I don't know. Like why I'm bleeding."

"The bleeding seems to have stopped. You are dehydrated. You drank alcohol last night?"

"It was my first night out. What do you think?"

"Answer the questions." Kate glared at him as she interrupted, her arms crossed, her jaw set. "And tell her about the other thing with your head. He needs a blood transfusion. He lost a ton of blood."

It was hard to be angry at her when she was so damn sexy.

"What's wrong with your head?" Villanueva asked, wiping the crook of Val's elbow with an alcohol pad. It took her two stabs, better than most, the second barely hurt. In danger of becoming a heroin addict he was not. He watched the tubing fill up with red.

"It was bleeding from some funny places," he said, looking away from his arm to lock eyes with Kate, daring her to say anything else.

The doctor looked from one of them to the other. "If you choose to tell me, of your free will, you will feel better about it. Letting me know everything can only help you. I'm going to need to do a drug test." She let the implication hang there as she unstuck his arm, picked up the two vials he'd filled and left the room: the drugs will come up on the blood test, might as well tell me about them now.

"As if you needed to lose more blood," Kate said.

"She thinks I've been snorting coke." He closed his eyes.

"You look tired," she said.

"I didn't sleep so well. Someone was distracting me half the night." The other half, well, the other half wasn't so restful either.

"You've mentioned."

"I'm joking, you know."

"Yeah. I'm tired, too." He wanted to tell her it was all right, no one would find TJ, but he wasn't so sure. Villanueva came back and told him she'd put the sample in for testing and he should have his results within a few hours.

Kate looked at him. Cleared her throat. "Did you tell her about the hum in your head?"

"It's gone." He didn't want to talk about this here.

"All last night he was complaining of this hum," Kate said to the doctor. She turned to Val.

"Like a low frequency ringing in my ears."

Villanueva pursed her lips. "I'd like to do some other tests. A CT scan. Just to be safe. A lot of ex-convicts have a hard time adjusting to life on the outside."

"I haven't been out long enough." Val knew he was snapping, but he didn't want to be here anymore. This place seemed too sterile and too clean, with its white walls and white countertops. A different kind of pressure pushed in on him, but this kind he knew was a panic attack. He knew how to hold them off. You couldn't melt down like that in prison. They'd be on you like a pack of hyenas on a limping antelope.

Inhale, count to eight, hold for four, exhale counting to eight. Color started to creep back into the room.

"It happens faster than you think," the doctor said. "You've been in a structured routine for years. Now you're drifting."

"Why don't I take a rain check on that CT scan?"

"I don't think that's a good idea." She checked some paperwork. "We could have you in by two this afternoon. By the time we get the blood work back, we could have you in for the scan."

"I think I'll be all right," Val said, standing. "Thank you for your time." His fight or flight mechanism was kicking in, jangling in his hum-free brain, and he didn't want to start punching anybody, let alone a lady doctor trying to help.

He let Kate deal with the paperwork; he'd deal with the bill later.

Back in the car, Val said, "Can we stop at the Tire Warehouse? I want to get my truck back on track. As charming as it is to ride around in this thing all the time, I'd rather not."

"Yeah, sure," Kate said. She looked far away and pensive.

They didn't talk on the way to the store. Val picked up two used tires, and as he started to move them to the car, Kate made one offhand comment that he shouldn't be doing heavy lifting after his incident. After he politely told her to blow him, she leaned against the yellow hood of the car and watched him, looking surly, sexy and distracted at the same time, chewing at the skin around her fingernails.

Val popped open the Daytona's little trunk and tossed the first tire in. He tried to ignore the dried Hershey's stain that could be nothing but blood. He placed the tire over it, for optimal coverage.

"Is there blood?"

He willed her not to talk about it, but answered, "A little. Looks like old chocolate."

She chewed on her lip, and it made him want her. Easy, down boy. He got in on the passenger's side of the car. He bet she wouldn't let him drive after being in the ER.

"Why didn't you tell her how bad the hum is? It's been driving you crazy since you've been home."

"It's gone now. Been gone since the bleeding stopped."

"So what was it?"

"I don't know," he said.

Kate headed back onto SR-179, through Lott and into the desert to the south.

The pavement ended and they passed a small brown sign informing them they were nearing the Lincoln National Forest.

It started in harmony with the Daytona's engine. At first he thought something was wrong with the motor, it whined a bit louder now. A belt wearing out? He tried in vain to come up with automotive solutions, grasping at them like a drowning man, but as it got firmer and settled around him like a glove, he knew the hum was back.

8

"I've got to go and see my mom." After Val woke up from his nap, an innocent conversation about nothing escalated into crazy monkey sex on the kitchen counter, the kitchen floor, and finally the couch. This, Val thought, was how it was supposed to be. Except for the fucking hum in his head. They lay there now, Val on the inside of the couch.

"Do you want me to come with you?" she asked.

"No."

Kate's lower lip stuck out. Not a deliberate pout, he knew, but a sure sign he'd annoyed her.

"It's not another woman, it's my mother."

"Your mother is another woman." She tried to make it a joke, but her sulky tone shone through.

"I can only see her for an hour."

"Do you want me to come along for the ride?"

"Sure," he said after a moment. He wanted to be alone. However, after so much time with so many other people, being by himself was one scary thought. He would go crazy out here without her. "Thanks for asking."

"I'll drive if you want," she offered.

No fucking way. Now that he changed his flat, he wanted his truck, wanted to drive. "I got it. I want to put some gas in the truck anyway."

"You can drop me off in town, and I'll catch up with you when you're done."

"Sounds good," he said, running his fingers through his hair, leaving it standing upright in a shocked mess. He reached onto the coffee table for his T-shirt.

"You're not wearing that," she said.

It was an *Operation Ivy* shirt, stained, faded and full of holes. Val stood up, and the blood rushing to his head caused the hum to accelerate like a chain saw. He grimaced. After a day, he was starting to get used to it. He collected the rest of his clothes, went down the hall to his bedroom and opened the closet. Everything was so old. He opened his mouth to call to Kate, to have her pick something out, but instead he sung under his breath a bit and selected a worn button-down black shirt. He sang the song in the same pitch as the hum. They played off one another, a pleasant harmony in his skull.

He heard Kate go into the bathroom and close the door behind her. Back in the living room, Val dropped onto the couch to wait, running his hands through his hair in an attempt to make it lie flat. While he waited he laced up his boots.

Kate emerged from the bathroom a moment later, and Val retrieved his black Stetson from the back of the couch and plopped it on his head.

"Kate," he said.

"Yes?"

"I love you."

Her face lit up as she followed him out.

Rain pelted down from the sky and as they stepped out onto the wooden stoop, lightning flickered somewhere in the distance. Kate ran for the pickup, while Val chose to walk and feel the rain. You didn't get to appreciate nature on the inside, not like this. After slamming the truck door behind him, he paused a moment and listened to the rain drum the metal roof. The engine coughed once then roared to life. The CDs in the visor seemed like a museum exhibit, untouched for so long. The truck, with its sparse layer of trash on the floor, felt like a time capsule. Coke had changed its bottle design at least once since the plastic bottle in the cup holder.

He turned his music up, an early *Suicide Machines* album, and it pumped through speakers worth more than the truck itself. Val cranked his window down so he could feel the cool, wet air on his face. Cleansing rain, good tunes, and his best girl...he could almost trick himself into thinking that things were looking up.

9

With a clap of thunder, Val realized the hum was gone. He wasn't sure when it left him, but everything in his mind felt sharper, clean—as if the rain had scraped away the muffling fuzz. A stray patch of sun in the storm lit the Nassar Valley Hospice. Dark, wet pavement indicated he'd missed the rain here, but not by much. Val parked in visitor parking.

He turned the truck off and sat with his fingers on the keys. He could leave. He could come tomorrow. What was one more day of putting things off? Ignoring the temptation, he pulled the keys from the ignition and stepped out into air that smelled like hot, wet asphalt and clean rain.

He walked to the glass doors, taking as much time as he could. They'd told him his mother would be dead before he got out of jail, so he'd spent a great amount of time preparing himself in case he never saw her again. It didn't happen, but his mother's letters eventually stopped coming, replaced by updates written by Angelina Warder, a nurse at the hospice. Angelina was a pretty name, and he'd always pictured her to look like the actress.

Still, he really didn't want to go in there.

Feeling the sun on him, he stopped walking and acknowledged that he could head back to the truck and go. His mother, in and out of consciousness, would never know.

The sun looked both sickly and bright in contrast to the dark storm clouds surrounding it. The hospice was named for the valley it overlooked; the land below was dark with rain.

Apparently they wanted you to have a nice view as you died.

So much goddamn brown. Val, though born here, spent most of his formative years in leafy green Massachusetts, and a slight longing for all that foliage and the ocean pawed at him. Anything, though, was better than the institutional gray he'd faced for the past few years.

He crossed the threshold into the air-conditioned hospice. As the doors slid shut behind him, goosebumps covered his skin in the cool air and he paused to look out a huge picture window overlooking Nassar Valley.

"I'm here to see Caroline Slade." He pulled off his hat and ran his hand through his hair in a final attempt to make it stand down.

The receptionist clacked on her keyboard and slid a clipboard across the desk to him. "Sign in here, please."

"Room 127," she said, looking back to her monitor.

So no one would be going with him? He had to go and face this alone? He didn't know what to expect. Stomach cancer, he knew, but that was about it. Could she talk? Would she know him? The prognosis had been so bad for so long, he sometimes wondered if this was all some manner of psychological prison abuse. Angelina, in her letters, suggested Caroline was waiting for Val.

The receptionist looked back up at him. "Yes?"

"How is she?" he asked. "Is Ms. Warder here?" Nurse Warder? Miss? Mrs.?

The girl clacked on some more keys. "Angelina will be in at five."

Val looked at the clock on the wall. Four-forty.

She looked at his name on the sign in sheet. "Are you her son?"

He nodded. That's me, the son who's never been able to visit his dying mother because he got busted for banging his underage girlfriend. He felt a dark cloud of guilt.

"Sir?"

"Sorry, what?"

The receptionist had been speaking.

"Why don't you go ahead and I'll send Angelina down as soon as she gets here."

"Thanks," Val mumbled, and headed down the hallway, reading door numbers much slower than necessary. His fingers trailed along the wall as he walked. Why put all the numbers in the hundreds for a single story building? He turned the hat over and over in his hands. He should have left it in the truck.

Room 127. A neat hand lettered sign, the ink faded, read: *Caroline Slade.*

The door stood open. He hovered outside it awhile, took a few deep breaths then forced himself through the doorway.

Instead of cold water, medicinal smells and the sounds of the *Home Shopping Network* washed over him. White walls, white bed sheets—adrenaline pumped through him and he wanted nothing more than to run. Out of here, away from her, away from the white, back to the hum. He gulped in a mouthful of air, then another, then remembered what the prison shrink told him. He closed his eyes. Deep breath through the nose. Just like that. Okay.

Caroline looked more like a mummy than a human, her slight form a petite mass under thin blankets. She looked eighty instead of fifty and wore a blonde wig which removed, instead of added, dignity.

He wanted to turn, go back to the desk, explain to the girl that they made a horrible mistake, this wasn't his mother. But there, on the night table was a picture of him with his cousin, standing outside the Boston Museum of Science. This was the picture she chose? He and Kevin were about ten at the time, and they'd both made horrible faces at the camera. Somewhere, at his Aunt's insistence, there was a corollary photograph where they both smiled mom-friendly smiles.

"Mom," he tried to say, but nothing came out. He swallowed, aching for a glass of water, and said it again. She turned to him so slowly he could almost hear her tendons creak.

"Valentine?"

"Yeah." He stepped closer, setting his hat in a chair. The life support unit sat at her side like a sentinel, looking white and futuristic in the artificial light.

"I thought they had you," she said.

"I got out. This morning," he lied, not wanting her to know he let twenty-four hours pass before he came to her.

She smiled. Her eyes looked so dull. They were blue, like his, but much darker. When he was younger, she'd called his eyes husky-blue.

"I thought they'd never let you go."

Not sure how to answer, Val said, "They did." He floundered for something else to say. "And here I am."

She touched his hand with one of her own: hot, dry and delicate like paper. Her nails were painted a light pink and it looked like a sick joke.

"I thought once they had you, they'd never let you go."

"But here I am. My lawyer's pretty good. He wouldn't let them keep me any longer than the six years I promised them."

"You promised them?" Caroline looked worried, but a minute furrowing of her brow was all she could muster.

"Well, I was sentenced."

"You poor boy." She squeezed his hand. "Did they hurt you?"

"No," he lied again. "It really wasn't all that bad." And he closed a door in his head, keeping the memories at bay.

"They hurt me when they took me." At first he thought she meant one of the times she'd been picked up before he was born, once for drunk and disorderly, three times for DUI, and once for prostitution, which had been thrown out of court for lack of evidence. He should have figured it out sooner. She meant a much different *They.* The kind of *They* that warrants a capital *T.* He guessed if she still had her alien fantasies, the drugs couldn't have her too far gone. Val's attention was pulled by the next question. "You haven't seen that girl, have you, the one who got you in trouble?"

More lies. They got easier and easier. "Nope," he said, sliding his eyes down to his hands.

"Good."

"I might look her up, though."

"The girl's trailer trash."

"She can't get me in trouble now."

"Girl like her can always get you in trouble."

Val tasted Rich's shotgun again and suspected his mom might be right.

"I, uh, got my law degree," Val said, staring at her hand in his. *Not that I'll ever be able to use it for anything.*

"You'll make a fine lawyer," Caroline said. "Like your uncle."

Nope, Val thought, *I sure won't.* He smiled. More gently than was probably necessary, he patted her hand.

Blaring from the TV, a woman on the *Home Shopping Network* advised them to call now since only fourteen gold plated brooches with synthetic garnets remained. Outside, fat raindrops plunked against the windows. Alternating rain and patches of sun mottled the valley below.

"Knock knock," someone called. Nurse Warder. Angelina. Who, at possibly four foot eight looked nothing like the actress Val had likened her to. "You must be Valentine," she said; her voice an abrasive coo, and extended a chubby hand up to him. He relinquished his grasp on Caroline and shook.

"Val," he said.

"It's so nice to finally meet you," she said, going to check Caroline's vitals.

As the nurse made small talk, Val wondered if it was appropriate to discuss his mother's condition with her here in the room. He didn't want to talk about her as though she wasn't here, but he also didn't know how much she knew. What if she thought she was getting better? Fuck. He hated being around sick people. Of course she knew what was up.

Val stood, half watching Angelina as she ran through the machines, making small talk with Caroline, who told the nurse Val was back from his Aunt Sally and Uncle Dick's place back east, half looking out at the valley.

"Mr. Slade? Val? May I have a moment?"

"Sure." He followed her into the cool, sterile hall, with its New Mexico tones of brown; brown and turquoise.

"She does know where I've been, right? Sometimes it feels like she does, sometimes it doesn't. Like just now she said I was back from Dick and Sally's. It seemed like she thought I'd been somewhere else."

Angelina smiled a smile she'd probably rehearsed for hundreds of patients and family members. It carried the slightest edge of condescension, and Val decided he did not like this woman, no matter how kind her letters had been while he was in jail.

"I upped her morphine," she said, as though she were speaking to a child. "Your mother has some rather peculiar ideas."

Val said nothing.

"In her lucid moments, she knows you were incarcerated, and she knows why. As you noticed, sometimes she thinks you were still in Connecticut—"

"Massachusetts."

"—with your family. But sometimes...she has this notion." Angelina made a clucking noise. "That she's been abducted by *aliens*." She paused, waiting for a reaction. When she got none, she continued. "And she seems to think you'd been abducted, too."

"Yeah, I know all about it. The book?"

Angelina smiled like a sphinx. He wished he hadn't said anything. But he did, so he plowed forward.

"Did you read it?" he asked. "I actually haven't, but I've heard all the stories. I really appreciated that they didn't use her real name when it was published. Most folks around here know the story."

"Which book do you mean?" Angelina asked. He couldn't tell if she was playing dumb, or thought she was being polite.

"*Trinity*, of course. The book about my mother."

"I skimmed it. I can only imagine she was in quite a state when she wrote it. Alcoholism is a terrible disease, and even then she probably had some of the early symptoms of the cancer."

He rubbed a hand across his face. No one in the jail knew about his mother's book, and he was thankful. He'd told Felix one night, a nocturnal admission of secrets. By the time Felix walked out of there, Val had told him every minute detail about his own life. That was why it was so weird to see him again. Like a walking journal uprooted from its context.

His mother's fantasies always managed to follow him.

* * *

He remembered a night when he was younger, five or six, maybe. Fueled by Aftershock or some other cinnamon scented liquor, his mother had grabbed him by the meaty part of his upper arm and hauled him from his bed to the driveway. She thrust an unsteady hand at the sky, pointing. The only light came from the trailer's kitchen window, a comfortable gold rectangle on the gravel driveway, and the stars glowed bright in the sky. He remembered no moon that night.

"Up there." She jabbed a finger at the sky. "They're coming for you."

He remembered trying to run, but her hand was a cool vice on his bicep, digging into his skin. He started to cry and she had called him a baby, cinnamon-stinking breath in his face. If he thought this was scary, she told him, just wait.

"When they come?" She laughed. "You'll wish it was dear old Mom. No one's going to hear you scream, not out here."

They stood in silence, Caroline watching the sky, Val watching Caroline. Five-year-old Val didn't know how long, somewhere between ten minutes and eternity. When her fingers loosened, he took his arm back, rubbing the red skin where she held him.

He tried calling her name, but she didn't answer, so he went inside, closed the door behind him, and started watching an old monster movie. The creature's dead eyes scared him, so he switched to re-runs instead, even though it meant getting up to change the channels.

The next morning he woke up on the couch, the TV still on, to find Caroline slumped in the easy chair. The bottle of Aftershock—it was Aftershock, that was the one with crystals in the bottom of the bottle—lay on its side in the middle of a dark puddle on the carpet.

Not long after, he'd gone east.

"We've tried every combination of medications we

can think of," Angelina was saying, "but nothing stops the delusions."

"How long does she have?"

"I don't know. No one knows. Six months ago I would have said less than six months. I don't know how she's hanging on; the cancer isn't going into remission. It's stabilized, like it knows how much it can take and let her stay alive."

"So she could go at any time."

The nurse nodded. "All we've been doing for months is making her comfortable." She said some more things Val didn't understand then waddled down the hall to another patient's room.

He went in to say goodbye to Caroline, but found her asleep. He picked up his hat and headed out to his truck, careful not to disturb her.

EXCERPT #2

from *Trinity* by Judd Grenouille ©1988

At first I thought Adrienne was crazy when she told me that she'd figured it all out.

"The ones that look like people call themselves the Tylwyth Teg."

"Adrienne," I said. "The Tylwyth Teg are fairies. It's an old Welsh name for them."

She ignored me, though. "They want our children. They've always wanted our children. That's why they took my first." She was quiet a moment. "They let me see her."

This is common; the visitors often let mothers see their taken children. (See *Intruders*, 1987, Budd Hopkins.) Kathie Davis, the subject of Hopkins' book, reported seeing her daughter several times.

"I don't remember, though. I remember that I saw her, and everything in my heart was so wonderful. I don't know what she looked like, or where we were, or anything. Will you hypnotize me again?"

It has been eight months since I have last seen Adrienne. She is wearing a white dress; her hair is down, cascading over her shoulders. She looks innocent, like a girl herself. I don't smell alcohol on her this time. She claims she is making an effort to turn her life around.

"Tell me your theories first," I coax.

"They aren't theories. I'm tellin' you what they told me." Now she looks wary instead of innocent. "The gray ones are the Sangaumans. The Tylwyth Teg want their mind powers, but they can't find a way to breed with 'em. So they've traveled the galaxy for years and years—millions of years—looking for a third species to do the mix with. And they found us."

"Why do the Sangaumans take you to their ship?"

Adrienne sighs, like I'm slow. "Because the Tylwyth Teg are trying to make a human/Sanguaman baby in me. And they have. They made two of 'em, but the second one must nota worked 'cause they let me keep him."

"What will you tell your son when he asks where he came from?"

"The truth."

"Good," I tell her. I wish more of the abductees that I work with could reach Adrienne's level of openness.

"The Sanguamans like to make regular check-ups. It's the Tylwyth Teg that really do things to me. My Earth doctor told me I can't have more babies. I think they did something to be sure I don't have any accidents, human or alien. Please hypnotize me, let me find out about my baby girl?"

I pull out my pocket watch, and set it spinning. Adrienne stares at it hungrily, drinking in the way the light from the open window plays on the gold of its surface. It spins, and as she slips under, her shoulders slump.

The following is an actual transcript of our conversation:

JG: Tell me about seeing your daughter.

AG: No. (She shakes her head violently.)

JG: What day did you see her?

AG: Two months ago.

JG: Tell me about that day.

AG: No.

JG: About the afternoon. Tell me everything that happened.

(AG relaxed as she talked about going swimming at a reservoir, going home, smoking some dope, and going to bed.)

AG: When I woke up my bed was surrounded in white light. I thought, gosh, the neighbors must be real mad about all this light, I'm going to wake them all up.

JG: You are or the light is?

AG: The light is here for me. I'm rising out of my bed. I'm floating. I don't mind when the gray ones take me, but when the Tylwyth Teg come…I know it's not going to be good.

JG: Relax. You're safe. Where are you now?

AG: The ship. I'm with them, I'm in a big dark room, but it isn't an examination table, it's a room. I'm not strapped down or anything. (She sounds surprised.)

JG: Are you alone?

AG: Um…no. They are there with me, dark, humanoid shapes. They have something little with them, little and white. What is it? (Her voice is guarded, cautious, almost disgusted.) It's white and fat and crawling…oh my God. Oh my God! It's her! It's her! It's her!

JG: Tell me what she looks like?

AG: They let her crawl to me and her face is beautiful. Her eyes are like theirs, though, big and black, taking up too much of her face, but her hair is the finest, silkiest blonde. She doesn't have any nose, slits like they got, but her mouth is perfect. She's shy, she sits down aways away from me. She must be cold up there, naked and crawling on the floor. I tell her I'm her mama, I tell her I love her, and I want to go to her, but I can't. I don't know what they'd do. So I talk quiet to her, and look at her, plump little baby body, she looks healthy, but pale, you can see right through her skin, all blue veins. I reach out my hand but she don't move. We stay like that. Mighta been a few minutes. Mighta been all night. (AG swallows, tears welling up in her eyes.) Then I'm back in my bed. And I cried, and cried and cried.

10

Kate stood in the street outside Woodstone's Saloon, breathing in the scent of air wiped clean by the rain. She didn't want to go in, go drink, and slip into all the old patterns. Like most American downtowns, Lott had seen better days. The historical society did their best to spruce it up. They had succeeded in bringing a few businesses in, a new restaurant, a coffee shop which seemed to be doing well, and a sports bar. But there were still empty storefronts, a few of them boarded up with plywood where kids had thrown rocks through the glass.

She couldn't ask Val what he intended to do about his dying mother. That seemed crass and tacky. She couldn't stay here, but she couldn't leave him, not alone, not after waiting for so long. Santa Fe was big and sprawling and anonymous. Even now Kate dropped her head in hopes of avoiding being seen. "Papa" Guerrerez, her brother's old dealer, sauntered by with a girl who looked like she wasn't legal.

If Papa noticed her, he didn't give any indication. She looked up and watched them stroll into Woodstone's.

She stood and went to the new restaurant. The old restaurant, Rosie's, was where she'd worked all through high school. Rosie's daughter owned it now, Kate had heard. She didn't want to see any of those people.

No one in the new restaurant—Loco Cabana! according to the menu, exclamation point and all—knew who she was. A new crop of bored, zit-faced high-schoolers worked the tables, and Kate saw herself in the dejected looking blonde who asked her if she wanted anything to drink.

Kate ordered an iced tea.

From where she sat she could see the street through the big windows, tinted to keep the sun out. A young man wandered in, gazing around as if this wasn't quite what he expected, and set himself in a booth across from hers. She kept her eyes out the window; the sun was out now, baking the rain off the street. In her peripheral vision she couldn't help but notice how straight the man sat, the prim way he held his menu. Something familiar about him? Perhaps they were two people alone in an empty restaurant. Kindred spirits?

That wasn't it.

He didn't look like the type of fellow to sit alone in a restaurant. His sweatshirt, UNM, was preppy but grubby, he looked like a frat boy, and those, she knew, never went anywhere without a pack in tow.

He ordered water, lots of it, and she listened in to his peculiar speech patterns when she saw Rich, wife in tow, strolling down the street. He still wore his uniform, must have just gotten off work.

She regretted the seat by the window. They were tinted, so maybe he wouldn't—Rich saw her. She looked away, but he changed his trajectory. He let the tinted glass door swing shut behind him so Maria, his wife, had to catch it and let herself in.

He filled the table across from her, and Maria dropped

to the chair on her left. She was trapped.

"Where you been?" he asked.

She shrugged.

"You seen TJ?"

Act appalled. "TJ?" She curled her lip up, raised her eyebrows, as if the thought of her seeing TJ was the most ridiculous thing she'd ever heard of.

"Uh huh."

"Why would I see TJ?"

"Where's the child molester?" Steamrolling over questions was Rich's specialty, and Kate wondered how he functioned as a State Trooper, where much of his job included asking questions and listening to the answers.

"With his mother." There was no point in lying.

"One drunk loony deserves another."

"Rich, lower your voice." Maria spoke softly, with a voice that didn't get much use. Raised in Mexico, she spoke with a lovely, lilting accent. She was also deadly, Kate knew. Back when Rich rolled with a third-rate gang, she'd been one tough bitch. He domesticated her, though, and it was funny to see her in clothes that looked grown-up instead of belly shirts and headbands. They'd been friends, kind of, but Maria's alliance lay with Rich.

Rich glared at her. The old Maria never would have put up with that shit.

"He is listening to you," she said, almost too low to hear. Maria would enable Rich until he died. Or she died, which was more likely to happen first.

Rich's head snapped up, and he looked around, his head swiveling on his bull neck. The frat boy still held his menu, but seemed to stare through it.

"We got a extra room you can stay in," Rich said, looking back at Kate, changing tracks so fast it made her head spin.

"I have a room in Santa Fe," she said, which at the moment was bullshit, but she could get one. "And Val's let me know as long as I'm here, his place is my place."

"You disgrace me, you know that?"

"How do I disgrace a drug-dealing dirty cop?"

He smiled a faux sympathetic smile.

She guessed she could scream. He wouldn't hurt her here, not in his uniform. She snuck a glance at Maria, but her attention was on the man sitting by himself.

Maria couldn't save her. And even if she could, Kate knew she wouldn't.

James Spencer came in then, wearing his own uniform, one of the deputies of the Otero County Sheriff's Department. He graduated the same year Val did, the year Rich should have. He had a working knowledge of the history between them all (he didn't know the whole truth—almost no one did. Maria certainly didn't) and so he took his hat off and pulled up a chair at the head of the table. Kate could have kissed him, bless his good timing.

"Afternoon," he said. With his round boyish face and thinning sandy hair, he didn't look like much to be afraid of. When Spence and Rich talked about wanting to go into law enforcement, Val had been with them for some time, thinking about being a cop, moving somewhere larger than Lott to do it. He'd thought about going east or west, LA or New York, and the idea scared her. Then he got the law school idea in his head. Poor Val.

And it was all Rich's fault.

"Get out of here, Spencer."

"Haven't seen you in a while, Kate. How are you?" Spence asked, ignoring Rich.

"Great," she said.

"Your brother bothering you?"

Kate opened her mouth to say yes, but Rich spoke over her again, as he liked to do. "I ain't seen her for a while myself. We're catching up on old times."

"I think we're about caught up," Kate said.

"How's Val?" Spence asked. "I hear his mom's real

bad."

"He's all right. He's with her now. It's the first he's seen her."

"Spencer, you got TJ Drinkwater down in your drunk tank?" Rich asked. Kate sucked in her breath, tried to mask it with a drink of water. Maria watched her for a moment, her brown eyes calculating, then turned her attention back to the frat boy.

"Nope. Haven't seen him in a while. Maybe Monday night at Woodstones?"

"He was supposed to come by this afternoon and didn't."

Spence laughed. "He's probably hung over somewhere, maybe up in Allenstown with his baby mama?"

"Don't think so."

Maybe he got sick of your bullshit and finally took off. It was what she should have said, but she was worried Maria would see through her, and know the truth.

"Give us a call tomorrow afternoon and we'll see what we can do." Spence didn't sound concerned. Excellent. Thank goodness Rich wasn't a classier guy with more upstanding friends.

"I can take care of it myself. I was curious."

"Sure thing. I think Kate wants to order some food, maybe you and the Missus should get moving along."

"I want to order something, too."

"Is he bothering you, Kate?" Spence asked.

"Yes," she said. Speaking out to her brother caused this knot in her gut. Pathetic. "Get him out of my face." It made her mouth go dry to speak it out loud.

"I'm on duty, Rich. I gotta do as she asks. You don't want to cause trouble."

"Not while you're around."

Spence frowned. "You don't want to cause trouble."

Rich mock saluted with an easy smile that drove Kate crazy. "Anything for you, Deputy." He used the word like a racial slur. Spence nodded goodnight as Rich and Maria stood. Rich followed Maria's gaze to the man's table. He sat with an untouched cup of coffee.

"You like what you hear, hombre?"

He looked up at him.

"I know not what you speak of."

"You know not what—where're you from? You some sort of...European retard?"

"Rich! For God's sake get out of here," said Spence, sliding his chair back and standing up. "You're officially disturbin' the peace."

"I forgot I was under the eyes of Otero County's finest. I'll be on my way, Deputy."

They left and Kate watched them stop out on the sidewalk, looking left and then right. Looking for Val?

"Don't blame you one bit for leaving. Bad kin's like a bad stain."

She chuckled. "I can't wait to go again."

"What's up with that guy?" Spence lowered his voice and nodded towards the man and his coffee.

"Maria said he was listening."

Kate glanced at him, over Spence's shoulder. He stared off into space, dreamlike. But not. More focused than a dream. Like a robot. What a weirdo. He turned to her, his head moving like it was mounted on clockwork, and they made eye contact. Kate looked at her place mat. He must be high on something.

"He's not bothering me, he's fine." Something about him was the opposite of fine.

"How is Val? Really."

She paused before she answered. She hated the way his eyebrows dropped with pity. Sympathy, probably, but it felt like pity.

"He's a little spacey. Haunted, almost. I think his mom's bothering him more than he's telling me."

Spence nodded. "He was gone for a long time."

"You're telling me."

Spence smiled, pointing out the window as Val's pickup pulled up. "Is that him? Still with the same old pickup?"

"Yup. He thinks I'm at the bar." She got up, went to the door and stepped out from the air conditioning into the sun. The pavement was dry now, and the sky gave no indication of the afternoon showers they'd had.

For a split second she was certain Rich would be lurking behind the door, waiting to take her, but the street was quiet until she called Val's name.

He looked to her as he slammed the truck door. His eyes looked red, high or crying, please let him have been crying. He crossed the street on a diagonal. Kate hoped Spence wouldn't bust him for jaywalking.

"How is she?" Kate asked, feeling obligated. The real subtext of the question was "how soon can we leave?"

"Eh," said Val. "Not well. She's not really with it."

"Is she in pain?"

"I don't think so. They have her pretty well doped up."

"I have a table inside. Spence has been sitting with me."

"No shit! Good ole Spence."

He followed her into the restaurant, taking off his hat like the gentleman he wasn't, and shook Spence's hand. The strange man looked up, and his gaze captured Val's attention.

"Hang on a minute." Val went to the man's table. "Do I know you?"

"I do not believe so."

He sure didn't talk like a frat boy.

"You sure? You look awful familiar."

"I am certain that I do not know you."

"Good to know."

Val came back and took the seat across from Kate,

where Rich had been sitting.

"You want to get dinner?" he asked.

"I'm not really hungry. You can if you want to."

"Spence? Hungry?"

"I'm on duty."

"And you can't eat?"

"I'll get something later."

"Well then what are we doing here? Let's go over to Woodstones."

"Maybe I do want something. A small steak, maybe?" She didn't want him drinking. He was being so strange and unpredictable, moods and bleeding. Some of it could be attributed to the stresses he'd been though lately. But not all of it.

"Okay then." Val gave her a funny look, then picked up the menu. She half smiled at him. He and Spence made small talk. When the food came her steak looked like a piece of a car tire with "authentic looking" flame marks. She wasn't hungry, she picked at her dinner.

Spence's radio went off, a crackling domestic disturbance in the trailer park at the south end of town.

"Sorry guys," Spence said, "I'll catch you later, though. Val, we should get a beer later this week."

"Sounds good," Val said.

"Oh hey—before I go. I heard something about a mountain lion out your way…most likely rabid. Watch yourselves."

"Ten-four." Val fired off a mock salute.

Kate gave her steak another hearty poke with her fork.

They sat, looking at one another. "I called Felix. Hoped maybe he could come out tonight, do something. I left him a message with your cell number. Let me know if he calls, okay?"

Kate looked at her phone. It was on silent, and she made sure she hadn't missed any calls.

"Shall we leave?" Val asked.

"If you want to," she said, clearly meaning yes. She caught frat boy from the corner of her eye, watching. He didn't even have the tact to drop eye contact when Kate met his gaze. She didn't look away, at first, but finally she dropped her eyes.

"You lost," Val said, not even trying to be discreet or keep his voice down. Maybe frat boy's bad manners weren't that astounding.

"He must be on something."

"Or a jackass."

"He's following us. Look."

And he was, wandering out of the restaurant, looking lost and inspired, all at the same time.

"Well, he can't get in the truck with us. No zombies allowed."

11

"Val!" A voice from across the street, from the parking lot of Woodstone's saloon.

Val's face lit up when he saw the man who'd called his name. He was tall and slender, almost pretty, with dark features that weren't quite Latino. Maybe they'd wave, and then they could head home, she thought.

Nope. She followed Val across the street. Kate racked her brain to try and remember who this guy was, no one she knew from school. Val let her catch up to him, then he took her by the shoulders and thrust her at the pretty-looking man.

"Kate, this is Felix. Felix, this is Kate."

Oh!

She should have known, and as Felix kissed her cheek, she blushed with embarrassment. Of course. Who else would have gotten Val to perk up like that? Maybe it was what he needed. They'd go out, have a few drinks, she could drive his drunk ass home if need be. It would be fun.

"You're as beautiful as he said you were."

She smiled as she met his chocolate brown eyes, but the smile died on her lips. Meeting his gaze, there was something about him she didn't quite like, something that made her wary. She didn't think she liked Felix very much.

He and Val embraced in a quick man-hug.

She was being stupid.

"How's life on the outside treating you?" Felix asked.

"It's been interesting," Val said, choosing his words.

"And your mother?"

Val let out a long breath. "Let's get some brews and head out on the patio."

They stepped through the wooden saloon doors with carved-antler handles into air conditioned air, darkness, and twangy pop country.

"Is this that fucking song," he shouted to be heard over the music and the din, "about checking for ticks being sexy?"

She shoved him playfully, and he slung a long arm across her shoulders. For the first time, he looked so happy. He and Felix ordered PBRs in cans, and she got a red microbrew they had on tap. As Felix and Val babbled about beer, Kate scanned the place for familiar faces. She didn't want to see any of them. The bartender was in a class a few years ahead of Val—she couldn't remember his name—and they chatted for a few minutes.

The beers came and they went outside to the fenced-in patio. Four of the ten picnic tables were taken, no one of any interest. She let out her breath in relief. Out here the Eagles were playing, which were slightly more up Val's alley. Kate sat facing the entrance to the bar.

"I'm sorry to be a jackass," said Felix. "But I have a thing. I really can't sit with my back to the door. It freaks me out."

"He's been that way ever since I met him," Val echoed.

"Not that I would mind sitting over there with you.

But I think your man here would punch me in the mouth if I did."

"I would," Val said agreeably, sitting with his back to the door. He held up his beer. "A couple more of these, and I'll punch anyone!"

Kate got up and moved around to Val's side of the table, and Felix took her spot.

"Shit's been crazy," Val said.

"It's only been a day. What happened?"

Kate knew Felix could see the look she gave Val, the eye daggers telling him to shut the hell up. But he told. He told everything. She kept watch while Val talked, making sure no one could hear them. What was he thinking? Felix looked sympathetic, appropriately surprised in the right places. She wanted to go home.

"Another beer?" Val asked her.

"No, thanks. I'll drive you home."

"Wonderful." He kissed her on the forehead, a wet, beer-smelling kiss, and made his way inside.

"How are you?" Felix asked Kate.

"Me?"

"Yeah, this has all got to be really tough on you."

"I'm fine. I want to get out of here. I don't like Lott."

"I'm renting a place outside of town," Felix said. "I think it's a cute little town."

"You didn't grow up here." She scanned the patio. "I can name all but three of the people out here."

Felix laughed. It seemed forced. "I get your point."

"I like Santa Fe. I like feeling lost there."

"But you're not leaving until Val's got some closure with his mother, right?"

"Right," she said, taking careful measure to keep the resentment out of her voice. Felix looked at her like he could tell she didn't care one whit whether Caroline Slade lived or died. Well why should she? The woman had always been a bitch to her.

"Be strong," Felix said. "Val needs you."

"I know. That's why I'm here."

* * *

About an hour later, they left Woodstone's. Felix said goodnight and headed off in the opposite direction. Val insisted he was fine to drive, and he sounded fine, so she let him. He blasted the music, as usual, until she turned it down.

Headlights flashed behind them in the dusk.

"What did you think of Felix?"

She didn't tell him she thought there was something off about him. Something about the protective way he watched Val.

"Seems nice," she said.

"He was my other half for five years."

"That sounds kind of gay."

"Eh, only once or twice."

She looked at him.

"I'm kidding. Ha ha, funny, joke?"

Sometimes she couldn't tell. They rode along for a while, turning off the pavement and onto dirt roads.

"Who do you think killed TJ?" she asked.

"I am trying my damndest not to think about it. We shouldn't have touched him, but now that we did, all we can hope is no one finds him."

"I should do something to make it look like he's out of town. Call Rich, or something."

"That's the stupidest thing I've ever heard. It's a sure-fire way to get it tracked back to us."

"I can do it so he won't catch me." One of those call scramblers, maybe?

"He's stupid, but he's got police training, some of which must have stuck." Val was right, of course. Rich had a terrifying clever streak. You couldn't call it smart, it was more like whatever force allows a terrier to relentlessly ferret rats from their holes. Tenacity, perhaps? Deep instinct?

"I think we need to leave it. The less we do the better. Rich will be looking for any reason to connect this to me," Val said, gazing out into the darkening evening. With each day, TJ's trail would grow colder, and they would be safer. Once they left Lott and melted into Santa Fe, it would all be better.

She thought of TJ as Val drove. Stupid, soft TJ, who in his awkward way, wanted to be loved.

A bump in the road brought her back to the present. The sky was a rich indigo, delicious and purple. Val turned down his driveway; the yellow headlights of the truck splashed the front of the trailer. Out on the road, a car passed the trailer. They didn't get a lot of traffic out here, particularly not at night. Probably some kids, looking for a place to park, or drink. Unless it was the frat-boy. The thought chilled her. He didn't look well enough to drive.

Kate stretched her legs as she got out; Val came around and took her hand. They paused a moment, and looked up at the sky. They let their eyes adjust to the dark. Black shadows became things: bushes, Val's mom's old Oldsmobile, gray and silent off to the side.

Something moved over by the Oldsmobile, a rustling, scraping sound of feet on loose stone.

TJ's killer? The rabid puma? Something else?

"We should go inside," Kate said, feeling very small and very quiet.

"It's nothing. Coyote or something."

"It's too loud for coyotes. And they would never come this close to us. Let's go in." She thought of the pistol in Val's drawer. Of Rich's shotgun, what had Val done with that?

"Okay," he said, turning his face to the sky. He never

bothered to lock the door, his mother never had, so Kate went in and found herself alone in the dark living room, waiting for him. *Come on, come on, come on*...she willed him in. There was another sound from out there, and she opened the door again, peering out into the yard. She wanted to call his name, but didn't want to call attention to herself. Feet on loose stone again—not feet but shoes. Why had he left the steps? She slipped back into the living room, and without turning on the lights, she went to his bedroom, went to the top drawer, rooted through folded boxers and paired socks—his mother's neatness, not his own—until she found the hard, cloth-wrapped lump. It was heavier in her hand than she remembered, the entire time she'd been in Santa Fe she hadn't seen a gun, hadn't seen anyone beat up, or threatened, or anything like that. Once she'd seen a drunk motorist shouting at a cop as she drove by.

This place was violence, the real Wild West.

She unwrapped the gun and its matte surface reflected no light. She ejected the clip and saw it was fully loaded. Leave it to Val to leave his gun loaded for six years in his underwear drawer.

It felt strange and alien in her hand; she hadn't used one for years. Like she'd seen in movies, she kept it pointed at the floor.

If there was something out there, it probably was gone by now. She hadn't been quick about getting the pistol.

She moved through the dark hallway, through the living room, and stepped out onto the wooden steps. They creaked under her weight. A slight breeze rustled the leaves on some of the scrub nearby, sang through the tall grass.

"Val." It was barely a whisper, lost in the breeze. The saliva was gone from her mouth, replaced with the sour, Chinese-soup taste of adrenaline. She said it again, louder. "Val." This one came out as a croak. Nothing. She stepped to the next step, feeling the wood flex beneath her. It would break and she would shoot herself in the foot, and then the killer would know where she was and finish her off.

She stepped down to the gravel of the driveway, scanning left and then right. She willed spit to her dry mouth, and called his name. Nothing happened, but there was a sound of rattling stones from somewhere. Was he (it?) killing Val right now?

Very aware that her back was exposed, she moved around the dark bulk of the truck. She raised the gun, repeating in her head the mantra, *don't shoot Val, don't shoot Val.*

Something tan moved in her peripheral vision. Without thinking, completely adverse to her mantra, she raised the gun and squeezed the trigger, the flash from the muzzle blinded her, and the recoil sent her arm wild, snapping at her wrist. The brass cartridge landed hot on her shoulder, and she brushed it off, afraid of getting burned. The sound was impossible, consuming everything, and leaving a ringing in her ears. Her heart pounded as she got her bearings in the darkness.

"What the fuck are you doing?" Val shouted from the direction of the Oldsmobile. It sounded like he was calling from the end of a tunnel.

He came out of the darkness towards her, a floating face and arms, his black shirt melting into the darkness behind him.

"I thought..." her own voice felt padded and far away, the ringing making conversation almost impossible.

Reaching over, he plucked the gun from her hand, fingered the safety, and popped the clip out.

"There's someone out here," Val said.

The relief she'd felt at finding Val, and the shame from firing blindly into nothing were replaced by the same sick fear that there was someone here.

"I think I scared him off, I made it around behind him, when he saw me he headed for the hills. It was that schizoid frat kid from the restaurant. Since you decided to shoot up the place, I bet he won't be back."

"That doesn't make sense. Why would he follow us?"

"I don't know. He's gone now, I guess."

"Do you think he killed TJ?" An even worse thought overtook her. "Do you think he saw what we did to TJ? Is he trying to blackmail us?"

Val hissed at her to be quiet. "Stop talking about it. If he is still here, we don't want him hearing anything. Let's go in the house."

Kate rubbed at her wrist, jarred from the pistol's recoil.

"Maybe tomorrow we can do some target practice. You're going to kill someone with this thing."

Maybe tomorrow we should pack up and go to Santa Fe, Kate thought, *where I won't have to kill anyone with this thing.*

12

Maria walked across the parking lot, holding the small bag of groceries. They made the parking lot too big, back from when they thought the town would boom, and she hated crossing it. She didn't drive, and didn't want to ask Rich to take her out for more rice. She should have thought of it on her own.

Her heels clacked the pavement, and she looked forward to taking her shoes off at home, maybe having a quick drink, and then cooking dinner. Rich wasn't home yet, who knew when he'd be around. He'd been deep and moody since Slade got out of prison, and Maria was ready for some kind of resolution, kill him, run him off, get over him...she didn't care which, stop mooning over it. She never said that, of course. Maria also had some suspicions about Rich's absences lately, but even if it was an affair, it came with a little relief. Let him bother someone else.

Shoes scraped asphalt behind her, and she glanced over her shoulder. A man walking a few paces back. Clean cut, dark, and very pretty. Not a threat. She was from the barrio; she knew a threat when she saw one. She could break that guy in half. In the dusk, the streetlights cast strange orange light, and the shadows overlapped on the tar, stretching one way, then another, disappearing all together in the dark holes between the lights.

The street was well lit, and it wasn't far to the house.

Drink then food.

While she knew a threat and this man didn't look like one, she also couldn't shake her sense of unease. Something here was wrong; it tickled the back of her neck, making her hair stand up there, making her feel primitive and animal. She looked around again, keeping her head up and her shoulders back. Nothing but the pretty boy.

It reminded her of the afternoon when her brother died—was murdered—back home. There'd been something going down all day, and while she didn't know what it was, she couldn't relax, could feel something coming. She wondered if Rich was all right. She was grateful to him; she had a nice house and nice things, but always a feeling of unease, of not wanting to tip the boat. If she left him, where would she go? Better to stay and to keep her head down.

She didn't want to look around again, didn't want to look uneasy, or give whoever might be watching a clue she was nervous. She kept her eyes straight ahead, slid a manicured hand into her purse and closed her fingers around the handle of her knife.

Rich told her not to carry it, that she should bring a gun instead, someone would take the knife from her and use it on her. He forgot, sometimes, who she had been before he took her over. She could handle the knife.

Feeling it in her hand let her walk taller, with more confidence.

Out of the parking lot and onto the street.

There were people here, and though she knew they had a habit of looking the other way, she felt better with them around.

A dry breeze began to blow, brushing her long hair back, making her large hoop earrings sway.

She turned down her street; it wasn't far to the grocery store, past house after house, all of them identical. America might be the Promised Land, but you gave up a lot when you came here, compromised big pieces of yourself. Better to be a little bit unhappy here than dead in Cuaron. She let go of the knife to pick up her keys, and the man behind her seemed to realize that. He was up behind her, close, on the doorstep with something hard—a gun? But it didn't feel quite like a gun—in her back.

"Let's go inside," he said in her ear, his breath pleasant.

From the corner of her eye she could see it was the pretty boy. She'd let her guard down, and here she was.

She admitted him into her home, turned to face him as he let the door click behind him.

"Rich isn't here," she said. What was he holding? No gun she'd ever seen, something new? Plastic? Was it some kind of dart gun?

"Not interested in Rich."

This was surprising.

"What do you want?" Maria asked, still fairly certain she could give this man a run for his money. She stepped out of her heels, feeling the cool clay tiles under her stocking feet. She kept her purse over her shoulder. She wanted the knife close. You weren't supposed to keep weapons in your purse; they were too hard to get to when you needed them. Back home she'd kept them in her tall boots, strapped to her leg under a skirt, on her wrists. But suburbia softened her. She accepted she might be paying the price today.

They stood in the hallway. If she could get him to the kitchen, she'd have a shot at the cooking knives.

"Would you like a beer?" she asked.

He laughed. "I hold you at gunpoint and you offer me

a beer?"

"That's not like any gun I've seen," she said.

"Nope, it's not."

She moved towards the kitchen, moving like a dancer, making no sound with her feet.

He took a few steps after her, keeping the weapon trained on her. She was afraid of it because he treated it like she should be. He respected it, chances are it was dangerous. It looked like a toy, but something told her it wasn't.

She would carve great lines down this pretty asshole's face.

"Where are you headed?" he asked, putting a hand on her arm.

"The kitchen. If you don't want a drink, I do."

"Easy there," said the man. "Why don't you stay right where you are? Or better yet, let's get out of here." He gestured towards the back door, the opposite direction from the kitchen.

"I was offering you a drink."

He smiled at her, a wide, teeth-whitening commercial smile. She carried her purse towards the sliding patio door and he followed. She put a hand on it to slide it open, but the smile dropped from his face.

"Wait," he said. "Don't open it."

She took advantage of his momentary confusion and plunged her hand into the bag. She could find her checkbook, lipstick in three shades—there it was. The switchblade her brother had given her when she turned twelve and some of the older guys in the neighborhood started giving her trouble.

She pulled it free and popped the blade in a single fluid motion, whirling on him. He stepped back—how could he be so fast?—but she got him with the tip, from chin to cheekbone. One hand went to his face and the other hand went to her wrist, which he slammed against the door jamb, knocking the knife to the floor with a harmless clatter. Pain shot up her arm, amplified when he squeezed, and she felt all those little bones grinding together. She didn't cry out.

"Drop the purse." Red oozed down his face.

She didn't, and he squeezed again. She opened her hand and it thumped down beside the knife.

Only then did he take his eyes off her and glance out the sliding glass door. He pulled her away, deeper in the house.

"When's your husband getting home?"

"I don't know."

This time when he squeezed, something broke. She let a hiss of air out between her lips, but nothing else. Everything went white for a moment, but she breathed through it. *I've been through worse, I've been through worse, I've been through worse*. The colors settled back into place and she felt much more grounded.

"When is he getting home?"

"I don't know! I think he's fucking his mistress."

"I'm going to let go of your arm. If you try anything else, you're dead."

The man's eyes slipped to the door again, to the outside where full dark had fallen. He was afraid of something out there. Absently, he wiped at the blood on his face. Even if he got stitches right now, that was going to leave a scar.

"What do you want?"

"I want you, sweetheart." He smiled at her.

"At least tell me your name."

"Felix. Nice to meet you."

Where had she heard the name before? Slade had a friend Felix. This must be Slade's doing.

"Rich will kill you when he finds out what you're doing."

"Yeah?" Felix said. "What am I doing?"

That was a question she couldn't answer.

He smiled, stretching the cut on his face, making it bleed a bit more. She looked down at the knife but he followed her gaze and kicked it away.

"I'll tell you what I'm doing. I'm going to give you a little present, and then I'm going to send you to keep an eye on Valentine Slade for me."

What? That made no sense. "Aren't you his friend?"

"In more ways than he realizes. The only hiccup to my little plan is that Val's protector is out there, waiting for us. And we don't have a prayer against it. I'd much rather it guts you than me."

What?

"Is this a joke?" *A joke resulting in a broken wrist and a sliced-open face?*

"Yeah, think of it as a joke. Go sit on the couch."

She stayed where she was. None of this made sense. If this was true why was he telling her? And did he really think that she would go along with his plan?

"Go. I need you to watch him. You need eyes, ears and legs for that, not much else. I can break your other wrist. Maybe an elbow? You certainly don't need your nose, and it hurts like a bitch when it's broken."

"I know."

"Your husband break your nose?" Felix asked. She went to the couch and sat down.

"Among other people."

Felix peered at her. "It still looks pretty good. Your husband is a sack of shit." He pulled a jar from his pocket. Something dark was in there, clouded by the shadows in the room. But it was moving, throbbing. It wanted to get out of the jar; it was like a leech, black and probing.

"What are you doing?"

"This won't hurt a bit. Uncomfortable, yes. Pain, no."

"No way."

Pushing him away, she punched him, as hard as she

could, in the ear with her left hand. Fast as a cat, he took her left wrist and brought his forehead down on her nose. Crack. The white came back. She reminded herself, over and over, as her eyes filled up with tears, that she'd been through worse. People had done crueler things to her, and she was still here. Tears slid down her cheeks, cooled by the air conditioning. She willed the white away, and opened her eyes. The jar landed on the carpet with a thud. The organism inside looked irritated and began thrashing. Had she killed it? She blinked to clear the tears out of her eyes so she could see. What was going on?

Felix straddled her, pinning her arms against the couch. "Move and I'll break your other wrist. I have plenty of time. I can play all night if I need to." He twisted on top of her, and picked up the jar. He opened it, and the turgid little thing plopped out onto his palm.

Then she cried out. She was ashamed, but it had surprised her.

"What is that?"

"Relax. You won't remember a thing."

Won't remember a thing? What was happening to her?

He set the thing on her face, rested it on her upper lip. She started struggling, but Felix let her go and stepped back, way back. That was a mistake. For a split second Maria cataloged all the ways she could get in the kitchen and get the knives, then the fucking thing pressed its way into her nose! All thoughts of Felix vanished. She couldn't breathe and the panic lambasted her, pressing on her ears and her face. Then her nose was clear again, but it was in her sinuses. She could feel it moving! She drew blood with her fingernails clawing at it. No, think of Felix, think of the knives. She was going to die, but she wasn't going to die alone. One hand pressed over her nose, she shambled to the kitchen, falling and breaking a vase filled with silk flowers. Felix didn't follow her; waited in the dark of the living room. She closed her hand over the handle of the butcher knife as a wave of…something…washed over her. Dread and adrenaline flooded her, electrifying every follicle on her body. Time was running out. If she couldn't kill Felix, she'd have to do herself. The big knife seemed to weigh a thousand pounds, and as she lifted it from the block, it caught the hall light on its blade. Then everything went black.

13

Felix could hear her slamming around in the kitchen. It would take a few minutes for the Beta to take hold. If she hurt herself that would be unfortunate, but not the end of the world. Felix needed someone to watch his back tonight. The frat boy would be there too, but Felix thought doing it this way was kind of a neat little joke. Take that, Rich. Sure, Maria might make it through ok, but he doubted it. Her job was to watch for the monster, and run slower than he did. This was when it would be at its most volatile, and having two Betas would be the most efficient way to handle it.

The sounds from the kitchen stopped. Maria rounded the corner, pressing one hand against the wall to steady herself, the other against her nose. She raised her head and looked at him, brown eyes devoid of everything that made her Maria. Pity. She would have made a fine Tylwyth Alpha. He liked them with some life to them.

When she pulled her hand away from her nose it came away bloody. He offered her a handkerchief to wipe it off. She took it, dabbing mechanically at herself, looking at the blood as though she was confused. She had nice lips, if you could get into humans. Sometimes, when you were stuck here for so long, you had to get into humans. Not now, though, it didn't pay to mix business and pleasure. He'd tried making it with one of the Betas once. It was like masturbating, but...clumsier.

Felix's car was parked at the grocery store a few blocks away. They should have time to make it there before the monster got interested in them, it had the frat boy to worry about, a much more pressing concern.

"Get some shoes on."

Maria obediently went to the closet and started to step into a pair of stilettos.

"No, walking shoes. Sneakers."

She rooted around in the back of the closet, but eventually she came up with them, and sat on the couch to put them on. She fumbled with the laces, but Felix could see her dexterity was coming back to her.

When she finished, she stared down at her shoes. She'd looked for so long that Felix was about to say something to her, when she raised her blank eyes to his.

"What next?" she asked, no longer speaking English, Felix realized, but her native Spanish. The Beta must have triggered some wiring in her brain. Funny, the way the human mind worked.

"We go for a stroll, then we go for a ride."

"When do we deliver the Alpha?"

"Easy. It'll be a while. Tonight."

Maria nodded then headed for the door, her shoulders square and her joints moving mechanically and uncomfortably. That would wear off a bit, in time. Felix couldn't help but smile. If tonight went well, they could have the ship back here in less than a month. He could go home, and would be on the front lines of the great change that would sweep his people.

"All thanks to you, Val-ey boy."

Felix closed the door behind him as he and Maria headed for the car.

14

White again. White everywhere, with the camphor medicinal smell that pervaded his mother's hospital room. It surrounded him and held him like a sea, like a dense cotton blanket. Val reached up, trying to find something concrete, something in color.

Then everything changed, and the white wasn't soft anymore. An unblemished impossibly white floor—no one could keep floors that clean—stretched out before him under his bare feet. Why wasn't he wearing shoes? He hated going without shoes. The white made his legs look less pale, but the dark hair on them stood out. Was he wearing a dress? No, a hospital gown. A white hospital gown like his mother's. Was he okay? He felt himself up and down, through the thin cotton, finding no bruises or cuts, nothing hurt. He slid tentative fingers to his ears and his eyes, but there was no blood on them this time. Thank God. A cool breeze ruffled the open back of the gown. He reached behind to hold it shut and tears of embarrassment and fear burned in his eyes.

Fuck, fuck crying. He blinked them back, looking around. A room larger than the eye could see was impossible, but it seemed to be where he stood. No walls, no ceiling, just white light. It reflected off the floor, hot in his eyes. That must have been where the tears came from. He took a step forward, a tentative baby step because his knees were weak. He felt drained, kittenish, his muscles atrophied and barely useful. He wiped at his eyes with his hand.

"Hello!" he called. "Is anyone there?"

Because there was nothing for his words to bounce off of, he wasn't even met with an echo.

He took another step, stronger now, and then another.

Then he felt it, a tug at the back of his throat, at his nose. He reached up and his fingers met a clear, light plastic tube. It was supple and delicate in his fingers, and he gagged as he pulled it from his nose, broke the little piece of tape holding it in place. His stomach roiled as he pulled, and pulled and pulled, and still the tube came.

getitoutgetitoutgetitout...

It tore at his throat because he was pulling too fast, and he screamed around it, the scream breaking with gags as the tube touched his uvula on its way past.

He sucked in great gasps of air when he finally reached the end, looked down at eight feet of tube, spittle and stomach acid and god knows what else soaked, lying in a loose coil at his feet. Only then did he think to follow the tube to its other end. Up.

It stretched up as far as he could see, devoured by the white.

The time for screaming past, Val whimpered, a tiny sound from his ravaged throat.

15

Felix knew what was happening inside Val's head, god knows they drilled it enough times. He chuckled, a little rusty sound, tugged away by the night breeze. There he went, talking about god again.

Assuming everything was working properly, and so far he had every reason to believe it was, the Alpha should be getting its bearings, tapping into Val's nerve endings. There were fifteen Alphas trained to command the procedure, Felix himself was the fifteenth. Watching Val's slack face, Felix knew no one could survive fifteen penetrations. With luck he'd only need the one.

Val's eyes opened, blue and piercing. Nothing of Valentine Slade remained behind them. If Kate were to see him now she would know in an instant it wasn't him; that something was smothering the man she loved. Val's fingers flexed, then his toes, he rolled his neck, stretching his muscles. These were the actions of the Alpha as it got to know its host, the most important host any of them would ever inhabit. And maybe the last host. Felix caught himself crossing his fingers. He really didn't want to be here anymore.

"I'm in," Val said. Val's voice. All the inflection, the wit which made Val a damned good cellmate for five years was gone.

"Get to it. There isn't much time."

The girl hadn't been able to create for them. They weren't sure if it had to do with stress, or lack of gravity, or the wrong mix of nitrogen in the air she breathed. So Val got to stay on Earth. Lucky him.

Val took several deep breaths. He closed his eyes, opened them. Never once in all his life had Val knowingly harnessed his Sangauman talents. Sure, stuff happened, mostly light bulbs breaking, glass shattering. Sometimes their cell door would stick. No matter how many times they moved, or changed cells, when Val was pissed, or upset, or scared, the door would stick. He never knew what he was doing. The trained Alphas knew the strings to pull, the buttons to push.

About ten feet away, in an open patch of desert, something began to happen. This was the piece none of their mock-ups could predict, how it would happen. Each of the fifteen Tylwyth Teg knew the plans for the new body inside and out, down to the DNA structure. Tattooed into their consciousness, they knew every curve and bone and atom.

At first it looked like a dust devil. Particles caught up in the air moved and swirled. But it shimmered. Like the twinkling stars overhead, where a home would be. Felix realized his mouth hung open in a huge, gaping grin and he closed it.

He pulled his gaze away from his future and scanned the night horizon. With two Betas, if shit went down, he should be able to recover the Alpha if he needed to. Even though the monster was here to protect Val, if it sensed he'd been compromised, it wouldn't hesitate to tear him to bits with those god-awful claws. Getting the Alpha out was job number one. Felix rocked back and forth on the balls of his feet.

Watching the swirling, changing thing before him pulled his thoughts from the monster. It was like watching something being born, but no, bigger than that. This was the birth of an entire new race, there would be no more living as a parasite now, no more searching for host bodies. The shape coalesced. At some point, the Alpha would transfer its consciousness to the new form, and poor Val's body would die. For ever after the Tylwyth Teg would see him as a hero, worship him as the father of their race's renaissance.

The frat boy Beta raised his arms in the moonlight. That was the signal. Felix went to Val's side, shouted "pull back, get out of there". He looked to the shifting thing, saw it freeze, then it melted away, leaving a moist smear on the dirt below it and the smell of ammonia. The Beta was tussling with the monster, Felix could hear grunting and moving around, shuffling of feet on dirt.

He tried to hold back the thoughts of despair, there wasn't time. He could mope later. The Alpha disengaged, and Val collapsed on the ground. Felix held open the jar, allowing the Alpha to crawl back in; forcing itself from between Val's closed lips. Betas went down with the ship, the Alphas you busted your ass to save. Felix checked Val's pulse, still strong, and then took off at a sprint for his car. He hoped Maria would follow. She was still of use to him. But if she didn't, oh well. This wasn't the end of the world. It would have been a miracle if the test had worked. Val was ready. The next step would be to get him up to the ship, get him off Earth, away from the fucking Lharomuph.

The only thing Val had to worry about here was Rich. In a day or so, they could come get him, in the meantime, Felix would put some Betas out to watch him.

Everything would be fine.

16

He was too scared to wake up screaming, but was alarmed to find himself underneath a huge, black sky riddled with specks of starlight and a deep blue to the east indicating the rising sun. His heart pounded in his ears, rippling and coordinating with the hum. It pressed against his face like a sinus infection. He sat against a rock on the cool desert floor, next to a patch of scrub brush. Same spot he'd woken up last time. Perfect. God damn that hum. The back of his throat and his nose felt thick and stuffy; post-nasal drippy, like he was getting sick. That was just what he needed.

He breathed. Once. Twice. Just a dream. Like last time. One more deep breath. He knew he needed to reach up, to touch his face, to prove he wasn't tethered to infinity via his spleen, or wherever that hell tube had reached to, but what if it were real? What if his fingers touched soft, silicon-like plastic?

It didn't hurt to swallow; hurt up in his nose. He tried it a few more times, concentrating on it so hard it kind of did start to hurt.

Better to know than wonder, right?

Right?

He reached, moving like he was underwater. He was dressed, not wearing a hospital gown—that was a good sign. He wore the boxers and T-shirt he'd fallen asleep in. His legs were as pale in the starlight as they were in the dream. He looked at the deep blue sky and wondered how long he'd been sitting here, not touching his face. His index finger bumped against his nose, and he poked its tip...nothing hurt, nothing pinched or pulled. He explored his face, finding nothing out of the ordinary.

The cool night air made his muscles ache when he stood up. For a moment he felt weak, like in the dream. He stretched, not liking the even pulsing in his head. It was worse out here. Stretching felt good as he got his bearings, and made his way home. Like in the dream, like the previous night, he wasn't wearing shoes, and each step hurt his delicate feet. He supposed he'd have to start sleeping in his boots, if these nighttime excursions were to become the norm.

He made it to his dooryard, and paused. On the rickety steps there was a big bundle of something.

A person.

Jesus, did Kate come looking for him and lock herself out?

He called her name, feeling like a jackass. She looked so uncomfortable.

She looked so uncomfortable because it wasn't Kate. It wasn't a woman, and whoever he was, he wasn't alive. The red that soaked into the wood of the steps gave credence to that. No way someone could lose that much blood and live. Ignoring everything he'd learned from *CSI*, Val took the fellow by the shoulder and flopped him over, crumpling him against the door. Nope. Not alive. It was the guy from the restaurant...the frat boy. The one who'd been lurking out here.

And whatever killed TJ was very much alive and well.

Whatever killed TJ. He looked down at himself, at shallow cuts on his wrists and forearms. Shallow, bloody gashes on his legs that stung once he noticed them. There are a lot of nasty plants in the desert, they have to defend themselves. Did frat boy get a chance to defend himself?

Could it be a coincidence that Val was wandering in the desert for two nights in a row, where there happened to be gruesome killings in his neighborhood? Either he was very, very lucky or...

How? It was impossible to think he could be going into fugue states, and killing people with a giant machete or samurai sword—it was sharp as hell, whatever it was—and hiding the weapon during the day. And how did he keep the blood off his clothes?

He did it naked. Or in something like the hospital gown from his dream.

Or, more realistically, he didn't do it at all. Then what was this guilt feeling that gnawed at him.

He went around behind the trailer, where the scrub met right up with the house. That was where the back door was, the one they never used. It stuck when he pulled on the latch so he thought it was locked, but a final tug pulled the wood free. Swollen from the afternoon rains? Kate was up, in the hallway, in a shooter's stance wearing nothing but black panties and a white mostly see-through undershirt. She held the Desert Eagle before her, in two hands this time, God, please let her have forgotten the safety, have left that on. He held out his hand to calm her, he felt his pulse quicken at the sight of the gun. They needed to practice with the thing; she seemed hell bent on using it. If he was a killer she should drop him like a dog, here and now.

"Easy," he said. "It's me."

"What are you...where have you been?"

He resisted the urge to swallow, to clear his throat,

anything like that. "Sleepwalking," he said, as matter-of-fact as he could muster. "And that frat kid from last night?" Kate nodded. "He's dead on the porch."

She blinked at him, and only then did she lower the gun. He still couldn't see if she had the safety on or not. He hoped she wouldn't shoot herself in the bare foot.

He waited for a reaction. Gave it a beat, then a second beat. "If we had left TJ, I'd say we should call the police, but we didn't, we hid TJ, so I guess we need to hide this one, too."

She shook her head. "You're kidding."

"No."

She kept shaking her head. "I can't—there can't—" she let her voice trail off. "Did you," she paused for a moment; Val could tell she wanted to ask if he did it. "See anything?"

He shook his head. "Nightmares. Like last night."

"We could call Spence."

"And there'd be an investigation, and they'd know we got rid of TJ's body, and—"

"But there's nothing linking us to this guy. He's a no one."

"He isn't no one. A State Trooper and an Otero County Deputy saw him stalking us."

"What if it happens again tonight?" she asked. She turned to the bedroom, came out a moment later, with jeans on and one of his T-shirts. Like she didn't want him looking at her.

She didn't have the gun when she came back. He doubted it would fire a second time. He'd left the clip in it; it was sure to jam.

She took a few deep breaths. "Did you do it?" she asked. "Either of them?"

He wished he could get mad, bluster at her, be appalled she would even suggest such a thing. Anxiety pooled in his chest.

"I don't know. I don't think so; they were both big guys, and I think I'd be showing more damage if I'd done it."

"Unless you snuck up on them."

"No one snuck up on TJ. This guy either."

"So it wasn't you."

"I guess not." Though there was guilt that held him.

And she looked at him like she didn't believe him. She moved wide around him in the hall, towards the front door. "Are we going to hide this one, too?"

What else could he do? Helplessness washed over him like a sea, building, mixing with the hum. It was softer now than when he woke up. Kate headed for the door. If she opened the door, the dead frat boy would tumble right into the kitchen floor.

He almost caught her in time, but she hauled the door open wide, and was rewarded for her efforts with a dead frat boy flopping face-first onto her feet. Her toenails were painted red, now the tops of her feet were smeared with tacky, rust-colored blood.

Her scream was almost enough to wake the dead. Almost. The fellow on the floor lay still.

Blood pooled around her bare feet and she stepped back, leaving half a crimson footprint on the linoleum. She looked down at it, drawing in her breath in great gasping whoops.

Val tried to think. Corpses weren't supposed to bleed. But this wasn't bleeding. This was gravity.

He took her to the sink and wet a paper towel for her feet, knowing he needed to get the blood off the floor. This would never hold up against those lights they can use to see blood, would never hold up if they brought dogs in. The pool stopped spreading, at least. The blood would never come out of the crack by the doorjamb.

They had to hope the cops would never make it this far.

Kate calmed herself down, holding the damp paper towel to her foot as though she'd been cut, looking at the body. She poured herself a glass of water and drank half of it in one gulp.

If he was the killer, he wasn't doing it in his right mind, which would make him nice and easy to catch.

He couldn't be doing it; his arms would be sore from all that slicing and stabbing.

"What are you thinking about?" Kate asked. She sounded like she'd been running.

He looked at her.

"How we're going to get rid of this."

She offered him the water, and he took a drink. It tasted like chlorine, the well got like this sometimes when it hadn't been used enough.

"He's leakier than the last one."

Kate's look told him he wasn't funny. He shrugged.

They stood a while longer.

"Are we doing this?" he asked.

She looked at him, and he wasn't sure if he read too much into her stare, but it looked like she was accusing him.

"Why don't you call Felix and tell him about this, too?"

Yow, where did that come from?

"We haven't killed anyone. Just hid the bodies."

"One body. We need to make it plural before the sun gets too much higher. He's going to start to stink, and I don't want anyone seeing."

"We use your truck this time."

"Wrong. We need the trunk. There's already blood in there; if we go down for one we're already fucked for both."

"I don't want that in my car," she whined. Before she had stared at the body, now she actively looked away from it. "TJ was different. I knew him."

"And I'm sure this was a hell of a guy. Get your keys, back it up to the stoop. At least he's lighter than TJ."

"How can you be so crass?"

"This was your idea to begin with. You found TJ. You were the one who decided not to call the cops."

"I didn't know there would be more of them."

"Get your keys. We can mope about this later."

She glared at him, but only for a moment. Then she turned away, a turn that said more than her glare, and got the keys. She stepped over the body and disappeared from sight. Val stared at the corpse's milky corneas as the car started with a roar and a backfire.

So much for subtle.

The Daytona's brake lights lit the kitchen as she backed up to the stoop. When she killed the engine it died with a sputter. God, he hated that car.

She parked the car so close to the body that she needed to reach across it to unlock the trunk. At least they wouldn't have to lift it too far.

"You get the head. I'll get the feet."

Val nodded. As she reached, he interrupted her. "Gloves." It didn't matter, though, because he'd already touched the thing.

He grabbed some dish gloves from under the sink. That was it. Last pair. He'd be in trouble next time a body rolled around. The body's head flopped and a little more blood dribbled out as he groped for purchase on the meaty shoulders. This guy was sturdier than TJ, but about as big. TJ had a lot of nice, light fat. This guy was all muscle. Val grunted, tried to lift with his knees, and not with his back. Kate had trouble with the legs, and when he paused to look at her he saw she'd been crying. If it wasn't his fault, why did he feel so guilty?

The body left a crimson smear against the paint on the lip of the trunk, ketchup to the car's mustard color. They'd have to clean it before they went anywhere. While Kate went into the house to get a rag, Val looked at the steps, the old, dry wood stained blood colors. He needed to get rid of the steps anyway; it might make a good afternoon project. To get his mind off the bodies, and off his mother. A sneaky little voice in the back of his mind wished to be back in prison. The thought stabbed at his heart, but it was a little bit true. He'd known which end was up. During his time there, he hadn't disposed of a single corpse.

They looked in at the body for a moment before slamming the trunk on it.

"Shall we?" he asked.

She went without speaking, to the driver's seat. He got in the passenger side.

"If you want to blow up at me, do it." She could sulk for days before she let go on him. They didn't have time for that bullshit.

She started the car and took a deep breath. She didn't squeal her tires or anything dramatic, which was good considering their cargo; she pulled out of the driveway.

Neither of them spoke on their way to the mine.

As they drove, the pressure in Val's head increased with the ticking of the odometer. By the time Kate stopped and he got out to pull the gate aside, it pounded like surf behind his ears. By the time she stopped in front of the mine's gaping mouth, it felt like he was a hundred feet under water. Was she pausing for dramatic effect? Go, he thought, massaging his temples.

"Are you okay?"

"Pressure on my head. The hum is a million times worse. I guess it's the stress."

"Or the mine," she said.

"Can't be. You'd be feeling it, too."

Kate shrugged, her face lit by the green of the dashboard light. "It happens when we're here."

"So let's do what we have to do, and then get away."

She drove slowly, gravel crunching under her tires,

and gradually the shadow, then the darkness, overtook the little car. Kate looked to him, her face still green.

"Can you do this?"

"I don't have a choice."

She opened her door, leaving it open behind her. He wished she'd shut it; the light blinded him. She opened the trunk, and they saw this body had left behind a dark red stain in a different spot than TJ.

They were fucked if anyone found this car.

Val started to think how he could burn it, make sure the fibers from the carpet burned up, while still making it look like an accident. Thinking helped—if he let his mind go blank, the pressure seeped in even deeper.

The body tumbled into the darkness without ceremony. It had been special when TJ went, but the second time was a do-over.

Val felt hot blood on his upper lip. Nosebleed again.

He was concentrating on that when Kate grabbed his arm, her fingers like a vice.

"There's something else in here."

He tried to listen through the hum, tried to use his senses, but everything was dull and flat; only the monotony of the vibration stayed in focus. The car lights killed his night vision, and he could barely hear Kate speak. Like she was talking through a thick, down comforter.

She pointed, and he followed her finger, tasting his own blood on his lips, down the back of his throat. He wiped it with the back of his hand.

Maybe he saw something move where she pointed, a hallucination? He wanted to get out before his eyes started bleeding again, before more blood vessels burst.

"Let's go," he said, his own voice sounding like he wore ear plugs.

"Did you see that?" she asked.

"I don't know."

"There!" she said, pointing somewhere else, and that

time he saw a swish of tan. A rabid cougar? Something that looked like a rabid cougar, but killed people? With a machete?

"Yeah, let's go," he said, his knees feeling weak, as if the air was too heavy. Sweat covered his body; he could feel the cool air against it, and he shivered, the sudden movement agitating the hum.

He wiped again and his hand came away with more blood.

Kate stared into the darkness, not moving. Paranoia wrapped him like a glove, as he saw movement from the corner of his eye. He pushed her—if she didn't go, this place would drop him to his knees. If that happened, the thing in the dark would come for him.

She stumbled and he reached for her, but his hand came up short. If she fell it would go for her. She caught herself against the car's fender, steadied herself, and opened the door.

"Go!" he shouted, and ran for the car.

It was like gravity had been increased, like moving through molasses. Something snapped inside his head. It should have hurt, but it didn't. He couldn't turn around—moving his head that distance would take everything he had left—but he could sense it right there. As he slammed the door, he expected something to stop it from closing, something to block his progress.

But the door closed with a muffled click.

"You're bleeding!"

It was too much work to tell her to go. So he closed his eyes, feeling the car come to life under him, feeling it turn, and accelerate, and before he left the world behind, the darkness behind his eyelids turned to light. He probed at himself, what had snapped? Something...something inside him. And then he passed out.

17

The hum of a revving engine brought Val out of his doze by the television. He felt feverish, definitely better than when he'd been at the mine that morning—which didn't say much. He spent the day oscillating between dark spells of fearing for his sanity—*someone* had killed those people—and feeling like he needed to get his act together. A job. Something to break up the isolation he felt. So he'd found a marathon of cheesy eighties and early nineties horror movies, and camped out on his couch. He switched off "Fire in the Sky", though. Made him think too much of his mother, and that silly book. He'd also spent a lot of time thinking he ought to go and see her, but what would he say to her. "Hi Mom, glad to see you look as awful as yesterday. At least you don't look worse!"

"That's Rich," Kate said. She'd been dozing, too, but recognized the engine.

The revving stopped. Doors slammed.

The door to the trailer was unlocked.

Val tore the steps up that afternoon, and burned the pieces, so it would be one big uncomfortable step for whoever came in through the front door. He got to his feet, but could hear the sound of a hand on the knob. Come on, door, be locked.

The door rattled. It wasn't much of a door. One good tug would pull it right off the hinges.

Val's headache came back with a vengeance. He was sure he hadn't locked the door.

But it was locked.

Fists pounded on the door, and there was Rich's sweet musical voice: "Let me in, you sonofabitch!"

"No one's home, come back tomorrow." He wondered if he should get his gun. He settled on a baseball bat instead.

The flimsy door strained against the pounding.

"Where's my fucking wife?"

Val and Kate looked at one another.

"What's he talking about?" Kate asked. Val shrugged again. *Oh Christ. Did he have her? Did he do something to her?* If so, he'd had a busy night last night.

Val reached to open the door, unlocked it, as Kate hissed at him not to.

Bat in hand, Val looked down upon Rich, who stood looking fat and out of breath on the ground below. "Where is she?" He raised his pistol up into Val's crotch.

"Fuck if I know." Val said. Rich jabbed the gun at him, rapping his balls through his jeans. Val clenched his teeth and took a step back, letting his molars grind in tune with the hum.

"Where is she?"

"Who knows? Search the place if you want."

Rich hauled himself up into the kitchen. Sweat beaded on his scalp, visible through his crew cut. Val caught him looking around. Maybe remembering the time he'd spent here? It all looked the same, maybe less shit piled up everywhere. Probably looking for his wife. He turned his attentions on Kate.

"Where is she?"

"I don't know. We've both been here all day."

"She's gone. You're back. I did the math."

"You really think I could take your wife? She's more man than I am," Val said, and mostly meant it. Maria was a tough lady. She'd told him she killed someone once, back home in Mexico, and Val believed her. He'd seen her handle a knife, and had serious doubts he could take her if she was armed. And unless she'd been completely domesticated, she was never unarmed. "You've got one *chica loca*."

"Have you called her?" Kate asked.

"Voicemail," Rich said, staring at Val.

"How long has she been gone?"

"Don't fucking ask me questions like I haven't thought of that shit."

"I'm trying to help me not get shot. I don't have her, I haven't had her. If you don't trust me, listen to your sister."

Rich looked at her and laughed. "She isn't even family any more. She gave that up when she tossed in with you."

Some of Rich's initial anger seemed to have dissipated. Knowing Rich as well as he did, he suspected the worst was over, this time. Rich was still a serious problem, one he wanted to get away from at all costs. He had a bad feeling about Rich—it would end badly for one of them. But now he seemed too distracted by the missing wife to be concerned with Val.

"You tried calling home?" Kate asked.

"You think I'm dumb?"

Val decided not to push his luck, and kept quiet.

"Look around. She's not here."

"I will."

And Rich did. He moved like a whirlwind, one room to the next, throwing the mattresses off the beds, tearing clothes out of the closet.

"What about the old mine?"

Oh. Fuck.

"Where we used to go and shoot up."

"Yeah, I know the one."

The hum pounded in Val's ears in time with his pulse. This time he didn't look at Kate, willed her to look cool, to be cool.

"What about it."

"Is she there?"

"Why would she be there? I haven't been there since the last time I was there with you. That place gave me the creeps." *And, funnily enough, it makes me bleed out of my eyes and ears, these days. So please don't make me go there.*

"Do you think maybe she left you?" Kate asked. Was she trying to antagonize him?

He spun on her, glaring. The topic of the mine seemed, for now, to have been forgotten.

"She wouldn't leave me."

"Because she's scared?"

Now she pushed it, getting him mad in a different way. In a complete role reversal, Val placed a cautionary hand on her wrist. He missed being a mouthy prick.

"Scared? She isn't scared of nothing. I saved her from her shit Mexican life."

That was one way to think about it.

Rich stared at them, his eyes looking small in his red, blotchy face. Was he going to cry? That would be an absolutely amazing event to behold.

"Crawl space under the house?"

"Be my guest." Val and Kate followed him outside, making the hop down to the ground. Val pulled open the little hinged lattice door. Rich gave him a baleful look before he squeezed in, taking up most of the opening crawling through. Val wanted very dearly to shut it behind him and lock the door.

Val's heart shot to his throat when he heard Rich yelp.

"Ah, fuck!"

He found her, Val thought. *I killed her and he found her.* There was nothing to yelp about the other day, when he was hunting for the hum. Had he put a body there? He looked down at his hands, looking for blood, scratches, anything.

They were clean and looked fine. Calloused from weight lifting in prison, a delicate paper cut on his index finger from his release form.

Rich exploded out of the little door, some of the flimsy lattice wood pieces cracking and breaking off against his bulk. Dust plumed where Rich's boots scraped up the dirt. He looked pale, his eyes bulging against their sockets. *Bloody fuck, he's going to have a heart attack.*

"Get out of here," he said, hustling to his Jeep. He turned his back on them, a very un-Rich thing to do. When as many people didn't like you as didn't like Rich, it wasn't wise to turn your back on anyone.

Val and Kate looked at one another, then at the gaping black maw. A mini-Olympus Mine.

Kate rushed to her brother. "What is it?" she asked, catching him at the door.

"Something down there. It was eating."

"What do you mean?" she asked.

"Get out of here," he said again, hauling himself behind the wheel, firing up the engine. "Claws as long as my arm."

Val and Kate stared at him. Rabid mountain lion?

"I fucking hope it gets you," Rich exploded, punctuating his word by flinging his Wrangler into reverse, spraying gravel from the driveway, and leaving them in twin plumes of dust.

"He knows about TJ," Kate said.

"What the fuck spooked him?"

"He was on something."

Val shook his head. "He can't, not with his job. He had

his uniform on. He's dumb, but not that dumb."

Val stared at the gaping black hole under his trailer. Next to it was the spigot for the hose. All perfectly normal. Yet something down there reduced him to jelly. That haunted look in his eyes.

"I gotta go check it out."

"Are you crazy?"

"I want to know what's so terrifying under my house. Besides, two seconds ago you said he was on drugs."

"Take the gun."

Was that a good idea? Man, that would be loud down there. Couldn't hurt to bring it along. He went in the house for it, very aware of the floor, wondering what he was walking over. *Claws as long as my arm*. Maybe he was on drugs.

The weight of the Desert Eagle wasn't comforting; it was a lump of steel. Maybe he shouldn't bring it. Maybe he should go down there, and let whatever happened, happen. He set it on the counter. He'd take a shovel. Not a lot of room to swing a shovel. Maybe this was best.

The late afternoon sunlight only reached so far under the trailer before its golden light faded from gray to black. The hum held him tight, felt like a helmet around his skull. Pressure from all sides. Cobwebs stuck to his face and in his hair, pine needles crackled under his hands. He let his eyes adjust to the darkness, and scanned the crawl space.

Rich had been here, so worried about Maria that he wasn't interested in kicking Val's ass. Or killing him, as Val worried things had escalated to. So strange. He knew Rich loved his wife, in the strange way Rich had of loving anyone. Not his fault, not entirely, things had been rough for him as a kid, both he and Kate were in and out of foster homes, then back with their drunk mom when she married a rich guy who had the house in the nice development. He died a few years later, heart attack. Val sometimes wondered, a little bit, if maybe Rich had something to do with it. You never knew. He'd voiced the concerns to Kate, and she'd gotten pissed, denied Rich would ever do such a thing. It brought them to the cusp of a fight and Val had backed off. Why did she feel like she needed to defend him?

A sound. Flies. Now that he noticed it, it swelled so that it rivaled the hum. An orchestra of flies. He crawled towards the sound.

A coyote lay in the pine needles, a sunken eye wide, white and staring.

Three deep gashes tore it most of the way into pieces, he could see white bone and red meat turned brown.

Was this what scared the shit out of Rich? Impossible.

Had he done this?

The coyote's body was stiff, and its soft parts had been something's lunch, the white fur of its belly bloody and stiff, surrounding a black hole of ichor. Val slid the shovel under its haunches and crawled backwards, dragging the body with him. It kept sliding off the shovel, and he had to stop and reposition himself to get it to come along.

Above him, in the kitchen, the phone rang. As he scooted backwards, dragging the coyote, disturbing the flies, beetles and maggots, he heard Kate's footsteps, soft on the floor above him. He heard her say "Hello?"

He brushed a fly away from his face as he paused to listen. Dirt and cobwebs stuck to his sweaty skin; there was a shower in his future.

"He's here, I'll get him," he heard her say, clear as a bell through the thin trailer floor. He hurried with the coyote. He'd miss the open space, but it would be nice to go to Santa Fe, to be in a city, and have people around, and no dead animals, and a house that was better constructed than this POS fire trap. He heard the screen door slam, and her jump down from the missing stoop.

"Val?"

"Yeah, be right there."

"Phone's for you."

"Thanks," he said.

He burst out into the warm sun, pleased to feel it beating through his shirt and warming him. He couldn't go back, even if he was doing this. He looked at the coyote, balanced on the shovel, lilting headfirst towards the ground. There had to be another option, a way to tell if he was the killer, a way to make himself stop.

Kate extended the cordless phone to him. He looked at his hands, at the dead coyote, wiped his hands on his pants, and took it.

"Hello?"

"Valentine Slade?" A woman's voice, the lilt of an accent. Maria?

"Speaking." It seemed like too much effort to be wise or snarky.

"This is Doctor Villanueva. How are you feeling?"

"I'm all right."

"Are you still experiencing the vibration in your head?"

"Is that the technical term?"

"I'm not sure there is a technical term. Are you still experiencing it?"

"Not all the time."

"Is that an improvement?"

"I guess so," Val answered. "Are you calling to check up on me?"

"No. I'd like you to come back to my office. I'd like to run some more tests."

"Why?"

"I couldn't get anything definitive from your blood work. The samples came back contaminated."

"How so?"

"It happens from time to time, careless lab workers, perhaps I made a mistake drawing it. I would like to see another sample."

"How was it contaminated?"

"We don't check. Once we see the results are off, we throw the sample away. What an odd question, Mr. Slade."

"I don't think I'm going to be coming back in. I feel fine, and I don't have any insurance."

"I would really like another look at you—"

"Thanks for your time and concern, Doc."

And he hung up, the hum resonating louder than ever with the dial tone.

Contaminated.

Deep inside, he didn't think it was a mistake, or carelessness. He was contaminated, he could tell on his own from this hum, and he was dangerous.

He took the phone inside, hung it up, then went back out to the tall grass where he could dig a hole and bury the coyote. *Contaminated.*

18

Kate went to the grocery store the next afternoon. Val stayed in bed, and there was no body the next morning, not on the front step or in the road on her way to town. She'd asked him to come with her, asked him what he wanted, but he replied with a listless melancholy that got under her skin. It wasn't him. Who had come back from prison?

She'd asked if he was okay one too many times, and he'd snapped at her, and she'd been clumsy and somehow knocked a glass off the counter. That was when she left.

She headed back to the trailer with two plastic shopping bags full of mac-and-cheese and other crap—she didn't have a lot of cash and she'd panicked, not knowing what to buy—along the forested road, tall pines standing by like sentinels on either side. Something moved on the side of the road, hidden in the trees except for a few flashes of color. Something pink. A person. A woman. Kate cranked the Daytona's wheel, pushing the car onto the dirt road. The car didn't have good tires, so when she braked hard she skidded forward, already formulating her defense. *She stepped right out in front of me. I wasn't even speeding.* Hopefully they would be able to examine the skid marks and see she hadn't been speeding, braked as soon as she could...but if they did they would see the blood in the trunk. The thoughts flashed like lightning, taking only a few seconds to surge through her brain. She didn't want to think or worry anymore.

She didn't hit the woman.

When the dust cloud settled all around them, she saw Maria looking at her.

In her surprise, she let the car stall.

Kate cranked down the window. Maria peered at her like a zombie, and moved on towards the other side of the road. She looked like she was in shock, like a disaster victim.

"Maria!" Kate called.

She didn't respond.

Kate threw open her door and hurried toward her, leaving the door open. The car sat cockeyed in the road from her skid.

Maria wore a stylish silk blouse, though it was dirty and torn, black leggings that showed off the rose tattoo on her ankle, and...sneakers? Maria had never worn sneakers. She was short, liked the extra height of heels; always said after so long in heels, flats bothered her feet.

"Maria," Kate said again, taking her by the shoulder. Her skin was hot under the blouse, feverish.

She turned her head to Kate slowly, her eyes not seeming to register, her left pupil much larger than the right. That wasn't a good sign. She cradled one of her wrists, and her hand flopped at her side. Broken?

"Are you all right?" Kate asked. "What are you doing out here?"

Maria responded in slow Spanish. Kate picked up a few words, "nothing" "watching" and "going" and then Maria turned to go again.

"We have to call Rich. He's worried sick about you!"

She spoke again, and Kate struggled to understand it. She didn't care for him anymore, something about light? She'd have to bring Maria back to Val's and have Rich come get her. Or she could take her to him. Was he at work?

Kate pulled her cell phone from her pants pocket.

The next word Kate understood loud and clear, a sharp "No," and Maria slapped the phone out of Kate's hand. It bounced against a rock.

"What did he do to you? Are you running away from him?"

A head injury might explain her reverting to only speaking Spanish. If Rich had done it then it would make sense she wouldn't want to go back to him.

"I can call Spence. He'll make sure you go someplace safe."

More Spanish and she turned away again.

There is no place safe, not from the light? Kate had to be translating wrong. Her Spanish was really abysmal.

"Maria—" Kate moved after her again, but Maria turned and shoved her, planting her hands on Kate's shoulders and pushing her back. Kate's ankle caught a rock and she dropped back, landing on her tailbone.

Maria moved away into the pines, determined and methodical.

"Maria!" Kate called, standing up, not putting much weight on her left ankle. It hurt, her tailbone hurt. But she couldn't leave Maria out there in the woods.

Picking up her phone, not bothering to check to see if it was broken, she limped back to the car. She'd ask Val. They could call Rich, call the real police, though the idea of the police anywhere near this car, even Spence, worried her.

Maybe having something to do would snap Val out of it.

Back at the trailer, she jumped from the car calling his name. She found him inside, on the couch, watching Oprah of all ridiculous things, a bottle of Jack Daniels by his feet. He hadn't gotten far into it, but it rankled her how much he looked like his mother. Some subtle lines of his face, his nose and chin and cheekbones, but his posture mimicked Caroline's perfectly. The whiskey only helped the illusion.

Anger flared in her. She didn't know what he had to do with these killings but she wasn't going to let him look like this. On screen, Oprah held hands with a young black man, and they were both crying.

Kate turned the TV off.

"Hey—"

Then she grabbed the bottle of Jack. It crossed her mind to pour it down the drain, but she capped it and set it on the counter. He looked up at her, dazed and irritated.

"There's something going on out here. I saw Maria in the woods. I think Rich roughed her up. Like worse than ever before."

"What do you want me to do about it?"

"Stop whining or I'll slap you."

He stood up, one hand going to the small of his back, the other going to his temple. "Stop whining and do what?"

"Help me find her! She's out here in the woods and she needs a doctor."

"I don't particularly care what happens to her. I hope she falls in a whole nest of rabid pumas."

"What happened to your compassion?" she asked. She knew the answer, though, could read it in his flinty blue eyes. The past six years had stripped it from him.

"Call Spence. Get him and his guys looking for her."

"They can't be out here! What if she goes to the mine?"

"Then we're fucked." He moved to sit on the couch. She let the air out of her lungs in an exasperated whoosh.

"Fine. I'll go look for her by myself."

If Val didn't take this bait, it would mean he was fundamentally changed, no longer the man she'd fallen in love with.

From the couch, he sighed, a dramatic, pitiful gesture, and stood up again, this time both hands going to his temples.

"What are we going to do if we find her?"

"Put her in the car—your truck—and take her to the hospital."

He sighed again, and she wanted to smash the bottle of Jack over his thick, stupid skull. But he pulled on his boots, took his sweet time lacing them up, and walked over next to her.

"You look like the fresh air would help."

"I don't know what would help. At least no one died last night."

She followed his gaze to the doorjamb. True, it could have just been dirt, but they knew the dark spot between the linoleum and the wood of the sill was blood. He followed her out the door, hopping to the driveway below.

"Where did you see her?" Val asked.

"Sort of by the mine. I think she was coming this way."

"Hold on," he said, and hauled himself back up into the house. He came back out with a bulge in the back of his jeans, under his T-shirt.

"What do we need that for?" she asked. He didn't seem well enough to be carrying a weapon. Not to mention he'd be headed back to jail if they caught him with it.

"Something out here is doing a whole mess of damage. Maybe I can solve our little problem."

"Are you sure?"

"You heard Spence. There's a rabid puma in these here hills."

They trudged around the woods and the rocky scrub land for two hours. Sometimes Val seemed okay; sometimes she would catch him massaging his temples, a sick look on his face. The gun, she was pleased to see, never left the waistband of his pants.

The sun sank lower into the sky, and hung above the hills, casting long shadows, by the time they got back to the trailer.

"Do you want to go out tonight?" she asked, even though she'd bought food. Going out might raise Val's spirits, and it was bound to be better than macaroni and cheese.

"No," he said.

Then he raised a hand, silencing her.

"What?"

"Shhh."

She searched the shadows, by the Oldsmobile, the Daytona, by the truck. She didn't see anything. She stood a step behind him, and focused on the gun in his pants. Why didn't he get it out?

"Stay here." His voice was breathy whisper.

He went to the trailer, picked up the shovel he'd used on the coyote, hefted it in his hands like a weapon.

Kate stayed.

Something moved. Something tan. In the rocks by the Oldsmobile. Call out to him?

The thought was plundered from her mind by a keening scream.

Maria, in her filthy, ripped fuchsia blouse, erupted from the long shadows of the remaining wall of the barn and hurled herself at Val, wailing at him.

He caught her by the shoulder, but she swung at him, Kate saw the sun catch the glint of a switchblade in Maria's left hand. She was clumsy; her right hand drooped at her side. Something was very wrong with her.

It looked like he'd dodged it, but she couldn't tell from here.

Movement from the rocks caught her eye. The rabid

puma stood there, front paws on the rock, watching. She blinked at it; strained her eyes. Shadows obscured most of its tawny hide.

Pumas don't have tails like that.

Or mouths.

Nothing looked like that.

The thing flexed a front paw. Pumas don't have claws like that. A scream percolated in her throat, it all made sense…TJ, Rich freaking out. *This thing was under the house.* Its eyes were like two diamonds, Spiderman eyes, glassy and black, catching the pink from the sunset. What would it do if she ran? What would she do if it ran?

There was a heavy *thunk*, the sound of something hitting meat, and the wailing stopped.

Val… She took a step towards the house, and the thing stayed still, watching, superior in its silence. Then it turned and melted into the desert shadows, like a quiet trickle of water over some rocks. She blinked into the darkness once, twice, even took a step towards where she'd seen it. Val.

She ran to Val's side, slipping in the loose dirt of the driveway, her ankle complaining where she'd twisted it when Maria shoved her.

Val stood over a slumped form, all fuchsia silk and tangled black hair. He held the shovel like a baseball bat. Blood and hair matted the blade.

The skin on his knuckles was white from gripping the handle. Tendons stood out in his arms and his neck.

She put a hand on his shoulder and it was like touching high-tension wires clad in cotton.

"Don't touch me," he said; his voice a growl.

"Is she?"

Val shook her off, lowering the shovel.

"I did it. This proves it. I did all of it."

The gravel underneath Maria's hair was turning red and wet.

The sun disappeared behind the hills.

"Val, I saw something. I don't think you did it."

When he turned to her, his eyes were dark and devoid of emotion. For a moment they were the thing's eyes. Black pools of nothing.

"Look at this. Look at her. What don't you get? I'm a killer."

He threw the shovel. It lodged in the dirt of the driveway with a *thunk*.

She watched him head into the house. He took the big step into the kitchen in one stride. The air outside was still, the rocks where she had seen the thing were deserted.

The claws. It had to be what had killed those people. Had to be what Spence thought was a rabid puma.

Kate held the gun out in front of her, using both hands, since her wrist still hurt a little bit from the other day, and took a few steps closer to the rocks. It had been there, for all the world to see, watching Val and Maria.

Maria. Another body to hide. If only they hadn't hidden two others, perhaps this one could be written off as self-defense. She should have called the police when she found TJ. No, she should have ignored him, turned around and come back. Maria looked more like a clump of dirty rags than a person. Rich would kill Val for sure. He might kill her, as well.

They had to get out of here, and soon.

She couldn't move Maria without Val's help. The trailer was dark, he hadn't turned any lights on inside. It was night now, and without any light pollution the stars glittered from above. There was no tell-tale blue glow from the TV, maybe he'd gone to bed? A job would help, but he couldn't get one until they got to Santa Fe, 'til his mom died. What would he do for a job? He couldn't be a lawyer or a cop now; she didn't think he'd make it very long as a paralegal.

Taking one last look into the dark for the monster, she

went to the trailer. The pink of Maria's shirt made a light spot on the black driveway, Kate guessed she'd go into the Daytona, and then to the mine.

She grunted taking the big step up to the trailer. They could build a new stoop tomorrow. It would be a fun project, something to do. Anything to avoid thinking about the human puddle in the driveway. It was dark in the kitchen. The microwave clock glowed the time, after nine, and the house was silent. The couch was empty.

Maybe he was in his room?

She pushed open the door, stepped inside and froze.

Val sat on his bed in the light of one dim lamp. Maria's switchblade hovered in front of his face. He looked up at her, and she could see more blood vessels burst in his eye.

She held out her hand.

The door slammed shut behind her.

"This proves I did it. Did all of them." The blade hovered. If she tried the door, would it be locked?

"I don't think you did. I saw something outside—"

The phone rang and it stopped. All the tension and energy fled from the room. The darkness left his eyes.

It rang once, twice, three times. Each time Val twitched, like the ring was inside his skull with him.

Val cleared his throat, coughed, and said "Can you get that? Please?"

The door opened agreeably for her, and she went, reaching the cordless phone on the coffee table on its fifth ring.

"Hello?"

"Valentine Slade, please."

"He's..." *gone crazy* "...asleep. He isn't feeling well. Can I take a message?"

"Wake him up. This is Angelina Warder. Tell him his mother has taken a turn for the worse, I don't think she'll make it through the night. Have him come now."

She hung up. These people were supposed to be

trained to deal with this shit.

When she turned to deliver the message he stood in the door, looking gaunt and haggard.

"Is it my mother?" he asked, his voice sounding normal, like gravel.

Kate nodded.

"Is she dead?"

"No. They don't think she'll make it through the night."

"I have to take a shower."

Kate just nodded.

EXCERPT #3

from *Trinity* by Judd Grenouille ©1988

When I next see poor Adrienne, she looks much worse. We meet in the activity room of the Chaves County Mental Heath Institute. The administrators were not thrilled to admit me, but Adrienne insisted upon it.

"Cal's gone." Her voice was scratchy and haunted, and there were dark circles under her eyes. I sat silent, encouraging her to continue. It turned into a waiting game, she stared at the floor, and I examined her. Her hair looked to be in need of a wash, her fingernails were gnawed past the quick, giving her fingers a stubby, blunt look.

She and I sat together on a couch. An orderly hovered at a desk across the room. I wondered how much he could hear.

"Where did they take him?" I asked. I'd heard nothing about a missing boy. It went very poorly for parents of abducted children. The law never seemed to understand.

"He's in Rhode Island," she said.

How oddly specific…

"My sister's got him. Everyone thought it was for the best." Oh. I understood now. This was the first she'd spoken of his travels there, and I had, for a moment, feared the worst.

"Can they get him back east? Is he safe? I thought maybe they couldn't find him there."

"They can be very persistent. Did something happen?"

"Something happened all right. And you don't even have to hypnotize me." She settled herself into the uncomfortable institutional couch. This was fairly common, the Visitors could tamper with our memories, but often didn't think to interfere with us when it was our loved ones in danger.

"Everyone thinks I'm crazy," she said. "Or high." She smiled wistfully, as if longing for a drink or a fix. "I'm kinda on a different high in here, though. They've got me on so many pills." I let her go on. They treated her fairly here, now that she was behaving more reasonably. When she first came in she'd been in the throes of detoxification.

"When did your son go east?" I asked. "How did that come about?"

"I called my sister Sally after..." she let her voice trail off and she looked around. "They don't like me talking about the Visitors," she said. "They think it was drunken crazy talk. They don't know it's real, not like you and me do."

I nodded, patting her hand.

She swallowed, looked around again. "I'm going to get a glass of water."

I waited for her, looking around the big, sunny room. The windows opened on a nice patch of desert as yards are too expensive to maintain. A few benches sat here and there, for any patients who wanted to brave the sun.

Adrienne came back with a paper cup of water. She sat, and gave me an earnest smile. Her eyes were glazed, probably from her medication.

"I was in the living room. I was a little—a lot—drunk. I couldn't sleep otherwise. I'd have nightmares, terrible dreams about the light and them reaching up inside me. Some weren't dreams, but by this point a lot of 'em were. I don't think they cared about me so much, both kinds were dutifully checking up on me. I was watching something, a late talk show rerun, maybe? Kinda staring at the TV. Then I saw a man in my hall. He was one of the Tylwyth Teg, I know it from how he walked. He was in my house, silent like a cat. I stood up and I looked down the hall, he went into Cal's room. So I ran, I ran down there, tore the room apart, ripped everything out of his closet, under the bed, he's six, a little guy, and he started crying. But he was afraid of me..."

I grappled with myself for a long time debating whether what Adrienne saw was a drunken fantasy or was a legitimate encounter. Based on other information concerning Cal and the Visitors, I elected to keep it in this book. I believe she saw someone in her home that night.

"A few mornings later he looked tired. I asked him if he was sleeping, and he told me there was a boogeyman in his room at night. At first—God, I was so stupid—I told him there was no such thing, that he was perfectly safe. How I didn't see it was really them I surely don't know." She rubbed her face with her hands, her plastic patient bracelet winking in the sun. "It wasn't until...he came to me one night. I was asleep—" I wanted to ask if she were under the influence, but something in her downturned eyes told me she was. "—and my door swings open. Real slow, creaky on its hinges. The sound wakes me up, and I look, and little Cal is standing there, in the doorway. We always kept a nightlight in the hall, for when he had to get up and go to the potty. I couldn't see his face, it was all dark, in shadows. He stood there. I said his name. Said it again. His head was down, his little shoulders slumped over. I flicked on the light, and he fell, crumpled into a ball. The front of him was all blood. I run to him, picked him up, and he said 'White.' I asked him what he was talking about, got him laid out on the floor and he said 'It's all white, Mama.' The doctor said he poked a hole in his nose with a pencil or something, and that's what got him the nosebleed. But I don't leave none-a that shit where he can get to it. The doc said then he musta done it with his finger."

This is not the first time I'd heard this type of story. The nasal tracking implants they put inside us—usually in the sinus cavity—don't always take, and sometimes work their way free. It seems more common in children.

"A few days later, though, he said the strangest thing to me. 'They put a slug up my nose, Mama. It burned and then I woke up.' What does that mean?"

"A slug up the nose?" I asked. I'd not heard that before. "That may be a dream, is he afraid of slugs?"

"Not especially."

"A boy at daycare tormented him with one perhaps?"

"Not that I heard about."

"I've never heard of an extraterrestrial slug being used on anyone," I said. I vowed I would look into it, and through all my research, and the research of several colleagues, I could find nothing on the topic. I have dismissed it as a childhood dream.

"They took him again after that. I guess it was like with me, where the Tylwyth Teg came first and the Sangaumans came second. To check up on him. We couldn't help them. We weren't going to be the key to their interbreeding, so I don't know why they won't leave us alone." She started to cry. The orderly gave me a nasty look, like I'd done something to her. "He's got a really nice new friend in Rhode Island," Adrienne said. "His name is Max."

"That's good. I'm glad to hear it."

We chatted a bit more about how he was adjusting,

then I left her, hoping not too much time would pass before we met again.

19

Val let the steaming hot water pour over him, almost scalding him, turning his white skin bright pink. He leaned against the shower wall, breathing in the steam, the drumming of the water harmonizing with the hum in his head. He stared at a bar of soap, a thin little bar, taken from a motel somewhere.

If he tried, he could move it with his mind.

Because he was contaminated.

He lifted it, just a little bit above the tray where it rested, then let it splash back down.

He had to pull himself together to see his mother off. Then he would evaluate the next step. Keep his shit together for the rest of the night, then he could lose it. Maybe she'd have some answers for him.

He'd spent so many years telling himself his mother was crazy, that she was a drunk. Which was why she sent him east with Dick and Sally.

It explained how he could kill those people without getting hurt.

He wondered what Kate had seen, what she was talking about. She probably didn't want to hurt his feelings.

Maria was still in the driveway.

They'd get her into the Daytona, and then Val would have to go. Maria could wait, Caroline could not.

He toweled off, goose bumps rising on his skin after the heat of the shower. Having a list in mind of things to do made him feel better. He pulled on his jeans, aware that he would need to do laundry sometime; these jeans were ready to stand up and walk around on their own. That grown-up thought conflicted with everything going on around him. He found a T-shirt, and his hat, not looking at the sharp knife that lay on his bedroom floor. Instead of kicking it under the bed, he gave it a shove with his mind. Pressure squeezed his head, the hum intensified, and the knife scooted out of sight.

Wild. Maybe it would be okay. He had a feeling, though, that it wouldn't, it couldn't, there were too many bodies and too much left unexplained.

Kate stood at the screen door, looking at the pink mass in the dark driveway. The Daytona was parked closer to the body. Kate had moved the car. She had the light on over the stoop and moths crowded around it, *thunking* into the globe and the screen.

"Hi," he said.

"You look better."

"We'll get her in the car, then I'll take the truck."

"That's what I was thinking," Kate said.

They both looked out into the night. A few bats fluttered around in the sky, supping on the insects drawn to the light.

"We can't keep doing this."

Val started to speak, to tell her he'd get it figured out.

"They'll find us. The cops are smart. Maybe Spence isn't, but he'll bring in the state cops, or the FBI and they'll find us. We haven't been that careful. No matter where we go, they'll find us."

Even in Santa Fe, they couldn't stay lost forever. And once he ceased to check in with his parole officer (which he needed to do in two days—can't forget that no matter how crazy shit gets) he'd be fucked.

Val nodded.

"We gotta go. Let's move her."

Since they'd run out of dish washing gloves, Val grabbed a blanket off the couch to wrap her in. If the bodies were found they were fucked. If they weren't, they had a shot. At this point, gloves didn't really matter one way or another.

Getting her in the car was easy, compared to the frat boy or TJ. She wasn't a small girl, but she seemed light by comparison. The shovel had crumpled the left side of her face, shattering the bones around her eye, flattening her nose. Val did everything in his power to not think about it.

"Should we take her to the mine? Get it over with?" Kate asked.

Yes, thought Val, but he couldn't stand the thought of going there, of feeling that strange pressure. "We don't have time." Leaving the body in the car was the most dangerous thing they'd done. It meant her scent would be heavier in the car if they brought dogs, though she was less bloody than the ones that had been ripped apart. She was still bound to leak into the car.

He noticed Kate scanning the edge of the light where the driveway melted away to blackness. Looking for something.

Val wondered about burning the car; how he could do it without attracting suspicion.

"Do you want me to drive?" Kate asked, as they walked towards the truck, after the trunk of the Daytona was slammed shut.

"No." Bless her heart, she didn't argue. The driving would cleanse him, ease his thoughts. Center him.

At the same place as before, he noticed the hum was gone. Without it filtering, sounds were crisper; the colors of the night were sharper. He pulled over to the side of the road.

"What are you doing?" Kate asked. Her voice was wary. Tension radiated off her, though she tried to seem calm and relaxed. She didn't trust him, and that made him sad, though he didn't hold it against her. He could stroke her hair while he held the wheel, though that didn't seem like it would win him any points.

"I want to try something."

"Are you being intentionally vague?"

"No." He cranked the truck's wheel, spinning its new tires in the dirt, sending it back towards his mother's trailer. He might not have time for this, but he had to know.

"I think the hum is geographical."

"What?"

"It always stops in the same spot. Right now I don't feel it at all."

He drove, and it came in like before. At first, even though he watched for it, strained for it, he wondered if maybe one of the belts in the truck was starting to let go, then realized it was his hum, back again.

"It's back!" Discovering something, anything about it gave him a sense of elation and power. It couldn't be in his head if it had borders.

He made a clumsy K turn in the middle of the road, and headed away from home towards where Mom was dying. Did he want her to be dead when he got there? Was he stalling in hopes of putting off conversation?

The hum melted away like an early frost as he passed the same spot, easily discernible by a bluff of stratified red rock that had been partially blasted away to make way for the road.

"It's not in my head."

"I saw a monster. This can't all be in your head. It had

claws, huge claws! It can't be a coincidence."

A monster? Claws? And telekinesis? "But I actually can move things with my mind?"

Kate looked uncomfortable that he'd posed it as a question to her. She fidgeted in the vinyl seat her eyebrows rising.

"I guess it makes sense," he said. "Didn't the military used to keep pet psychics? Competing with the Russians in the Cold War, who were much more excited about their pet psychics."

"I don't know," said Kate.

He wasn't sure if it was true, or if it was what pop culture wanted him to think. He seemed to remember a MacGyver episode about a Russian psychic but it may have been debunked mid-episode as a hoax.

They got to the hospice much faster than Val expected.

"I'll stay in the car," said Kate. "Get some sleep. Think about some stuff."

Val didn't like the tone of that last bit, but it made sense and he nodded. Then he kissed her cheek, and she stiffened under him. He gave her a sad smile, not meeting her eyes.

The same girl worked the desk. The lights in the lobby were low and soothing, the reception area was empty.

With no pleasantries, he signed in and went to his mother's room. The girl watched him go. She didn't say anything, and he interpreted that to mean his mom was in rough shape.

He didn't want to wake her if she were asleep and tried to keep his footsteps quiet. The dark voice in the back of his mind hoped she was asleep, maybe unconscious, then he could sit dutifully by her side, maybe switch the TV over to something interesting, and maybe they'd kick him out when it got to be too late, he could regretfully sigh and politely say he'd see them tomorrow.

Caroline was awake.

Whatever the previous night had sapped from the son it added to the mother.

Caroline looked worlds better propped up on some pillows and sitting up. Her face brightened when she saw him.

I thought she was dying. I thought this was it. He felt a little duped.

"Valentine!"

"Hey," he said, wondering if it were appropriate to tell her she looked better. Would that draw attention to how crappy she'd looked the day before? He settled for "How are you feeling?"

"Better," she said, not sounding addled like she had the day before. She took him in with her eyes. "You're so tall," she said, and he nodded, even though he hadn't grown in about ten years.

He sat on the chair next to her bed. He wondered if it were appropriate to ask *why* she was feeling better. Angelina hadn't made it sound very likely when she'd called.

After "How are you feeling?" the questions dried up in him.

"What did you do last night?" She asked. "Is it nice to be home?"

Two days, he thought. *You don't want to know what I've done.*

He could ask her about the aliens, he guessed. But she looked so normal. Like a mom, not drunk, and not ranting.

"It's weird. Stuff's changed, but a lot hasn't."

"Did you see *that girl* last night?"

Maybe it was better when she was delirious.

"Her name is Kate. I did see her. She's doing well."

"You were such good friends with her brother."

He dove into the topic on his mind. "Tell me about the aliens, Mom." Anything to get her off the topic of the Fultons. If she'd wanted him to have a nice life, with nice friends, she should have left him with Dick and Sally.

"The what?" she asked, her face growing dark, and he panicked for a moment before he realized she was stalling.

"Aliens."

"You're ready to listen, finally?" she asked, her tone laced with strychnine, her brow furrowing.

He opened his mouth for a gentle rebuttal, but she bowled him over. "You would never listen before. You never believed me. Now you're just humoring me."

"I'm not humoring you. Tell me your story."

"Have you read the book?" She was proud of being in that thing.

"I always thought it was crap before."

"What did you see?" she asked, looking curious and afraid beneath the blonde wig. He shouldn't have brought it up. He didn't want to upset her.

"I asked you first."

He didn't like the proud smile she gave, stinking of "*that's my boy.*" "Judd wrote a book all about it. I was on the Jerry Springer show."

Val shook his head. She was an embarrassment.

"They've been to see me." He swallowed past a knot in his throat. Should he show her his trick?

"Tell me."

Against his better judgment, he said "look." He just did a tissue on the night stand. Her eyes went wide and she started to cough. A frog in her throat. *Frog…or something worse?* Val thought of chest-bursters, and then of the thick feeling he'd had in his sinuses when he woke up that morning. Fear pressed against his sternum.

He let his hand hover over the call button.

"Do I need to call someone?"

"No."

His hand dropped.

"Fine."

She composed herself, regarding him like a cat watches a mouse. She seemed fine again. What had Angelina meant when she called, saying this looked like the end? Maybe he could even take her home, if she continued to feel this good…though the thought of sharing the trailer with her wasn't one he liked.

So he let fly with the million dollar question, not expecting an answer. Any one of the answers she'd given over the years could be the right one, though he suspected none of them were. Who had contaminated him?

"Who's my father?" he asked.

When she laughed it came out as a hollow, croaking sound.

"I knew you'd ask," she said, her tone condescending, as though he asked a frivolous question.

"Funny, I'm still curious after all this time. You'd think prison would have made me forget about that." He glared down at his hands.

"You were in prison?"

When Val looked up she looked cloudy and far away, like she had yesterday. No, she couldn't lose it, not right now, not when she might give him a real answer.

"When were you in prison?" she asked, her voice sounding like it came through a tunnel.

"For a drunk and disorderly," he said, the words coming in a torrent. *Like you.*

"Poor boy," she said; the role of mother seeping back in.

He should have humored her, shouldn't have talked about aliens. Not here. Shit. He rubbed at his eyes.

"Are you all right?" she asked.

He smiled a panicked shark's grin at her. *See, look how nice my teeth are. Everything is great.*

"Knock knock," Angelina called, like the other day, so much like the other day Val wondered if this were some kind of hellish time loop. She wore her own jack-o-lantern smile, he noticed. It must come with proximity to the dying. "Hi, Caroline, how are we today?" The word *we* made Val grit his teeth.

"Good, Sally," Caroline said. "Did you know Val spent a night in jail?"

The nurse made a *tsk*-ing sound and he wanted her to choke on it.

"Mister Slade, may I speak with you outside?"

"Yes," he said, wondering how she could backslide so fast, if she'd been as lucid as she seemed, or if maybe he'd seen what he wanted to see. "Call me Val."

"Your mother has taken a turn for the worse," Angelina said, looking up at him with a doleful expression. "I'm pleased you made it in time."

In time? Whoa, what?

"She was better. A few minutes ago. She was clear and talking, and she remembered stuff."

Angelina nodded, and checked the chart by the door. "We'd given her a shot. The shots clear her up for a few minutes. She had a bad night last night."

Didn't we all, Val thought, then regretted the selfishness of the thought. "So give her another shot. I need to talk to her."

Angelina shook her head. Somehow she made even that wordless gesture seem condescending. "It would kill her. That's powerful medication." She fired off some clinical terms at him, but he didn't understand.

"None of that means anything to me," he said. "Is this, like, it?"

Pursing her lips, Angelina gave a little half shrug. "In any other patient, I'd say yes."

"But?"

"Her condition has been so strange, so up and down, I won't say for sure."

Val let out a pent-up breath.

"I think she was waiting to see you again before she

died."

She didn't even like *me,* Val thought.

"Should I stay?" he asked. He didn't want to. He didn't want to alone, anyway. Kate was in the car, he could bring her in, but being alone was for the best. He wouldn't want to be held captive while her mother died. He chastised himself for every insensitive thought. He wished he could shut his brain off.

"I would," Angelina said. Of course she would, she'd elected to spend her life around the dying. "We can make exceptions to visiting hours in these kinds of situations."

"Okay," he said.

When he went back in the room Caroline was asleep or unconscious. Her breath was steady and her machines made a rhythmic beeping that replaced the hum in his head. He picked up the remote control and carried over another chair to prop his feet up on, careful not to make a sound. *Predator* was playing on one of the movie channels (she got HBO, Showtime, and Cinemax, and still she watched the shopping channel?) and he settled in to watch.

The beeping stopped right around the time when former Minnesota Governor Jesse Ventura's character got mangled by the Predator. He registered something was different in the room, but it took another second and muting the film to register what it was. The light over her bed went out, the light bulb winking to darkness, and as he stood, almost knocking over the padded hospital chair, the TV remote clattered to the floor.

Just like that? He thought, panic seeping around the edges.

He mashed on the call button, while repeating "Mom, it's me, wake up," over and over again in a low voice. Hers not being the first dead body he'd seen that day, he knew she was gone but his mind had gone all flighty, touching on thoughts before lifting off again to perch somewhere else.

At least he hadn't killed her.

He couldn't even hold his tongue for the little time they'd had together. Angelina came in and took his hand in her own chubby one.

"Aren't you going to do something?" he asked.

She turned to him with tears glistening in her eyes, and squeezed his hand. "No, dear."

"Can't you do CPR, or give her a shot or something?" He thought of movies where people were resurrected by an adrenaline shot to the heart. Surely they had something that could help her kicking around here.

Now she took him into her plump arms. He accepted the hug, standing still and limp, unsure of what else to do. She was warm and smelled medicinal, making him think of all sorts of medical experiences. "That's not what we do here, love." She laid her head against his chest, and he wanted to shove her off.

On the muted television, California Governor Arnold Schwarzenegger smeared mud on himself as he prepared to battle the Predator.

"You're going to let her die?" Val asked; the volume and pitch of his voice climbing.

Orange light from the street lamp in the parking lot shone through the window, casting Venetian blind stripes across the wall, dark in the low light after the bulb had blown. Had he done that?

Funeral arrangements. Who would he call? Who were her friends? Did she have friends? His T-shirt grew damp as he realized the nurse was crying on him. And what, he'd been putting off checking, was the money situation? He'd sell the trailer and the land as fast as he could, move in with Kate in Santa Fe, but he needed to buy a headstone, a casket, cremation…fuck.

"I need to sit," he said, pushing her off and dropping to the chair. She kept a hand on his shoulder and it sat there, warm and moist. Christ, all he wanted in the entire world was for this woman to stop touching him.

"Is there someone you can call?" she asked.

Call? For what?

"I'm fine."

"You're not fine."

"No, I really am fine."

"I can't imagine what you've gone through these past few days. You're a brave boy." *I'm not a fucking boy!* "At least you got to say goodbye."

But he hadn't. He watched a crappy old movie and let her die right there. He wasn't holding her hand when she went, wasn't telling her he loved her; he was captivated by the alien on TV, picking off the Army guys one by one.

Asking this woman for help was the last thing Val wanted to do. But he didn't know. He couldn't leave her here. He wanted to head to Cochran's Liquor Store on Main Street, get a handle of tequila, and disappear into it.

"What do I do?" he asked, his voice a whisper.

"Poor dear," she said, and his skin crawled under her sympathy.

He waited a moment for her to answer him, he didn't want to repeat himself, didn't want to feel indebted to her kindness, which infuriated him. "Where do I start?" He racked his brain, thinking of all the television shows he'd seen where someone died. "Calling a coroner?"

Again, she took him into her repulsive arms. Together, Val and Angelina began to make arrangements for his mother.

20

The truck was the only vehicle in the visitors' parking lot. Not much light came up from Nassar Valley, some streetlights here and there, but most of the housing developments were dark. The sky loomed overhead, and Val wondered what watched him from above. There was a certain inevitability to it, something that could traverse galaxies…could you even try to fight it? Why him? He guessed *why Caroline* was the more important question.

Caroline who was dead.

Val looked in the window of the truck, saw Kate there, curled in an uncomfortable ball on the vinyl seat. One foot touched the window near his face, and he put a hand on the glass.

He could leave. Then none of this would be her problem ever again. He could disappear into the night, walking across the desert.

She stirred in her sleep, and he opened the door.

His mother was dead.

The sound of the door woke Kate up. She uncurled, stretched like a cat, making a little mewling noise and rubbing at her eyes.

"How is she?" Kate asked.

Val was suddenly robbed of his voice. He shook his head, unsure where this emotion came from, where it had been hiding.

"I'm so sorry."

He shook his head again, a lump crawling into his throat and nesting there, setting up shop, all comfortable-like.

Val wanted to get drunk. He bought a handle of tequila at the liquor store, making it in minutes before they closed. He set it on the floor, sealed, until he pulled into the dooryard. He passed the place in the road where the hum began, and it did so, starting with just a tickle, and building to a steady vibration. In the driveway the Daytona mocked him, yellow with its evil load. Not tonight. He couldn't deal with it, couldn't deal with the body, the mine, any of it.

Standing under the stars in the warm night, he looked around, feeling a light breeze on his face. His mother used to have wind chimes hanging by the front door. He was glad they were gone; their hollow, musical tones unsettled him. Unbidden, he heard them and saw a great white light. What was he?

"I need to go." His voice sounded like it hadn't been used for a thousand years. His lips were dry. The tequila would wet them. It would block everything. It would reduce him to nothing.

"Where?" She sounded startled, and her eyes shot to the yellow car.

"I can't do it. Not now. I have to go." He paused, rubbed at his unshaven face. "Away. Anywhere."

"I'm calling Felix."

"I don't care."

"Please don't go anywhere."

"I got to be by myself. I need to think." *And drink.* He didn't want anything left. He unscrewed the cap, saw her lips purse—she was unsure whether or not to let him.

"I have to go," he said again, bringing the bottle to his lips and taking in the fire of the drink. It burned his throat, like the red sea it parted for the lump of grief there, and respectfully went around. He left, touching Kate's hair with his free hand feeling crazy and free.

Out in the night, under the mantle of stars, the sky threatened to suffocate him. So big, so black…it was everywhere. Somewhere deep inside he longed for four institution-green walls, eight feet by eight feet of security. They meet your needs in prison. In prison you start to see everything through a nicked, scratched sheet of Plexiglass. When everything was kept at arm's length, nothing could hurt.

Had he even loved her? Here was the nexus of the problem. If he could answer yes, then the guilt would melt away. He hadn't been a good son, and she hadn't been a good mother. She started it. It wasn't his fault.

A second gulp of tequila bolstered him.

Wasn't his fault.

Why was his face wet?

Aw, fuck.

He'd been a bad son and now it was over. It sickened him that he was feeling sorry for *himself* as opposed to his dead mother. In a way he was angry at her for leaving him like this. He *was* angry, mad at her because he felt so shitty.

He should be missing her. But you can't miss something that's never been there.

Val wandered, for the first time awake and wearing shoes, through the scrub brush and rocks, onto national forest land. He was not aware that he headed for the Olympus Mine. His current path would not bring him to the entrance, but it did lead him above the deepest shaft. When he got there, he knew it was time to stop.

He fell to his knees and unscrewed the tequila bottle. It felt like he was deep under water. The hum was all around him, like cotton tucking him into a box for safe-keeping. He held the bottle up to the moon, and saw the worm's still form bobbing around. He took a long pull and wondered what the point of living was. Common sense suggested lots of reasons, but he elected to ignore them in favor of self-pity. Another slug of tequila and he stared up at the stars. There were a few clouds in the sky, and stars peeked out from behind them, glittering in the night. He exhaled, and it turned into a sob. Fuck. He didn't want to cry anymore. Too late. Finally alone, away from everything, Val emptied himself spiritually there on the rocky ground, setting the tequila bottle down on a flat spot as he cried and howled and felt pathetic.

Val didn't realize he was no longer alone in the desert. It came on silent paws and sat on tawny haunches. It watched. It flexed and un-flexed its three-foot claws, then put them away, watching, curling its furry crocodile tail around its feet like a cat.

Finally, when he felt empty and used up, Val raised his eyes. He was too drained to feel afraid when he looked at it, but it registered that this was what had killed TJ and the frat boy. The thing Kate saw.

Its body was covered in sleek, sorrel fur and shaped like a lion. Thick legs, thick neck. The way it sat obscured its claws, but he could see them, great knives tucked away beneath it.

Fine. Let it kill him. That would be a peachy end to a great day. He was shit. He'd been a shit son; he was a shit boyfriend; so much so that he went to jail he was so shitty at it. He wouldn't even taste good to the thing sitting there before him. Shit pickled in tequila.

"Do you mind?" he slurred at the thing. Space Puma. That was what it looked like. Some kind of freaky mutant radiation space cat from the Alamogordo blasts.

It cocked its head and opened its mouth in a silent cry. Its mouth was a perfect circle lined with little, nasty teeth.

"Sorry," he said to it. "You're a dream. I can't even fucking sleep. Let's have one big pity party for me." Val took a long slug of tequila. He sighed and looked at his feet. "Do you have the answer?" he asked the thing. It opened its mouth silently again. "You got some ugly teeth, cat."

Val talked to the creature and it sat still as a stone, watching him. Protecting him? Presently Val's talking gave way to more crying, which he hadn't thought possible, and when he stopped again the worm didn't have much tequila to float in. He sat in silence, watching his new imaginary friend. He wasn't sure if it was real or not, but after all this time he was pretty sure it wouldn't hurt him. That didn't mean he was going to reach out and pat it, but they had a connection. They were pals.

It unfurled claws the length of its front leg. He noticed it walked on the outsides of its wrists, that the spots were calloused and black, and its claws looked very sharp, like glistening white bone in the starlight. How did it walk like that? Val was too drunk to be afraid. He was fascinated by the way its joints worked, how could its wrist still be so limber after taking the animal's weight for running? It had three claws per foot. Its back feet looked more puma-like, more dog-like, really, the short claws didn't seem to be retractable, and regular wear and tear from walking kept them short. It reached out to him, the claw tips wavering in front of his face. It touched him, a gentle caress that didn't break the skin.

He stood up, his joints stiff from sitting for so long. The thing stood with him, and stepped back, looking startled and wary. "Sorry, didn't mean to jump you. I'd best be going. I'm glad we had this talk. I'll look you up next time my mother dies."

Leaving the animal behind, he stumbled home.

21

There was a flat *pop* as the tire went dead.

Of course, in the rain. Always in the rain, only in the rain. Gabriela Correa cursed and eased the car to the side of the narrow dirt road, careful to avoid the deep gully which the downpour had filled with rushing water. She didn't need this. Eddie sat in the back seat, oblivious and quiet. He wasn't feeling well. Not since the rest area outside Lott. He'd let her drive in peace, no yelling, singing, talking. When she asked him about it, he gave sullen, one word answers. She'd been thankful for the quiet at first, now she felt bad about that. One more thing to worry about.

The rain didn't look like it would let up any time soon. She got out of the car, looking away from the headlights, unable to see in the dark after the brightness of the car's dome light. The rain beat her back with its downpour.

One of the back tires. Of course it was the one on the edge of the road. She fought back tears as she used the key to pop open the elderly Civic's trunk. Work-roughened hands pushed aside the trunk's carpet, revealing the jack and tire iron beneath. Fate told her this was a mission she shouldn't be taking. But even if she was deported, she'd made damn sure Eddie was born here.

They'd passed a trailer a few minutes ago, she hoped she could do this herself; that she wouldn't need to go and wake anyone up to use their phone. She couldn't afford a tow truck.

"What happened?" he asked in Spanish, from right behind her. She jumped and knocked her head on the open trunk, dropping the tire iron. It clattered down on top of the spare tire, clanging in the night. He stood in the road, shoulders stooped; his yellow rain slicker unzipped.

"Get back in the car, sweetie," she said, also in Spanish, pulse pounding in her ears. "It's too wet out here."

"What are you doing?"

"We had a flat tire. Go sit down, I'll only be a minute."

The boy didn't move. Looked past her, down the dark dirt road. Away from Mexico. She went back to the tire, pulling on it, wrestling it from the floor of the trunk. Rain dripped into her eyes, stinging them. She blinked it away.

"Eddie," she called.

The yellow of his slicker caught her eye, yellow against the darkness. "Get back in the car! We don't have time for this."

He didn't listen. Didn't stop. Kept walking. Again, she set the tire down, and stepped after him.

"Eddie!"

He didn't even turn his head. Gabriela left the keys dangling from the trunk lid and went after him.

Gravel from the road skittered somewhere, audible under the sound of the shower. A deer? Did squirrels come out at night?

She strained her ears, looked out into the wet blackness beside the car.

Maybe there was more out here to be afraid of than being deported.

She went back to the car and picked up the tire iron, the metal cold and slick with rain.

Something stepped out of the rain. It advanced on her son like a tiger stalks its prey, one foot in front of the other.

What was it?

What was wrong with its feet?

"Get away!"

Her voice seemed so loud, even against the downpour. She ran for her son, who walked on, oblivious.

It pounced, its feet unfolding, revealing knives in its paws. Knives? Claws?

They were on her son, but she brought the tire iron down on its shoulder, a blow that strained her muscles. It turned to look at her, its eyes were deep black pools, shaped like diamonds, reflecting the yellow light of the car's blinker. It opened a circular mouth full of needle-sharp teeth, but didn't make a sound. She swung again, hitting across its face. It looked at the boy—oh god, so much blood—and back at her, then disappeared in a tawny flash.

The night was quiet again.

She scooped her son up in her arms, able to see pink meat under his yellow slicker, so much blood all over it.

There was a driveway back there, wasn't there? A trailer tucked back from the road?

His face was so white, even his lips were white.

She scooped him up in her arms, tugging the slicker closed over the slices in his leg and his belly. Cradling him like an infant, she left the tire iron behind as she struggled down the road to where she hoped she'd seen a trailer.

22

The rain started after he staggered back into the trailer. He didn't feel drunk anymore, not really, more mystified, empty and sad.

Kate had waited up for him, but he'd only barely acknowledged her before falling into bed.

He woke up from a white dream, the room seeming all the more black in comparison. The hum made his head feel crowded and muffled.

Something struck the side of the trailer hard enough to make the windows rattle. Kate was awake. They both turned towards the sound, and when she turned back he was staring at her.

"What was that?" she asked. "The wind?"

It was never the wind. Why couldn't it just this once be the wind?

"Doubtful," Val said.

And he was right. Wind didn't forcefully pound on a door, screaming words muffled by a wall and the rain.

Val stood and pulled on his jeans. "If that's your goddamn brother…" He opened the drawer of the bedside table. "Damn. Gun's still in the truck. I guess I won't shoot him." Kate followed him into the hall, pulling on a pair of sweatpants.

"Why is the gun in the truck?" Kate asked, trailing after him.

"I took it with me tonight. Just in case."

"In case of what?"

Val went to the door, paused a beat. The pounding, accented by the driving rain, continued. He put a hand on the doorknob, took a knife from the nearby drawer, and threw open the door.

A woman stood on the ground where the steps should have been, drenched and non-threatening, holding a crumpled, bloody, humanoid mess in her arms.

"*Ayúdeme,*" she breathed. Kate and Val blinked at one another. He stood there, staring through the screen door.

"Let her in!" Kate snapped, and Val opened the torn screen door and held it for the woman. Setting the knife on the counter, he took her wrist and helped her inside.

"*Ayúdenos*!" the woman brayed, thrusting the mess at Val, a child, an offering.

Kate swept a few beer cans off the counter, and the woman lay the child down. Val still stood, holding open the door, looking like a deer in headlights. Kate called his name and he let it bang shut.

"What happened?" Kate asked.

"*Un animal. Con las garras.*"

Claws. Val thought of his new friend. Those were the biggest claws he'd ever seen.

Lightning lit the sky, followed by a window-rattling crash of thunder. Had the first bang been the woman, or thunder?

"Puma?" Val asked. He took a step away from the door. The off-white Formica surface of the counter turned pink with blood and water.

Kate reached for the phone on the wall. The line was dead. Out here the phone went out whenever the wind blew. At least they'd had the sense to bury the power lines. She went to the bedroom and pulled her cell out of the pocket of her jeans. She came back to the kitchen, dialing 911.

The child was a boy, maybe seven years old. They'd removed his yellow rain slicker and his pants. Ashen gray on the table, he lay there in a soaked T-shirt and colorful briefs. Val stared at him a moment, those deep gashes; the red making his skin look even more lifeless. Val whipped the leather studded belt out of his pants and fashioned a tourniquet at the boy's groin. He'd seen it in a movie.

"They've got me on hold," Kate said, her panic barely contained.

"Fuck!" Val started CPR on the boy. The woman kept coming up to Val, standing too close, looking down at what he was doing and praying in Spanish. Blood spurted from the wounds in time with Val's beating. Someone answered the phone and Kate told them where to come. It would take at least half an hour from Lott to get here, worse if any of the roads had washed out. She explained the boy wasn't breathing, and someone was doing CPR. The operator asked to be given to Val.

"Looks like his femoral artery is slashed. He's bleeding all over the place. And the slices in his stomach…I can't do anything about those. I've got compresses on them. He's lost a lot of blood. I—I got his heart going again. I don't know if it will last." Val was silent, listening. He wiped his bloody hands on his pants. "They look like claw marks. She says an animal did it. They showed up at my door, I'm the nearest house, I guess." He listened again, for a moment. "Big goddamn animal."

He pumped and breathed for the boy, ignoring the light pink whatever he was fairly sure was an intestine peeking out. Val hung up the phone and looked at Kate.

"He needs a million things I can't do," Val said. He applied pressure to the stomach wounds. "Hold this," he said to the boy's mother. She did, calling out after them in frustration as they left the room.

Val led Kate to the bedroom. "You need to get the gun out of my truck. Do something with Rich's Mossberg."

"What are you talking about?"

"He is going to die. The cops are going to come. And I'm going to get arrested."

"What are you talking about?"

"Hello. What did I just get out of jail for? What kinds of people aren't I supposed to be around?" He paced back and forth, and she sat on the bed.

"But…they can't…"

"Sure they can. I had my mouth on his mouth— "

"To save his life."

"Which I'm sure I didn't do. That boy is going to die." Val lowered his voice. "Why didn't it kill me? I sat right there with it, tonight, and it looked at me. It's killed everyone else, why not me?" He began to pace. "Should I run? If you think I should, I will." Before she could answer, he rubbed his eyes and said. "No. That would be stupid. I'm not smart enough to run from the cops. I can't keep my mouth shut about anything. Fuck, Kate. I don't want to go back there."

The mother called from the kitchen, panic in her voice. Val bet the world the heartbeat was gone.

"He's gone," Val said. "Get the gun, do something with it. Something smart so hopefully I can find it again." He ran for the kitchen.

No heartbeat, too much blood. He started CPR, the boy's lips like cool, flaccid rubber under his own. He lost himself in the rhythm, keeping time in his head with the song *Another One Bites the Dust*. Kate stepped out into the rain, as the hum and *Queen* resonated in his head.

23

Kate stepped out the screen door into the rain. It lambasted her, flattening her hair to her head, soaking her T-shirt and pressing it against her body. She ran to the truck and jumped in on the driver's side.

When she slammed the door, the dome light went out, and everything seemed very, very black. The rain drummed on the metal roof. She opened the glove box and she reached over, groped around, and picked up the gun. She looked at it in the low light, little more than a blacker spot in the dark.

Would the police look in his dead mother's room? Above the drop ceiling in her closet? Would they look anywhere at all? Should she move her car? She looked over at it, yellow and inauspicious in the rain. There would be no reason to look in the car. Right?

The kitchen lights were long and distorted by the sluices of rainwater flowing down the truck's window. Darkness pressed from outside.

What if the thing was out here? She'd seen it, Val had seen it, there was no doubt that's what got to the little boy.

And TJ. And the frat boy. Why hadn't it gotten Maria? She looked out into the rain, trying to scan the yard for the animal.

It wasn't far to the house. She could make it there in time. And also before the police arrived, she mused. It wouldn't do to be caught standing in the driveway, armed and dangerous, when they arrived.

Everything exploded in a flash of blinding white light and an accompanying crash. Across the yard, by the gnarled shape of some scrub brush, Kate saw something, a lithe animal shape crouching. Or a rock.

She might not be able to make it inside after all. She chewed on her lip and stared as hard as she could at the corner of the house, but the lightning had destroyed her night vision.

She had a gun.

She could shoot it, if there was something out there. That could at least slow it down, and let her get in the house. She thought of the flimsy two-ply door, and wondered what good it would do. Stupid Val. This was all his fault. Except it wasn't. All he'd done was get out of jail. And he wasn't stupid.

She groped around on the dark floor. Opening the door for the dome light was an option. Then her antagonist would have a clear view of where she was, and the little bit of vision that came back would be gone. She opened the door.

Feeling the rain blowing into the truck, cool wetness in the warm night, she ran. She held the gun in her left hand then she threw the truck door shut with her right and sprinted across the gravel driveway in her bare feet. And nothing happened.

She sort of tucked the gun under her soggy T-shirt and went inside. Looking between Val and the mother, she saw their faces were grim. They both looked at her. The mother dropped her eyes, cradling the boy's limp, wet body to her. Val wasn't giving the boy CPR anymore. He followed Kate down the hall.

"You might want to change your shirt."

"I think I saw something outside."

"Something?"

"Crouching over by the corner of the trailer, near the brush." She took the gun to the bathroom, wiped it down. She pulled aside the tile in the closet ceiling, and placed the gun up there. Val handed her the Mossberg, and she placed it next to the handgun. Over the wail of a siren, soft and faint, she replaced the tile.

"Too late, boys," Val said. "Seriously, change your shirt. Or don't. Maybe they'll be less likely to arrest me."

Kate changed her shirt.

The paramedics came in and started in on the boy, replacing Val's belt with a real tourniquet. They worked for maybe ten minutes, asked questions of Val, asked the boy's mother in Spanish. Kate couldn't understand what she said, but her answers didn't seem to be what the paramedics were looking for. Then the police arrived.

Spence hurried in, and Duane Harvey. Duane was two years ahead of Kate's class, but he and Rich had been pretty tight, smoking pot together and some pickup basketball games, and for that reason Duane had something of a personal vendetta against Val.

"Hey, Slade, why don't you get in the car?" Harvey asked, as the call to the coroner was placed.

"Can I grab a shirt first?"

"We're not arresting you. We need to talk to both of you at the station for questioning," Spence said, sounding kinder.

"No thanks," Val said, ignoring Spence and locking eyes with Harvey.

"Come on, Val. You don't even have to wear the bracelets. We want to ask you some questions about what happened tonight." Spence kept his tone even, like someone dealing with a skittish dog.

"Like why you got a dead kid on your table. I thought you weren't supposed to be around kids."

"I'm the only child he's ever molested and you know it," Kate said. Spence gave a half smile and Harvey looked her up and down. Kate crossed her arms over her chest, glad she'd gotten out of the wet T-shirt. She saw Val's eyes narrow, and she put a hand on his back.

"I don't know why Rich hasn't cleaned your clock," Harvey said, turning towards the paramedics and the boy.

She could see Val weighing the pros and cons of some smart-ass remark.

"I'll be right behind you in the truck," she said to him.

"You're serious," Val said to Spence, all good humor bleeding from his voice.

"Just for questions. Grab your shirt and some shoes."

"Can I sit up front?"

Harvey rolled his eyes and went to talk to the dead boy's mother.

"Yeah, you can sit up front," Spence said.

"Then why can't I ride with her?"

"I need both of you. If you come, I know she's going to come. If I don't bring either of you, it's something of a crapshoot. You hear me?"

Val let a long breath out of his nose. "I hear you. Okay." Val disappeared down the hall for his shirt, and Spence joined Harvey. Kate stood alone as the boy was gently placed into a big black bag, too big for his small body. His mother cried, and Spence spoke soothingly to her in Spanish. Kate picked up a few words, like *muerto* and *mi hijo*, but that was about it.

Val came out of the bedroom and chucked the truck keys at her. She barely caught them.

"Can we go?" he asked Spence.

Spence excused himself, and turned to Kate and Val. "Yeah. You following, Kate?" She nodded and fetched her own shoes.

Val got like this. She knew he would probably cry if he took a moment to say goodbye to her. The first few months visiting him in jail had all been like this, she reflected, heading out to the truck. He'd been keeping his own emotions in, and keeping her at bay.

It wasn't until the truck roared to life and the headlights came on, joining the flashing red ambulance lights and the flashing blue police lights that Kate remembered how afraid she'd felt out here not long ago. The truck's headlights were angled in such a way that they alone illuminated the scrub brush in the side yard. She looked for movement, any sign of life, but in the drumming rain, everything was still.

The police cruiser behind her turned around on the lawn, and headed for Lott, switching off its lights. Kate switched the radio to a country station Val hated, and followed. She pulled out her phone and scrolled through for Felix's number. Call him? Don't call him? Val wasn't okay, and regardless of how Felix unsettled her at the bar, he was Val's closest friend. She looked at the clock, and as the phone rang in her ear, debated doing this in the morning.

"Hello?" It didn't sound like she'd wakened him.

"Hi, Felix?"

"Yeah, who's this?"

"Kate Fulton—"

"Val's Kate?" Felix's tone changed.

"Yes, Val's Kate."

"How are you? Is Val all right?"

"I don't know," she said, keeping her tone cautious. She kept the red taillights of the police cruiser in sight. "His mother died. And…He's been taken in for questioning."

"What kind of questioning? About his mother? The police have him?" His voice was like syrup, or like butter, smooth and sexy, yet something about it still put her on edge.

"The sheriff has him."

"For what?"

"A boy was killed tonight, and Val tried to save him. The deputy we talked to told us he's just being questioned. I'm even being brought in for questioning, and I don't know anything."

"I'll come by. He's at the sheriff's office?"

Kate said yes, and they said goodbye.

They hung up and she sat in the dark for a moment, trying to pin down what she didn't like about him.

They rolled into Lott's downtown.

24

They made Kate wait for a very long time in a room with bare, white walls. She sat on a wooden chair, at a wooden table. An interrogation room. When they'd questioned her before, they'd done it in an office. She'd been a minor then, she'd been the victim. Now she didn't know what she was. An accomplice?

Kate sat back in her chair, swinging her feet, tracing her finger across the rough surface of the table. A cup of coffee, now cold, sat untouched in front of her.

Spence came in with a file and sat on the edge of the table. They looked at each other for a moment. Spence looked tired, and Kate knew she must look as rough. Her hair didn't like getting wet, then drying naturally; it tended to result in an unkempt, tangled, curly dark mass.

"No one is pressing charges. His story and the Mexican woman's story match up. She's saying some crazy things, but even Harvey doesn't think we can pin anything on Val. The woman's an alien, so at the moment, everyone is more interested in her than in Val."

"I'm sorry, she's a what?"

"In the country unlawfully."

"Oh. Right. You're letting Val go?"

"Not yet."

The tension flooded back, perhaps worse than before, a knot between her shoulder blades.

"There's a guy from Immigration who wants to talk to him. Should be here in a few hours."

"About the woman?"

"Must be. She must be some kind of big deal if they're coming this early. They asked us not to send him home, to keep him here so they wouldn't have to go looking for him."

Kate felt as though this should have eased the knot in her neck, but it didn't. Tonight. She'd demand they go to Santa Fe tonight. No more of this.

"The paramedics said he did an impressive job keeping the boy alive as long as he did. If the kid had lived, he'd be a hero. I want to get your side of things."

"But since he died, we're happy with not getting arrested."

"Kate, look. I know he's not a violent guy. I like him. I want him to stay out of trouble. He's had a really awful couple of days."

"We're moving to Santa Fe soon," Kate said.

"Good. Rich is toxic. This place is toxic."

"But you're still here?"

Spence smiled a little and shrugged. "I'm fine. My family's all here. I can't leave them."

Kate nodded, though she didn't understand. Family was something to run from. She told her version of what happened, omitting, of course, the parts where she hid the gun. She didn't like lying to Spence, didn't like lying to anyone, but it was all she'd done for the past few days.

"That's all I need to know. They've searched his trailer, found nothing linking him to a crime, nothing illegal or out of the ordinary. You're good to go back there." Spence said, organizing the papers into his file. "Oh, Kate, one more thing."

Oh, fuck. TJ. It felt like the color drained from her face, but Spence didn't react, so she assumed she hadn't gone white.

"Rich called in last night saying his wife was missing."

"Good. Took her long enough."

"He sounded kind of frantic. He suspects foul play from Val."

"Of course he does." Kate locked eyes with Spence, and felt like she surely was going to hell. "How else can he justify the massive coincidence of his best friend and his wife going missing at the same time? Knowing them, I bet they waited for Val to get out because they knew Rich would think he had something to do with it."

Spence studied her a moment. She could feel tears coming. Frustration leaking from her eyes—they were powerless, powerless against the monster in the desert. One slipped from the corner of her left eye, cutting a wet trail down her face.

Spence's face softened. "I hope you get to Santa Fe. Wherever TJ and Maria went, he'll be gunning for Val."

"Can I see him?"

"Sure. I'll take you there."

She followed him. She wiped at her eyes. Exhaustion covered her like a cape, heavy and muffling.

The walls of the sheriff's office were all the same, light industrial green, devoid of pictures on the walls. Val's interrogation room was two doors down from hers.

"Knock when you want to come out." Spence knocked once on the door and opened it, admitting her. The lock clicked as he closed it behind her.

"Hey," she said.

Val looked exhausted, great dark circles under his eyes, and his dark hair a disheveled mess. "You should go home and get some sleep. I can get one of these guys to give me a ride. I guess someone from Immigration needs to talk to me, this lady's run a few illegals across the border."

She nodded. There didn't seem to be anything else she could do.

"You called Felix?" he asked.

"Yeah, he said he'd be here. He was pretty vague about when."

"Here or the house?"

"I think the house."

"Yeah, go home and rest, wait for him, I'll be along in a bit. I can't imagine this guy will have much to say to me."

"How are you being so calm about this?" Another tear, this time from the other eye.

"Don't cry," Val said, and took her hand. "I'm on auto pilot. I'm exhausted. I'm going to cooperate, and then they'll let me go. They've got nothing on me."

His tone calmed her even as she stood sniffling. "Okay." She wiped at her eyes and nose. "You sure you're okay?"

"What can get me in here?"

"Don't talk like that. Please."

"Okay. I'm safer in here than I am at home."

"I want to go tonight."

"Okay. As soon as I get back, we tie up loose ends, and then we're gone."

The tension ball melted. They were going. They were going to be safe. Everything would go back to normal.

"Go home," he said again.

She nodded. Being tired made her so goddamn emotional. She hugged him, loving the feel of him through his old T-shirt. So he wouldn't see her cry she turned away. Like Spence asked, she knocked on the door and he opened it for her.

25

What the fuck was Felix doing here?

Val opened his mouth to ask that very question, but Felix, sporting a nasty gash on his face and wearing an official *Homeland Security* windbreaker, winked at him. Val forced a quick cough but remained silent.

Felix stuck out his hand and Spence took it. "I'm Albert Vargas with USCIS." It was a forceful handshake. Val suppressed a laugh. Felix and Spence would get along great. He had no idea why Felix was here under this guise. He trusted his friend. All would be revealed in good time.

"I want to take a minute of your time, Mister," Felix checked a folder, "Slade." Felix was good.

"Okay," Val said. This felt a bit like the role-playing activities the prison shrink tried to get him to do. He couldn't get over himself enough to pretend to be someone else.

"You need me for anything else?" Spence asked.

"No, thank you."

Spence nodded and stepped out.

"What are you—"

Felix put a long finger to his lips. He touched his ear then gestured around the room. It was bugged.

"Gabriela Correa had quite the little racket going. I need you to come with me to her apartment and look at a few things, see if anything jogs your memory."

"What?" This was stupid. Was Felix doing this to get him out? Because if Felix hadn't done whatever he'd done, saying he was with Immigration, Val could have already been home by now. This wasn't helping.

"I've gotten clearance to take you to her apartment, with your consent, of course." Felix winked again and Val smiled a queasy smile. "It's downtown, then I can run you home."

"Okay."

Felix strode over to the door, looking like a government type. It made Val's head spin, didn't seem right. This was his prison buddy, for heaven's sake. At his knock, Spence opened the door for them.

"You feeling all right, Val?" Spence asked as they passed him.

"Yeah, it's been a rough day. I'm going to sleep all afternoon." *As soon as I hide the body festering in my girlfriend's trunk.*

Spence clapped him on the back. "Get out of here, man."

"As soon as I can."

Val followed Felix to the car.

It was a navy blue Crown Vic with USCIS decals on the doors and government plates. Oh Jesus, did he steal this car?

Val got in on the passenger's side, and buckled in. He didn't want to get shushed again, so he waited to speak until he was spoken to. At least the hum was gone.

"You look like shit, Val-ey boy." Felix started the car.

"I am beyond confused, man. What the fuck are you doing? Did you steal this car?"

"Nope."

Val waited a beat, but Felix didn't elaborate.

The car accelerated, pushing Val back into the plush seat. Buildings blurred outside. The cops wouldn't stop a government car, even if he whipped through stop signs.

"Felix, what the fuck are you doing?"

"I'm really quite sorry about this."

Val looked at his face, intent on the driving. They left the little downtown behind and sped out of Lott.

"Sorry about what?"

"I have to take you in."

"In? I was in. What the flaming fuckbuckets is going on?"

Felix chuckled. "You've always had a way with words."

"Yeah, it's why you like me. Where are we going?"

"Home."

"What?" Something in Felix's tone suggested "home" didn't mean Val's trailer.

"You'll see."

"Whose home?"

"Mine. It's gonna be a long trip."

Panic trickled in. This was Felix, his trusted friend and confidant for years. He talked like a crazy person—and drove like one. They took the corner near the National Forest much faster than the recommended speed. If Val didn't ask any more, he wouldn't have to hear any more. Maybe Felix was bringing him home the long way. Maybe this was a joke. He opened his mouth to ask if it was, but when a bump made his jaw snap shut with a clack, he left it closed.

Whatever. He would hunker down, and he'd make it through. He'd survived jail with his humor intact, he could survive this.

Unless...

The dam holding back his panic burst. What were the

chances he would be in the same cell with an alien?

None. The chances were none. But it had happened anyway, because they'd planned it.

His seatbelt wouldn't come undone. The button depressed under his mashing fingers, but didn't give.

The door handle worked the same way, even when he unlocked the lock.

And Felix was smiling.

Val elbowed the window, unsure how that would help even if he got it open. At such speeds he'd be ground burger if he made it out of the car. The contact made his funny bone hum, sending vibrations up and down his arm. He cradled it, panting and sweating.

"You can't get out," Felix said. "And I am sorry. I liked you. You're an interesting guy."

"What are you?" Val asked, pretty sure he knew exactly where this was headed.

Felix turned to look at him.

"Watch the road!"

"We're fine," Felix said, keeping control of the speeding Crown Vic even though he faced Val. "I know these roads like the back of my hand."

Val had to break the eye contact. *Too weird, too intense.* He tried the seatbelt and the door handle again, even though the ground outside was a purple-brown blur in the building dawn.

"You're very special to us."

"Why?" Val was drenched in ice-cold terror…*special… why?* He was sure he wouldn't like the answer.

"You and your sister have some pretty impressive genes."

"Sister? I don't have a sister."

"Bullshit."

"I checked. There's no record of my mother having a second child. No one can even prove she was pregnant. I checked all the hospitals within a hundred and fifty miles of here."

Felix's grin widened, stretching the edges of his face and reminding Val of a snake detaching its jaw to swallow its prey whole.

"You would have had to look a lot farther away, buddy boy. You know how you've never known who your father is?"

He said nothing, would not rise to the bait.

"It's me, you fool. It's my DNA that knocked up your drunkard mother to make a pair of freak babies like you and your sister."

Val's heart stopped. It felt like it took a second to get it started again, for him to breathe. It was nice the hum was gone, but the sound of his pulse pounding at his temples was worse.

He tried to speak but only a whimper squeaked out. He tried again. "Really?"

Felix exploded with laughter, spittle catching the rising sun and splattering the steering wheel.

"No. Not really."

Val felt punched and abused and torn apart. He wanted very much to leave this car, wanted to wake up. Kate. Kate would have to notice he wasn't back, after a while.

And what would she do?

"Things didn't really go so well with your sister. Something went wrong. The enzymes didn't bond entirely right. I think—and I'm no scientist, mind you—it has to do with a lack of gravity and the artificial atmosphere."

Val's head spun. *Wake up, wake up, wake up*. This could not be real life. Felix was his friend. Why would he take his mother's side?

His mother was dead.

He couldn't get out of the car, but he could get Felix. He stared at the steering wheel, really saw it; examined the faux leather grain. And he pushed it.

At this speed it should have sent the car careening in

another direction, but Felix fought it easily.

If anything, Val's demonstration seemed to please him. "I knew you could do it. When did it start?" Felix asked.

"Last night."

It seemed to surprise Felix and he turned to look at Val again, still keeping the car on the road without even a wobble. "Last night?"

"Yeah."

"You're, like, the latest of the late bloomers in history." And Felix laughed again. "I always wondered, hoped, you could do it all along. That you weren't telling anyone." He paused, and turned back to the road. "And that was all you had? That little tug?"

It was like his worst fears of living in his mother's science fiction movie were being intermingled with some weird male performance high-school metaphor thing.

The car snapped to the left, down a dirt road camouflaged with the desert. The back end barely fishtailed.

"When did this start?" Val asked, knowing he set himself up for more mocking, but needing to know.

"When did it start?" Felix echoed. "Val-ey boy, this is your life. You were born with it."

The whir of tires on dirt road was the only sound.

"It's in your blood."

Contaminated.

Something wiped the smirk of Felix's face. Val looked behind and saw something in the car's dust, something tan and running.

Felix said something under his breath that sounded like a cross between a curse and a sneeze.

Ahead of them were chain-link fences, loops of concertina wire along the top. Val's chest constricted. It looked like a prison.

A monster behind and incarceration ahead. Was this even possible?

As the Crown Vic hurdled towards the wall, Val cast another look behind him. The creature was gaining ground. He silently spurred it on.

Ahead of them, the gates ground open, sliding on a track. The passenger side mirror folded in as they passed, and the opening snapped shut behind them. Val watched as the creature skidded to a stop, avoiding contact with the gate.

"Did it hit?" Felix asked.

"Hit what?"

"The fence!"

"No," Val said, very glad it had stopped in time.

"That fence would cook a rhino."

"The Space Puma is alive and well."

Felix let out a braying laugh. Val used to like his laugh. "It's called a Lharomuph. But that's as good a name for it as any, I guess."

Another fence loomed ahead of them, this one a tall cement wall. Another set of gates rolled open, smooth on their tracks. Inside sat a long, low building, single story, that at first reminded Val of his elementary school. Schools were welcoming, though. At least they tried to be. This one, the closer they got, reminded him more and more of the edifice where he'd spent those six years.

"You don't remember anything, do you?" Felix asked as he parked the car in a parking lot filled with similar nondescript cars, all sporting government plates.

"What do you mean, anything?"

"Us. Them. Any of your *contact*" Felix framed the word with air quotes "with extraterrestrial beings. Talk about close encounters. Yours is of the seventh kind, buddy boy."

"Why don't you tell me?

"Those gray fuckers took you on their ship."

"Sorry, *buddy,* but you'll have to start at the beginning."

"I know we gave you false memories, but I didn't know they were that good."

Val bit down on the inside of his lip. He didn't want to play anymore, this was stupid. Why was Felix teasing him.

Felix's smile reminded Val of the face a dog makes before it's about to throw up. Felix began to speak.

26

In the state of New Mexico, well-mannered prisoners are allowed to work on the state highways. Val fit this bill, and in September 2005, he and several other men had been assigned to a stretch of highway 380, about halfway between Roswell and Alamogordo. Felix Nasiverra was not a part of this road crew. Val remembered this, all except the part where Felix wasn't present. Were one to have asked Val about it, he would have assured you he and Felix did it together. That they'd sat together on the old converted school bus, painted white with the mesh windows.

Val worked the night shift. In all actuality he sat on the bus with a young Mexican man named Al who'd shot his wife after catching her with another man. Prison records stated Al was released in October of 2005, though if anyone had bothered to check the records, they would have seen he wasn't scheduled for release until 2016. And even though Al and Val, who thought it was hilarious their names rhymed, sat in the very back seat of the bus and wisecracked on their way to work every night, were you to ask Val about his buddy Al, you would have received a blank stare. Val had no memory of the man. He would tell you—or at least he would have told you—it had been Felix himself with whom he'd sat on the bus.

October fifteenth started out like any other night. The eight prisoners went through security and joked around, business as usual, Val got his place in the back, like he liked, and the ride to the site was encompassed by a con man telling racist jokes. Everyone laughed, even the Mexicans. They all had to stand lined up in their leg irons and listen while Assistant Warden Smiley explained the drill, his big German Shepherd, Zeus, at his side. His assistant, a deputy named Smith, stood off to one side.

He discussed how Zeus could—and had—bitten a prisoner's finger clean off while the man was trying to escape. Val stared off up at the sky, happy to be outdoors, somewhere other than the prison cell. The warden's words rolled off him like rain.

The work wasn't very complicated. They couldn't be trusted with backhoes, or sledgehammers, or things like that, so they mostly moved fill from one point to another. During the day a state crew did most of the work, and at night the prisoners came and shuffled dirt and rocks around. Val had a green wheelbarrow, and couldn't walk very fast due to his leg irons, so he sauntered around at a casual pace, whistling old punk rock songs to himself. Being out here and listening to the sounds of night birds made him happy.

But around three, the birds and crickets all fell silent. Val only had a second or so to notice before the sky opened up with light.

For the night work—especially since they were dealing with felons who hadn't yet been rehabilitated—they used massive banks of sodium halide lights hooked up to loud industrial generators. Those lights were bright.

The light that swallowed the site whole was even more radiant.

Everyone froze, blind. Hands went to shield eyes, and Zeus the dog began to pace and bark—a troubled, high-pitched sound.

Val's feet went out from under him. He started to fall, but he wasn't falling down. He fell up, into a dark circle which appeared in the center of the sky. The prisoners rose slowly, disoriented by the light until they were above it, and a floor appeared under their feet. The men tried to speak to one another, but there was a solid, steady hum that drowned everything out. Zeus looked like he belonged in a silent movie, mouth moving over and over again, no noise.

Everyone move in, closer together.

Val would never remember what happened next, not even under hypnosis. A large red arrow appeared on the blinding white floor, and the men and the dog followed it. Where else was there to go? What else was there to do? They stayed close, in a clump. Between the blinding white of their surroundings and the powerful low tone, touch was the only communication they had. The chains from the men's leg irons jingled noiselessly.

They followed the arrow, and a white door closed behind them. The white space in which they stood was smaller now. The humming became unbearable, one of the older men's noses started to bleed. The orange jumpsuits and the red blood looked strikingly out of place here, even more so when first one drop of blood, then another plopped fat onto the white floor. A rectangle opened in one of the walls. The rectangle was a door, and there was blackness behind it. The men imagined cool, quiet darkness. Zeus kept shaking his head, the way dogs do when they have ear mites. He kept his tail tucked between his legs.

A smallish gray shape filled the door, and each man knew what it was. Some of them, Assistant Warden Smiley especially, believed until the very end this was a test by the U.S. Government.

The gray shape was naked, smooth gray skin stretched across a humanoid body. Where its legs met was smooth and sexless; more gray-on-gray. Its head was large, as were its shiny black eyes. The nostrils were two slits in the center of its head, the mouth a little black smile. It held up a three-fingered hand and its words arrived in each man's mind.

Welcome. Please line up for testing now.

The door closed behind it. The return to the unblemished white walls sucked away at the morale in the room.

No one moved.

Welcome. Please line up for testing now. This time the men lined themselves up.

Not a one of them had the clarity to acknowledge that they'd been abducted by aliens, just like the cover of the *Weekly World News*. Instead, the collective thought, which the Sangaumanian doctor could hear quite well, was an agony over the hum. It started off annoying, but managed to eventually drive out all other thoughts. Just the way the Sangaumans liked it.

The doctor walked up to the first man in line. Evan Ringrich, a physician from the northeast corner of the state who'd had his license suspended for drinking but still continued to practice medicine, who was only four months away from a parole hearing he most likely would walk away from, stood tall under the scrutiny. He was a proud man, and had rehabilitated himself in prison. The little gray doctor pointed to him, and pointed off into the whiteness. A red arrow appeared, and a black rectangle slid open on the wall. A doorway. Ringrich looked at the other men with a questioning gaze.

Go, please. The being's mouth was an unnerving black line.

More than to any of the others, Ringrich looked to Smiley for his assurance. Perhaps because they'd all spent so long looking to Smiley for everything—when to eat, when to shit, when to work—the habit remained ingrained in the men. Smiley gave a little half-shrug. He didn't care what happened to any of these lowlifes, so long as that fuck-forsaken noise in his head stopped.

Ringrich followed the red arrow, and vanished into the black rectangle. This went on for seven of the eight men, pausing for a moment as Zeus dropped in a heap of black and tan fur, blood oozing out his ears. Smiley lunged for the doctor. They could do what they wanted with the men, but fuck with his dog, and that was the end. The doctor sidestepped as pretty as you please, and Smiley went down on his face. In the humming silence Val couldn't decide which bore more watching, Smiley and the doctor, or Zeus and the pool of crimson forming around his triangular head.

Smiley stood up and pulled his gun on the doctor. Its expression never changed, not even as Smiley silently fired his weapon. The doctor held up its hand with those three knobby fingers and froze the bullet. It clattered to the floor without a noise. Smiley let his gun slide out of his fingers and it dropped to the floor, discharging a bullet which began to ricochet. The doctor stopped that one as well, and then stopped Smiley, too. He stood dead still in his khaki officer's uniform, like something out of a wax museum, albeit not a very interesting one. The stain where he'd spilled his coffee earlier stood out in the harsh lighting and Val felt embarrassed for him.

The doctor pointed at the next man, a red arrow appeared, and a door opened. The man went, all the fight gone from him.

Val was last in line. Only Val, the doctor, frozen Smiley and dead Zeus remained. The doctor walked right up to Val and the little black smile expanded. It said something in its native tongue, and the original black door opened. Two more Sangaumans cautiously entered the room. They looked from Zeus to Smiley, then to Val. They crowded around him.

The same as many felt no remorse in slicing open rats in the name of science, neither did the Sangaumans from the planet Ye'Tunatal, feel remorse at the things they did to their prisoners from the Chaves County Correctional Facility. All except for Val. Val they nodded at, took a blood sample from, all the while chattering at him and one another in their own mental language. They measured him, weighed him, removed his cuffs and leg irons as if they were made of tinfoil, looked in his mouth, in his eyes, and in his ears, treating him with respect and gentle, cool, dry hands, and all of a sudden the hum disappeared and the hot white room vanished, and Val was on his hands and knees, bringing up the remainder of his dinner in a ditch on the side of 380. He rocked back onto his haunches and plopped onto his ass, covering his face with his hands and rubbing at his eyes. My god it seemed quiet. The crickets sounded so far away…someone was saying his name. He turned and peered though his fingers like a child, and there was Smith, a wet stain on his pants, Val noted with some amusement, calling to him, looking horrified. Moments later a Chavez County Sheriff cruiser rolled in, followed first by an unmarked army car, and then by a simple navy blue Crown Victoria.

27

Val felt as though he were sinking into the Crown Vic's plush gray seat.

"That didn't happen," he said, his voice cracking. He cleared his throat and said it again, with meaning this time. "That didn't happen."

Felix, not having been there on the alien craft, could only tell Val the parts he knew. That Val and seven other men had been taken onto the ship, and Val alone had returned. That Val had only been aboard for four minutes.

"They altered your memories. Now I told you it should all come crashing down. You should remember everything, in time."

"White," Val said. Like the dreams. Val felt like he was talking through a mouthful of cotton. His temples throbbed. Jail had seemed much simpler, and he rather wished he was back there. Maybe his incarceration here would be as simple.

White. It gnawed at him. He hadn't *really* gone up into a spaceship…

Except he had. He remembered blood on white. A white so polar pure it made the blood look black.

"Do you have water?"

"There's water inside."

"They're going to lock me up?" he asked, feeling very young. "You're going to lock me up?"

Felix looked at the gray leather steering wheel, with its rubber grips, black and gray. Like a certain smile. "For a while. Until it's safe."

"Safe from what?"

"Just safe. Come on."

Val followed, thinking of running, knowing he'd never make it past the fences and the guards, knowing even if there were no fences and guards he wouldn't run. Because he was a coward? He preferred to think of himself as an opportunist.

Inside he might as well have been in a hospital. A vacant looking pretty blonde with cherry red lipstick took his information and admitted him. Felix got him a glass of water in one of those conical paper cups.

"This snow cone sucks," Val said, drinking it all. "Can I have another one?" He knew he wouldn't get another one because his legs were buckling under him. They had drugged him. Felix caught him, slowed his descent to the floor, and as his cheek lay against cool white linoleum, his vision began to white out and Val's last memory was of being very, very afraid.

EXCERPT #4

from *Trinity* by Judd Grenouille ©1988

The next time I saw Adrienne, she was in quite an uproar. Her doctor said, not bothering to hide his disdain, that allowing her to see me was quite unusual, and it was only because she had had no other visitors that he acquiesced to her request to see me. She was not in a rehab this time, but a psychiatric ward.

I was searched before I went in, for she was on suicide watch, and they didn't want me smuggling in anything that she could use to hurt herself. She'd tried to end her life, but failed.

She looked dangerous when I saw her, but more self-possessed, like a Gorgon from mythology. She wore a shapeless white shift.

"There are triangles everywhere," she said, her voice so soft I could barely hear it. We met in a dark room because the light, she said, hurt her eyes. The single bulb from a lamp cast long shadows across her face, like when children tell stories by a campfire. "The Irish have their shamrocks. The Arabs have trifecta as a fertility symbol. The Father, the Son and the Holy Ghost. But the real trinity is us and them. Humanity, the Sangaumans, and the Tylwyth Teg."

I didn't speak, waiting for her to go on. What could I say? The glittering in her eyes that the doctors took for madness, I took for her unwavering certainty.

"One of them is in Cal's school. I can tell by the way Cal described him on the phone. You know what they are?"

Again I said nothing, content to let her talk.

"They're nothing. They're worms. Little parasites, who take over bodies. They can't have a world of their own until they make someone who can give it to them. And I gave it to them." She started to cry.

I stroked her wrist, feeling the texture of her scabs.

"They had nothing until a race with ships was unfortunate enough to land on their swamp planet. Then they gained hands, and that species' knowledge of ship building. They destroyed their home world, and then moved to another, then another."

She paused, turning away from me, facing into the darkness.

"Until I gave them what they needed to build a new race for themselves."

"A new race? How do you mean?"

'The Sangaumans can move things with their minds. Stop time, control the weather, all sorts of stuff like that. They can float me up to their ship, the Tylwyth Teg have to come down a ramp and carry me up. The Tylwyth Teg can't use the Sangaumans as hosts, so they've been looking for a species that can breed with them. They keep their Sangauman donors inert, frozen. They milk them like cows, and have been trying to find someone who can carry their babies to term."

She started to cry and I offered her a tissue. She took

it. While she talked, she'd scratched open one of her scabs.

"They said because I was on so much drugs I'd altered my chromosomes, and that's why they got two babies out of me."

'Why didn't they take Cal the way they took your daughter?"

"She didn't work out."

"What do they need these children to do?"

"Act as hosts. They can use the Sangaumans control over matter to build their new bodies and transfer their consciousness."

"And then what?" I asked. "I've never spoken with someone who knew this much…"

"The Sangaumans told me. They wanted me to know why it was important they not get to Cal."

"You said Cal was being watched."

"One of the girls in his class. I can tell by the way he described her. They're using her as a host to watch him."

I did some research on this girl, we'll call her Amelia. I could find no conclusive evidence, one way or another, that she was inhabited by the Tylwyth Teg. I am inclined to believe Adrienne because Amelia's parents moved to a new town a year and a half later, and the girl fell into a stream and drowned. A case of the Tylwyth Teg covering their tracks, or coincidence? I honestly don't know. I discovered there are two strains of Tylwyth Teg inhabiting humans on earth, there are Alphas and Betas. The Betas are disposable, used for scouting missions, etc. They have less defined social skills, and are often confused by unfamiliar objects. They only have their host's knowledge to pull from, and cannot form inferences based on new information. The Alphas are able to blend almost seamlessly with the hosts consciousness. They have personalities, and can leave a host once they inhabit it. The host will usually die at that point (it is my theory that the Alpha left the little girl when she was no longer useful, and they discarded the body—just a useless husk at this point—in a stream.)

"If they grow their own bodies, they'll be unstoppable. They'll take over resources even faster than they do as parasites."

Based on Adrienne's description, which she received from the Sangaumans, in their natural form, the Tylwyth Teg are about two inches long, and look like mottled, brown slugs. The Alphas and the Betas are indistinguishable. They reside in the sinus cavity of their hosts—the human hosts, anyway. They seem to be able to inhabit most any creature, except the Sangaumans. They then release two long nerves which tap into the host's brain.

"I have to get out of here so I can help my son," she said.

"It makes sense to them," I said. "Imagine, a vast intelligence, but with no way to implement it. No thumbs, no hands, not even paws. How long did they simply languish in the mud of their home world?"

"You're taking their side?" Adrienne asked, her voice like daggers.

"We can't know anything about them. We can't know what their motives are."

"I know. I've seen them. You don't know what you're saying. I want you out of here! And leave my son alone. All of you! Nurse! Nurse!"

An orderly came in and asked me to leave. Adrienne spit at me as I left. That was the last time we spoke. I shouldn't have said those things to her, as she was in a delicate mental state. But the way our three species, humanity, the Tylwyth Teg and the Sangaumans interact has made me really do some thinking on the nature of the universe. It is not a simple thing that we can ever hope to learn. All I know, as I look up at the sky, is that there are more vast wonders out there than there are twinkling stars.

28

The sun wasn't right. The thought vaulted Kate from a peaceful half-asleep state into full wakefulness. She lay on the couch, in the living room, still dressed in the clothes from the night before. The patches of sun on the floor were right under the windows, as though the sun was directly overhead. Noon. Really?

She rubbed at her eyes and tried to run a hand through her hair, but it got caught up in the tangles, and she decided to leave it alone. Where was Val? Where was Felix? Again, she looked at her phone, not at the time but seeing if she'd missed a call. She hadn't. So they went out for breakfast. Without asking her to come? Not likely.

It gnawed at her. Val was irresponsible and immature, yes, but not so much so he would vanish after a night like last night.

Although maybe he would. He'd gone through so much, between his mother and the boy, why shouldn't he be allowed to flake out?

Because there was a dead body baking in her car for the second day, that's why. The car was done. The next step would be to think of a way to trash it, to burn it up, before anyone could see the decomposed mess resting on the carpet in the trunk. And to do it in a way that wasn't suspicious.

Kate turned on the coffee maker, going through soothing morning tasks. It was hard to think about things like hiding bodies when you were doing something as mundane as making coffee.

She added sugar from a bag that looked like it had been there for a very long time. On a cursory inspection there didn't seem to be any critters lurking in it, so she dumped it in the coffee. There was no milk or cream. The fridge was empty except for three bottles of ketchup, a Tupperware container she would never open, and a few beers she'd brought over. When they found a place in Santa Fe—they could start looking today—they'd have a real home. With food in the fridge, they'd get jobs, and it would be blissfully mundane. No arrests, no monsters, no bodies.

She looked at her phone again while she waited for the coffee to cool. 12:20. Should she call the sheriff's office? To make sure he left…or he was still there? She could take the truck and see for herself. The Daytona in the yard kept drawing her attention. She expected to see flies swarming around the trunk, or blood pooling in the gravel under its tail pipe. But it looked like her car; her normal, shitty car.

Pulling the outdated phone book from its place under the house phone, she used her cell phone to call the sheriff's office. A prerecorded message picked up. If this was an emergency, she should hang up and call 911. If this was in reference to a parking violation or a traffic fine, she should press two. She mashed the zero button until a disgruntled woman answered.

"Otero County Sheriff's Daphne Maze how can I direct your call." The words spilled out in a monotone void of punctuation.

"Is Spence around?"

"He's on nights this week."

Of course, considering he was the one who came to the house in the wee hours.

"Can you tell me if Valentine Slade is still there?"

"This Kate?"

"Yeah." It was stupid to come to this town and hope for even a prayer of anonymity.

Daphne rattled some papers around on her end of the line. Kate wanted to ask her if she'd forgotten what she was doing, forgotten what she was looking for, but she figured as long as she could hear something on the other end of the line, Daphne probably knew what she was doing.

"He's not here."

Fuck.

"Do you know when he left?"

"You know it ain't my job to keep a tail on your boyfriend for you. Says here he left around five with one-a them boys from Immigration."

"He left with them?"

"Uh huh."

"Did they say where they went?"

"Not to me."

"Thanks for your time."

Daphne hung up without saying goodbye.

Kate stared at the phone in her hand for a moment then flipped it shut. She should have asked for a number to contact Immigration. She didn't even know where to begin looking that one up. If only there was a computer here, she could Google it for sure.

How would Felix have found him if he was out with Immigration? Val didn't have a cell phone; there was no way to get in touch with him. Did that mean he wasn't with Felix after all?

She would call Spence at home. Back to the phonebook, digging through the "S" section. That had to be him. God, did he still live in that same old place he grew up in? The desire to leave Lott welled up in her throat like acid reflux. It crossed her mind to go. Leave a note explaining where Val could find her. She couldn't take her car, though. If only there was a swamp somewhere where she could ditch the whole thing. It worked for that creepy guy in *Psycho*. He was only in California. That wasn't too far...

The phone rang in her ear after she punched in Spence's number."Hullo?"

Was that his mother?

"Hi," she said, stuttering a bit. "Is Spence around?"

"He's asleep."

"May I leave him a message?"

"Yup, hold on, I gotta get a pen." Spence's mom sighed as if Kate was really putting her out. "Go 'head."

"My name is Kate Fulton." She gave her phone number, repeating it three times, and making the woman spell it back to her. "Have him call me as soon as he gets up."

The line went dead.

What a charmer.

Now what?

She looked out at the zinc-yellow car in the driveway, then drew the shade so she wouldn't have to look at it any more. She could drive into town; see if they were at Woodstone's Saloon.

It seemed to make more sense to stay here and wait. She peered around the shade out the window. If she kept it drawn, then she couldn't see them (or anyone else) if they came down the driveway. She lifted the shade, and sat down on the couch, scooting over to the far side. She lay her head on her arm, settling in to watch.

When she woke up the phone was ringing, a popular R and B song playing next to her ear.

An unfamiliar number. No, Spence's home number.

She answered it, wondering how long she'd been

asleep.

"Hi, my mom said you called."

It was like a flash back to middle school.

"Yeah, I was wondering if you'd seen Val." Her mouth tasted like the coffee she'd drank. But in a foul, stale way, and she needed to brush her teeth before she made contact with another person, missing boyfriend or not.

"Yeah, he left around five with the guy from USCIS. Vargas, I think he said his name was."

"He didn't come back?"

"Guy said he'd run him home."

"He didn't." Kate struggled to kick the afternoon nap cobwebs. "Was he one of Rich's guys?"

"I hope not. Val seemed a little weird with him. I asked if he was okay, but he said he was just tired."

Kate exhaled into the mouthpiece. "You have any clue where they might have gone?"

"None. It's too soon to do a missing persons. Man, since Val's been back there's a lot of folks we can't quite keep track of."

She didn't laugh.

"Why don't you come into the station? I'm on in an hour, you can meet me there and we'll try and figure something. He seemed off this morning. I didn't really think anything of it, but it got my spidey senses tingling."

"He was supposed to meet his friend from jail. Felix. Felix was supposed to come to the house, but he never showed."

"So he's off with Felix?" Spence asked.

"I hope so. But I can't imagine he would be so excited to see Felix he'd forget to come see me." It sounded so conceited and snotty. Men did douchey stuff all the time. Even Val had.

"You think we should be worried yet?" Spence asked.

Kate waffled. "Yes? I think? It seems so weird. But between his mom and the boy..." And the monster and the bodies. It made her want to cry. She chewed at her lip. "Yeah, I am worried." Val would never leave her with a body in the trunk.

"Okay, come on down to the station when I'm on duty. I wouldn't look to Harvey for much sympathy on this one."

"Thanks, Spence."

They hung up, and she was alone again. She looked at the car. Could she drop the whole thing down the mine-shaft and report it stolen? She'd take a shower then head into town.

29

Val woke himself up screaming. After hearing all about his abduction (surely there must be a better word—encounter?), Val found he remembered his dreams, and the images gave additional credence to Felix's story. Miles of whiteness, broken up only by himself, his brazen orange prison jumpsuit and the petite gray aliens. In his dream they took his red blood with large, strange syringes. In his dreams he couldn't hear anything at all except a monotonous hum.

As his eyes popped open, Val saw white. Not a dream, then. White walls, white ceiling. But also, he noticed, as he took in deep gulps of air through his mouth—he couldn't seem to take in enough air—a bed, and pillows, too many pillows. Where was he? A red plastic cup next to his bed dropped off the table and startled him. Drenched in sweat, a loose fitting white shirt clung to his thin chest. What the fuck was he wearing? The sheets were soaked. He thought maybe his throat was bloody it hurt so bad. His pulse thundered in his ears. Fuck. He liked it better when he didn't remember.

As his heart rate dropped back down to a normal level, Val started to think about where he was. A hotel room. But...not a hotel room, since hotel rooms have windows and the doors aren't simply smooth on the inside. He wore strange white cotton clothes, loose fitting and comfortable. He looked like he belonged in a UFO cult. And what the hell, maybe he did. Val looked for his boots and saw no shoes of any kind. His feet were bare and cold. He didn't see much in the room he could use to harm himself, were he so inclined. Wherever he was, they had him on suicide watch. Great. He lay back on the bed, feeling the cold dampness of his sweat all around him. He didn't know the time, but his stomach gurgled. He hadn't eaten since some chips for lunch the day before. He looked around for a phone.

The walls, ceiling, and carpet of the room were a flat white. He wondered if they intended to make him feel as though he was back on an alien spacecraft. He wondered if that's where he was. Best to not think about it, nothing he could do if he was.

The walls were bare. Canned-smelling air blew in on him from a vent in the ceiling, turning his sweat cold. He pushed himself up off the bed and stood up on shaky legs. He peeked in the bathroom, and used the fallen cup to get himself a glass of cold water which slid down his inflamed throat like an incendiary. He rubbed at his eyes and looked at himself in the mirror. Damn. Not a pretty sight. His eyes were bleary and red and all the white in the room (and several years in prison) made his skin look pale and sallow. The collar of his shirt and the armpits were soaked a darker gray from sweat. Gross. The sweat made his hair look darker, too. He ran his fingers through it and it stayed standing up, and that made him smile a little. He turned away from the mirror. On further inspection of the room, he noticed a shiny white bubble in the corner. A camera.

"Hey," he said to it, his voice weak. He swallowed past the broken-glass feeling and repeated himself, louder. "Hey! I'm fucking hungry in here!" He gave the smooth surface of the door a few pounds with his fists, then dropped into a white chair. No TV, no books, no music. He'd been in the room and awake for all of five minutes and already he was petrified of being bored to death. He didn't expect an answer to his plea to the camera, but he heard a door open and close, then a pause, and then the door to his room opened. A bland faced woman with blonde hair came in, carrying a tray. She wore a white uniform, something like an old nurse uniforms, but somehow more modern, and let the door close behind her. She set his tray on the table. Eggs, sausage, toast and hash browns. And a glass of OJ to boot.

"Where am I?" he croaked.

She looked at him, Hindu-cow stupid, with large blue eyes.

"Where am I?" he asked again, each word dragging like fingernails down his throat.

He didn't even feel she was looking at him, yeah, her eyes were pointed this way, but they seemed dull and glazed and unseeing.

"Can you even hear me?"

She turned then, put her back to him, and as she touched the door, it opened on a smooth mechanical hinge.

"Hey!" He could tackle her. Or hit her. But her eyes… what if her skin felt as empty as her stare had been? What if he grabbed her and it was like holding nothing?

The food smell brought a wash of saliva to his mouth, but he didn't want to seem overanxious. He didn't want this minion to see him flapped, though the sweat on his shirt and his ungainly, spiky hair didn't help.

He let the door close behind her, and listened as a second door opened. Some kind of airlock? It looked as if it was held closed by magnets. Moving towards his food, he wondered if they were going to drug him again like before. He picked up his white plastic fork, and noticed fresh track marks on the inside of his elbows. It looked as though the tests had already begun, though his ass felt fine. That was where they probed you, wasn't it?

It didn't matter if they drugged the food, he was hungry, and letting it sit there, smelling the way breakfast should, wasn't an option. He ate, and afterwards he lay on the bed, drowsy, not due to medications, but boredom.

He used to think New Mexico was too brown. After all this white, though, there were a lot of shades of brown: reddish brown, dark brown, light brown, yellow brown, and more often than not it was matched against a big blue sky. Not green like the east, but he longed for it. He thought about his aunt and his cousins, and how when he'd turned fourteen his mother had called and said she wanted him back. Goodbye, cushy boys preparatory school. Goodbye ocean. Goodbye, sixteen-year-old girlfriend who had taught him everything a young man needs to know about pot, pills and punk. She hadn't been terribly popular with his aunt and uncle, with her black 1986 Plymouth Reliant station wagon. Val drifted in his memories, back eleven years. He started to doze and woke himself up. He didn't want to dream. The cool air blowing over him made it easy not to succumb to sleep. *My kingdom for a television,* Val thought. Or a book. Or even a note pad. He could play tic-tac-toe with himself, or maybe draw his Space Puma.

Val heard the sound of the airlock cycling, and a man stepped in, wearing a fresh black suit.

"Good morning," he said, extending a large, warm, clean hand. Val took it, wondering why he felt the need, in these circumstances, to feign politeness. They shook. The interaction left Val with a strong urge to wipe his hands on his sweaty white cotton pants.

"Where's Felix?"

"Is it too cold in here?" the man asked, the concern on his face looking like a well-executed façade. It set Val on edge.

"It's fine. Where's Felix?"

"Are you sure? We can tap it down a scosh if we need to. Say the word."

Scosh? Who says that? "Felix. Where is he?"

The man looked confused, as though Val said something he didn't compute. "Not here."

"Can I see him?"

"I am afraid not."

"Do you even know who I'm talking about?"

"I am afraid not."

It struck Val. No contractions. Like the guy at the diner. The realization rippled across his skin, and the tasty breakfast lurched in his stomach.

"How about your breakfast? That was good?"

"Yeah," Val said. He felt vulnerable lying on the bed on his back. He swung his legs to the side and sat up, rubbing at his greasy, tousled hair.

"I need you to come with me. We need to run a few tests."

"Don't you mean more?" Val asked, holding out his pale, thin arm and showing off the track marks there.

"We took a bit of blood while you were asleep. We also put you on a saline drip because you were dehydrated. It must have been a terribly traumatic night for you. I trust you are well rested? Aside from the nightmares, that is."

So they'd been watching him sleep. Not surprising, yet still not something he liked to hear.

"You can't keep me here." Val said this for something to say.

The smile got a little bigger. "Come with me, Val. The tests will not take long. We can get you something to read after."

This guy went for the big guns, it seemed. A bribe to

ease Val's boredom wasn't an offer to be refused. His other option was to sit here and stare at the wall.

"Okay," he said, standing. The man looked at the camera, and the door popped open. He gestured for Val to go ahead, and then he went, stepping off the carpet and onto smooth cold floor. The door closed behind them with a solid click before the second door opened. It confirmed his airlock assessment. A guard with a strange-looking rifle slung over his shoulder stood on the other side to greet them and escort the two of them down to a pristine white hall that looked a little too much like Val's dream for comfort. He could feel sweat beading on his forehead, despite the ultra-chill forced air in the building (*ship?*), and resisted the urge to wipe it away. He could smell himself as he walked and wished for a shower.

Val followed his nameless escort, with the armed guard at his back. The hall was empty, smooth walls stretching on for infinity in either direction. He wanted to touch it, just to stabilize himself, but he kept his hands at his sides. Would they walk down here forever?

"We're underground, aren't we?" Val asked, hoping this was the case. His escorts ignored him. The man stopped and waved a pass card, and a door in the wall popped open. He entered the room. Looking behind him, Val only got a moment's chance; he thought he saw another door, white on white, across the hall. Then the door behind him closed, and Val was brought face to face with a man sitting at a large white empty desk. There was one chair facing him. Val's eyes burned from the lack of color. His guy gestured at the one chair. Val sat.

The two men in the room could have been brothers, and they certainly shopped at the same nondescript tailor.

"Call me Jones," the second man said. He and Val repeated the handshake ritual, and this time Val didn't stifle the urge to wipe his hand. If either Jones or the first guy (Jones II?) noticed, they didn't let on. A spoon rested on the white Formica surface of the desk before them, reflecting a whole lot of nothing in its concave silver surface.

If the test had anything to do with vanilla ice cream, Val thought, he might scream. The two men smiled at him with little private smiles. Val smiled back, not letting it touch his eyes. He couldn't tell where the wall ended and the ceiling began. His heart beat faster. He teetered on the edge of an anxiety attack, and closed his eyes.

"Are you all right?" Jones II asked mildly.

"I'm cool," he said, his eyes still closed.

"Shall we postpone the testing?"

"No, let's get it over with."

"Open your eyes."

Val did. There. There was the line where the ceiling started. He wasn't sure if he'd found it, or if he'd merely tricked himself, but it served to center him a bit nonetheless.

"I need you to move the spoon."

"Move the…excuse me?"

"Without using your hands."

"Like with my mouth?"

"Like with your mind."

Val laughed; a huge braying sound in the white room. He could see a little dollop of spit that landed on the table near the spoon, and wiped it away with his hand. Why had he pushed the wheel when Felix was driving? If they didn't know about it, maybe they would let him go.

If he was crazy, he wasn't the only one.

"What do you mean?" Val asked.

"Use your mind," Jones said. "Move the spoon." His even, patient voice would have been at home on a self-help CD.

"What are you talking about? People can't just…move things. With their minds." He thought about the knife moving, all the things he'd seemed to move.

The smiles Val received made him feel about four

years old.

"Try."

"I did," Val said. "Nothing happened." A lie. He'd been thinking about overpowering these two yahoos, then trying his luck with the armed guard outside. Once he had the gun, Val reasoned, he'd be home free.

Jones' voice broke into his thoughts. "You did not. You were thinking about something else. Now relax your body, sit up straight so your spine can align itself properly, and try again."

Heaving a sigh worthy of a teenager, Val sat up straight. *Move, spoon.* "Nothing. I tried."

"Visualize. See it, and you can make it happen."

"I don't know who you think I am," Val said. "But you've got the wrong guy. I can't move spoons with my brain." He'd already told Felix. They must know.

"You know you were taken aboard an alien craft. That alien blood runs in your veins."

Contaminated.

"And they didn't do anything to me. They just looked at me." *Looked at me sort of like you are doing now* Val thought. *In a white room that looked an awful lot like this one.* The hairs at the base of his scalp prickled at the thought. He wasn't underground at all. The thought came as a certainty. He was above ground…very, very high above ground.

"Relax."

"Fuck relaxing."

The unwavering smiles did nothing to soothe him. He stood up.

"I can't."

"Val," Jones said. His eyes looked dry and red. It was the only thing that removed him from utter normalcy. "Did you ever take karate as a boy?"

"No."

"In the martial arts, they say there is no such word as 'can't'."

The contraction sounded, well, *alien,* coming from Jones' lips.

"Well, in the real world, where people don't have magical powers, there is a word called 'can't' and it aptly applies to this situation."

"It is not magical. Please. Take a seat and try again." Val hesitated. "Focus, Val, please."

"Sorry," he mumbled. He stared at his bare feet, pasty, but not white, not against the glaring colorlessness of the floor.

"Remember, this is a test."

"I must be failing."

"You are just nervous."

"Can't imagine why."

Jones laughed, but laughed like you'd imagine a robot laughing, when it detected a joke, and laughter was the appropriate response.

"Give it another try."

Val sat.

Move, spoon.

He wondered how much damage he could do with the spoon. Not enough to escape. Probably enough to annoy and anger them.

"Can I pick it up?" Val asked.

"Be my guest," Jones said.

Val picked up the spoon. He exhaled on the bowl and balanced it on his nose for a moment. It sloped a little too gradually for that trick, and slid off, landing on the floor with a loud clang. Val stooped to pick it up, looking at the two men's shiny, black polished shoes.

He set the spoon back on the desk. Maybe he should do this. He looked at the way the ambient lighting reflected off the bowl of the spoon. Or maybe he should tell them Felix was lying.

"Fuck this." Val stood up again. Jones and Jones II tensed at his sudden movement, like a pair of spooked cats. "Take me back to the cell."

"Val, it is not a cell. That is your room."

"Room? Those have knobs on the insides of the doors. That's a cell."

They frowned at Val, and that frown ignited an angry fire behind Val's sternum. "I'm not playing this game anymore. I don't know what the point of your little test is. Whatever you think I can do, I can't. I'm not your boy. Get me out of here."

"We can do that. You told us you can make things move. We need to see how advanced your technique is."

"No! This is garbage."

Jones II reached out to Val, to calm him. He jerked his arm away and stepped back, stumbling over the chair, which only served to make him angrier. "Don't touch me."

"Easy," Jones II spoke in a soothing tone. Coming from him, it sounded spooky and dishonest.

Looking around, Val realized he couldn't tell the size of the room due to the white walls and floor. Sitting at the table he'd faced away from the door, now, turning back to it, he couldn't make it out.

"Where's the door?" he asked, his voice lilting up at the end in rising panic.

"Relax."

"Where's the *door*?"

"Right behind you. Right where you came in."

Fuck, the room was small. It was like he was on top of the desk. He couldn't even think. The walls were closing in on him, they were already there. Left, right, behind him…nothing but walls. White. Everything white. Jones and Jones II even looked pale in their black suits. The sweat poured from his forehead now, dripping from his nose.

He placed his hands on the wall and faltered, it was farther away than it looked. It surprised him, a moment of nothing, when he trusted he'd meet the wall and met only air. Behind he heard a small clattering, and thought nothing of it because he saw a thin black line of shadow outlining the door. It grounded him, and he turned to face Jones and Jones II. They would let him out, and it would happen now.

They peered at him.

"We will take you back to your room now."

"Damn straight, you will."

"And I will find you some magazines."

The door slid open, and Val stepped into the hall, face to face with the armed guard. The guard's fingers twitched on the rifle (was it made of *plastic?*), but a look from Jones II stayed his hand.

They left Jones I behind, and resumed their walk down the long hall. It took less time to get back to the room than Val remembered. The guard stayed behind at the first door. They entered the space between, waited for the door behind them to close completely, and then the second door opened. Someone made the bed while Val was gone. He hoped they'd given him clean sheets. How did laundry work in space, anyway?

"Are you all right?" Jones II asked. "Do you need a sedative?"

"No. I'm good." Another sedative would mean more tests while he slept. It also meant more dreams. Neither one sounded terribly enticing. "What about TV? Or something to read. Anything."

"Magazines."

"Please."

"Anything else?"

"Clean clothes?"

Jones II nodded.

Val took a deep breath when the door closed behind him. He looked at the camera, and went into the bathroom. He closed the door, and turned on the shower, as hot as it would go. He braced his back on the door and slid down onto his haunches. Reaching up to the sink, he picked up a bar of soap and set it on the clean white linoleum in front of him. The white wrapper was a shade darker than the floor, and Val relished the contrast. The steam from the hot shower collected as a fine mist in the air.

"Move, soap."

When he'd made the spoon move, when he'd slammed his fists into the wall, he hadn't spoken aloud. Nor had he spoken aloud when he took control of Maria's knife.

The soap did not move. He was sure he'd made the spoon fall when he got angry. It couldn't have been a coincidence. And they'd expected him to be able to do it, and they'd let him go as soon as it dropped. When he'd moved the knife, he'd been in a blind panic. Thinking he killed all those people. Thanks, Space Puma. *Move, soap.*

He shoved harder, crinkling his nose with the effort. A warming sensation grew. He pictured the atoms. It had to have something to do with movement on an atomic level...right? It sounded good, anyway. He pictured the atoms, in his mind they were little white balls, and he visualized them moving, all together, and the soap, wrapper included, shifting its location in space. Go, soap, go.

It moved! He moved the soap!

But it felt like he'd moved a damned Volkswagen. His muscles felt all trembly, he felt weak like a kitten and his stomach churned. He'd seen it move, though, and it had made a faint scraping sound on the floor.

Great.

The bar of soap moved a quarter of an inch, if that. It wasn't even a cool party trick to do at the bar, because someone would accuse him of bumping the table with his knee, or something. He picked up the soap with his hand (much easier) and set it on the edge of the sink. He could smell his shirt as he stripped it off, reminiscent of onions, and he dropped it in the corner. He looked at himself in the mirror. Wondered if he could crack it, just by looking at it. It would put him to sleep to do so. His eyes were red and bleary; it looked like he'd burst another blood vessel in one. Reaching up, he rubbed at them for a good long time before tugging down his pants and boxers.

By the time Jones II returned with an issue of *Good Housekeeping* from October of 2004, a pair of khakis and a plain white T-shirt, Val, who lay on the bed in a towel, staring at the ceiling, had a plan.

He thanked Jones II, and took his spoils. He waited for him to leave, then dressed in view of the camera. They wanted a show? Val Slade could deliver a show. He even picked up the magazine, sat at the little table where he ate breakfast, and read about money-saving tips using household items.

It had become a waiting game, and the plan relied on him not being in this room. He found himself dozing off over an advice column about a woman wondering if she could, in good conscience, substitute dessert forks for regular forks at a dinner party. The answer, politely, was no. Val could hold out as long as they could. He was cold as ice. He had a plan. This whole thing was in the bag, baby.

Val's icy demeanor lasted until he finished reading the magazine (for the second time) and he woke up screaming from another white nightmare. He hadn't sweated nearly as much this time, but he'd fallen asleep in the chair with his head on his hands on the table, and he banged his knee on one of the legs when he woke up. He could still feel the screams dying in this throat, could see the little empty black smiles on gray skin. He shivered in the hum of the air conditioner.

The bounds of his ability were tight. He needed to figure something small, but effective. He could close off the aorta, just for a moment. The guard would pass out, and he could run. It nagged at him that he'd have to stick around to reopen the aorta and he would lose valuable time. But he wasn't about to go around killing any more people. No sir. Val Slade? Not going to become a killer. Though…were they people?

There wouldn't be time to stick around to rouse the guard, to rouse Jones II, or whoever was with him. Hell, he didn't even know if he had it in him to do more than one of them. He suspected killing one of them would diminish their hospitality, whoever *they* were.

He wondered what Kate was doing, right now. Since he had no concept of time, she could be doing anything. Was she worried? She must be.

He wondered what Felix was doing. That sonofabitch would pay. Val waited, head on his knees.

30

The little one-story adobe sheriff's office never seemed welcoming to Kate, and today was no different. She parked Val's truck in one of the street-side spaces out front, and threw all her weight into the parking brake. It tended to stick.

She sat for a moment, regarding the building. The sun was low in the sky, casting long shadows. The sheriff's office was front-lit, the tan adobe seeming to glow in the pinkish light. Locking the door behind her out of habit, she squared her shoulders and headed in. It was only Spence. And it wasn't as though she were driving the car with the rotting body inside it.

Daphne sat at the front desk behind bulletproof glass, looking blob-like in her chair; her hair dyed a glaring red never found in nature. Daphne had been pissed when they outlawed smoking in the work place, and her flabby jaws worked at a piece of gum.

"Haven't seen him, Kate," she said, barely looking up from her computer screen.

"Can I see Spence?"

Daphne did not look up, but raised her penciled-on eyebrows, reminding Kate why she'd left this shitty little town in the first place.

"Let me see if he's available." Daphne picked up the phone, started to dial, looked at Kate and said, "Have a seat." Kate sat, glad her taxes no longer went to this woman's salary. She picked up a new issue of *People* and flipped through the pages, not registering any of the glossy images before her. She peered over at Daphne, who had resumed a vacant stare at the computer screen.

There was a click of a lock, and the door opened. Spence popped his head out, and called to her. She resisted the urge to flip Daphne the bird, and followed him.

"Have you heard anything?" she asked.

A fellow in a blue FBI windbreaker hurried past them.

"What's the FBI doing here?" When a small town had three—four, if you counted Val—missing persons in a few days, she guessed the FBI would get involved.

"First National Bank stuff." Spence hurried her into the tiny office he shared with Harvey, who was mercifully not in at the moment. Was that what they wanted her to think? She sat, crossing her arms across her chest, hunching her shoulders forward. The old window air-conditioner blocked most of the natural light and hummed louder than most. Someone had placed a tray below it to catch its drippings.

"I haven't heard anything from him. I did wander into Woodstone's on my way in, and I didn't see him there. Rick Juarez was working the bar, and he said he hadn't seen Val."

"That'll set the gossip mill churning."

"Oh, probably. But my hands are pretty well tied until tomorrow. Because I like you—and because Val seemed so twitchy—I'm making a bit of an exception. All I can do is ask around. Have you tried calling this Felix back? See if he's heard anything?"

"No." She'd thought of it, but it seemed intrusive.

"Why don't you start there? Wouldn't you feel silly if Val was flaking out on you?"

Her face burned, and she knew she was blushing. She pulled out her phone, and kind of turned away from Spence. She faced Harvey's desk, which had a big "terrorist hunting permit" poster behind the desk. The number was third on her list of dialed calls, and she selected it. It rang several times, then a recorded operator said: "The number you dialed is no longer in service. Please hang up and try again."

She swiveled in her chair and looked back at Spence. "It's been disconnected."

"Let me make a call to USCIS. I want to speak to this Vargas guy."

Kate nodded and sat back in her chair.

Spence asked to speak to the guy then made a chorus of "uh-huh"s, and incredulous sounding "really"s. He drummed on his desk with a pen, the tempo picking up.

He returned the phone to its cradle with a click. "I think we have a problem. Officer Vargas wasn't working this morning. In fact, Officer Vargas has been out of the office for the last few weeks going through chemotherapy. For lung cancer."

"So who took Val?" Kate asked.

"An excellent question. I'm going to see if I can flag down Taylor. This'll tickle him much more than the bank bullshit."

"Taylor's the FBI guy?" Kate asked, the saliva draining from her mouth. What if they wanted to come out to the house? What if they wanted to search the car?

"Yeah, this is serious business."

She didn't want serious business. She wanted Spence, Val's old buddy. God, how to get rid of the car? Rich would know, but she couldn't ask him. Would you get red flagged somewhere for Googling "How to dispose of car"?

"Wait here," Spence said, hefted his not-inconsiderable bulk out of his chair and lumbered out of the room.

This was all way too much. She picked up her cell phone and tried Felix's number again. Same results as last time.

Spence came back with the FBI guy in tow. He was clean-cut and handsome, looking like an overgrown boy scout. With a firm handshake he introduced himself as Special Agent Taylor Anderson.

Then he perched on the edge of Harvey's desk, putting Kate in the middle, where she had to scoot her chair back in order to see both men at once. They filled him in on what had happened to Val, and he took a few notes into a smart phone.

"This guy is bold," Anderson said. "Did you guys check his creds?"

"When was the last time we checked yours? Cooper put him through, and I glanced at his badge, which seemed to be legit."

"Cooper will be lucky if he keeps his job. Did you see what this guy was driving? Can you give a description of him?"

"He had a Crown Vic."

"Who doesn't?"

"We use Impalas."

"Some of our guys are getting Chargers. Nice cars. Gives you a bit of an edge in a chase."

Kate wanted to scream at them. Who cares what they're driving! Cars, of course made her think of her own car, which she didn't want to be thinking of here and now.

"Did you get the plate number?" Kate asked.

"It was a government car. Blue plates."

"I wonder if Vargas is all right. We should check up on him." Anderson made another note on his phone.

"Kate, I think you can go home, at this point."

"I can't," she said. *We were supposed to have left by now.*

"There's not a lot we need for you to do."

"I can't leave..." she let her voice trail off.

"You might want to be at home in case he comes in on his own," said Anderson.

"Okay," she said, not relishing the idea of going back there and waiting. "You have my phone number in case you hear anything?"

And with that, they dismissed her. Daphne was gone for the evening and Cooper, the dumb hick shit that had let Val go with some imposter, sat at the desk. He waved at her and she ignored him, moving past without making eye contact. He was lucky she didn't fling herself over the counter and claw his eyes out.

The forty-minute ride out to Val's place gave her too much time to think. Pulling into the driveway, her headlights swept her car, the burned-out barn, and the yellow-green reflection of a pair of glowing eyes near the door. Something tan dashed away, too fast for her to get a good look at it. Could have been a deer. Nevertheless, she pulled up as close as she could get to the trailer. She tried to peer into the night, but the truck's headlights reflected off the siding, killing her night vision. She killed the engine, keeping her hand on the key in case she needed to get away fast. The engine ticked as it cooled, and she turned off the headlights. She peered out at the night. The shapes of the land, the dry brush and the big stones were familiar by day, but tonight they seemed alien, as though they only served to conceal the monster.

She could get a hotel room in town. It would break the bank, but she could manage. She'd be sleeping with the pistol under her pillow tonight. If she slept at all.

The night was barren and quiet, and the squeak of the door's hinges made her cringe. She sprinted, whether she needed to or not, reaching up (since there was no front step) and jamming the key in the lock, willing it to turn.

She stumbled into the quiet trailer and slammed the door behind her. She clicked on the light, listening to herself pant.

Now what?

31

Something stirred Val from sleep. The white of the room accosted him, and he realized as he awoke the lights were always on here. He rubbed at his eyes. It seemed he hadn't screamed himself awake, as his throat felt no worse than yesterday. He rubbed at it, wondering why he was up. Once again his mouth tasted terrible, and his stomach gave a malicious growl. Hungry.

He sat up, the floor cold on his feet. Goosebumps stood up on his chest and arms. From the other side of the airlock there was a muffled "thud." That must have been what woke him, though it didn't seem loud enough. Maybe Jones I and Jones II were roughhousing out there. Val went to the door, pressed his ear against it.

Nothing. Silence.

It should have sent him back to bed, nothing to worry about. But the silence had a weight, a texture to it that didn't sit right with him. Tiny hairs stood up on the back of his neck, and the primal region of his hippocampus—or whatever the fuck gland responds to threats—warned him of something out there.

A tiny, metallic tinkling sound came from the other side of the door, the sound of a delicate instrument clattering to the floor and instantly retrieved. Like bells, almost. It meant there was someone there, someone right there outside his door. He took a step back, and then another. Silence. Adrenaline began to pulse through him, he could taste it, bitter and metallic, drowning out the sleepy old-food taste in his mouth. Something smelled like burning out there. Oh, fuck, if this place was burning...He let it trail off, couldn't finish the thought. When he was in Cambridge with his aunt and uncle their neighbor's place burned down. He was at school, but one of the kids who'd stayed home sick tantalized them all the next day with stories about the elderly woman on the top floor. They couldn't get to her, and she screamed and screamed, too scared to jump out the window. He said it smelled like roast pork, but Val guessed he'd read that somewhere.

The upper left corner of the door flexed.

Just a little motion. So slight he almost couldn't see it. The shadow between white walls and white door grew a little bit bigger, that was the only clue.

He stepped back again, but he was pressed against the table, nowhere else to go. He could barricade himself in the bathroom, but that didn't seem very useful.

Val had no concept of how quickly or how slowly time was moving. He saw the corner move again, away from him. That shouldn't be possible. The table dug into the backs of his thighs, but he didn't know where else to go. He tried to control his breathing, but then the door pulled away from him a bit more.

Someone was peeling the lid back from a can; did that mean he was the treat inside?

He could see through to the airlock now, a sliver of dark. Before he'd had the thought he might be in space, what did this mean if they were pulling the airlock apart? Were all sorts of noxious gasses going to come rushing in, destroying him? He didn't want to die so far from home.

In a massive burst, the door peeled back, about an eighth of the way. The metal gave a demure little groan. The smell of heat was stronger now.

"Come and get me already!" he shouted, but his voice sounded rough against the quiet, and it made his throat hurt.

The door gained momentum. It gave another heave like the one before, and now Val could see shadows moving. There were things in the airlock, moving around.

The suspense pulled at him, it wasn't fun, it wasn't interesting, he was tired of being scared, what the fuck was behind the—

The door pulled back, so over half of the thick metal was peeled back like a can lid.

Two of the aliens, the gray ones, stood there, short, naked, peering at him with luminous almond-shaped eyes. They looked to one another, then to him again. Their little black mouths curled up into smiles.

They say once you see something it's automatically less scary than not seeing it. The sound, the implication is worse, what you can dream up beats what you can see any day.

These things weren't supposed to exist. But here they were. Campy little shits that looked too cheesy for even a Fox exposé or an *X-Files* episode. And he'd been with them, they'd taken him to their ship, they'd tested him. He was a part of them.

The stress made Val's leg muscles shake. Standing was too much for him. A weak gesture, he pushed out at them with his tiny little power. The exertion caused him to fall back, having to catch the tables for support.

The two beings looked at one another, and in simian, loping movements that were somehow dignified, they came over what was left of the door, using the sloped curve as a kind of a ramp.

He couldn't resist them. Even if he picked up the chair and tried to use it as a weapon.

Valentine. Come with us.

They didn't speak. The words were in his head. He blinked at them, from one to the other, and then back again, but they favored him with those secretive little smiles and those deep dark eyes, like pools to nowhere.

The corner of the table jabbed into his kidney, and he very slowly relaxed himself off it, not willing to look away from those beings that shouldn't be. One of them pointed at him with one of its three fingers, it felt too much like the movie E.T. and Val stifled a giggle.

Come with us.

It echoed in his mind, resonating like the hum, an omnipresent thing he couldn't control.

"No," he said, his voice still sounding out of place.

You don't need to speak out loud.

"Can you read my mind?"

Only when you direct something towards us.

He wondered if they were lying or not.

Come with us.

He couldn't tell which of them was speaking at any given time; their resounding mental voices sounded too similar for him to tell them apart.

You can't stay here, their voices chorused, bouncing around the inner places in his skull. Val brought his hands to his temples, a familiar movement since the onset of the hum.

Come with us, we can keep you safe.

"I want to stay here," he said, meaning Earth.

The little smiles flattened out into frowns. *You cannot stay here. This is not your home.* They made an unpronounceable sound, and added a possessive to the end – *men will be back soon. It wouldn't do to have them find us here.*

"Men? Is that the Space Puma?" He felt stupid saying it, but didn't remember the real name Felix gave it. He didn't think it was the same thing. Nor did he think Space Puma had a squadron of men.

You know him as your friend Felix.

"And what do you call him?"

They made the sound again, and Val gave up.

They come now.

Let us take you.

What else was he going to do?

Out of the frying pan, into the fire.

"Okay. Let's go. Take me home. I want to go home." He wondered if they would listen.

They advanced on him. Where were they going? Did they have a car? Felix used cars...these guys were a little less incognito than Felix, though. Strong, knobby, three-fingered hands clamped down on him, and time collapsed in on itself.

It felt like he was being pulled all directions at once, and as soon as the white room went black, he was in the sun. He covered his eyes, aware the aliens weren't touching him anymore. The hum was on him like an anvil, pressing at him, resonating in his head. He gasped, not exactly in pain, but surprise or maybe shock.

He was in his driveway. There was his truck, there was Kate's car—was Maria still in the trunk? He hoped not, but couldn't imagine how or when Kate could have dealt with it on her own.

"How—?"

We master our environment. As you are part of us, you can master yours as well.

He cleared his throat; cast a glance at the house. He didn't want Kate to look out and see.

You hold the trinity within your DNA. The Tylwyth Teg have searched for one like you. You must not go with them.

Val resisted the urge to parrot the alien's words back at them.

We wish to bring you with us, back to Ye'Tunatal, to keep

you safe from them.

"That's a planet?"

They nodded their smooth gray heads.

He would be the alien. The rest of his life in a cage. The rest of his life in a cage.

He must have thought it harder than he intended the second time, because one of them spoke in response. *It won't be like that. Our people will see you are a feeling, thinking being, as we are. We will do our best to make you a useful member of society, as your kind like to be.*

His head spun, and the hum rode it like a tilt-a-whirl.

32

Kate let the shower go cold as she rinsed her hair. It stung her with icy needle droplets but it also felt good, cathartic and punishing all at the same time.

Three days with no word from Val. Three days. Last night she'd even gone to look for Rich, to see if maybe he knew something—either as a cop or a kidnapper. Or a killer. His house had a vacant look to it, and even though she spent ten minutes knocking, on and off, standing in his nice upper class neighborhood, she knew no one was home.

She swung by his station, on route 82, and all the troopers were cool and wary of her. Hadn't seen him. He didn't show up for work today. Spence put out an APB on Val, on top of all of this he'd missed his parole meeting.

Val was fucked.

One more day. Tomorrow at dusk she was going to pack it in. It wasn't as though she'd be hard to find, both Spence and Val had her number. But she couldn't be here anymore.

She reached down to add some hot water to the mix.

The shower curtain exploded around her, wrapping her in a slimy, mildewy bear hug. The curtain caressed her face and she inhaled it, screamed, swung and kicked as a sharp pain shooting into her knee—the kind that made her nauseous and her eyes water—made her stop. She felt her weight slipping in her kidnapper's grasp as he fumbled and nearly dropped her. It allowed her a good feel for his size, and she called out his name. "Let me go, Rich!"

He didn't. Not right away. They turned some corners, her head banged off a doorframe, and she tried to keep stock of where they were. Definitely still inside. Then he picked her up a bit. And dropped her onto the fake hardwood floor. She landed on her hip and elbow. After the clobbering her head had taken, she could taste shampoo, mildew and blood. She spat, clawed at the shower curtain and pulled it off her head.

"Where is she?" Rich asked. His eyes were bloodshot. Was he on something? She didn't think so. This was what Rich looked like when he was bereaved. It happened when their foster father died in a truck accident. He devolved into a zombie. A violent zombie on autopilot. That time Rich tracked down the SUV driver who veered into Jim's truck, it had been Val, she realized, who got him down. He even convinced the yuppie not to press charges. Kate pulled her arms free, keeping herself covered with the shower curtain. It had once been white, but was now a thick brown color. Better that pressed against her skin than let Rich see her.

"Where is your fucking lowlife? It ends. Here. Now."

"I haven't seen him in days."

"Bullshit."

"I thought you had him." Kate eyed her bag, not ten feet away, her clothes in it. Then she saw a sparkle under the bed. Maria's knife. If Rich saw it, she was done. She should've sucked it up, done something with the car on her own. She never would have remembered the knife, though. Val, how could you leave me like this?

With a loose fist, Rich punched her in the temple.

White spots spun in her vision, and her stomach bucked. So this was what they meant by seeing stars.

He sunk his fingers into her wet hair and pulled her up. She lost her grip on the slippery shower curtain and it dropped as he pulled her to her knees. Rich made a sound of revulsion—oh thank god—and shoved her towards the bureau.

"Get dressed, you fucking slut. We're going to find him."

She pulled on jeans and a tank top fast, no time to worry about a bra or panties. He kicked her in the back while she was bent over, right on her "Valentine" tattoo. Fine. She could deal. She could deal with a lot when she had to.

"Where is he?" Rich asked again. "And where's my wife? Where's TJ? He took them all."

In the span of a few days, Rich's world had fallen apart.

Kate grabbed one of Val's button-down shirts just in time as Rich clamped onto her upper arm. He pulled her out of the bedroom and into the living room. The back door hung open, a bright patch of sunlight in the dark hallway.

She scanned the place for anything she could use as a weapon. Her hands were free, as she was lucky he hadn't cuffed her. He stank, and she hated herself for pitying him. Maria was a bitch, but they had a strange sort of mutual love. They meant a lot to one another. What would she be if she lost Val? Like if he was really gone? The thought sucker punched her, but the sight of the frying pan on the dish drain, where she'd left it after cooking herself some eggs for breakfast, gave her hope. She hadn't eaten them, but the cooking gave her something to do. As he shoved her again, towards the door this time—*watch the step down*, she reminded herself—she used her free hand to grab it and swing. Too bad it isn't cast iron, a cheap thing from Wal-Mart. It clanged against his crew cut, denting the pan then clattered to the floor. He let go of her arm and she ran, sprinting for the back door but he was on her, missing the waist of her jeans but snaking a hand around her ankle instead. She fell, but caught herself instead of smashing her face into the floor.

"You want to play, little bitch?"

He yanked her back up, and resumed their trajectory to the front door. "You're going to take me to him."

Rich picked up her car keys from the counter as they passed and thrust them at her. Oh no, not in her car. He would know the smell...oh no. She could use the keys and claw at his face, maybe hit an eye, but he was fast and he was inevitable. He was family and she deserved him.

He got a hold of her hair and kicked open the front door. Together they hop-stepped down into the dirt driveway.

And there was Val, his back to them. What was he wearing?

She opened her mouth to call to him, but another sound caught his attention and he turned and looked back at the house.

33

There was a sharp crack from the direction of the house, and Val turned to see Rich, coming out of his house, holding Kate, using her hair to control her. He whipped back to the aliens, but they were gone. Did they see?

"Val, run!" Kate cried. Her face was red and puffy, she'd been crying, and it looked like she had a bruise on her forehead. That fucker had hit her.

Before Val could charge, Rich reached down into a holster and pulled out a little silver pistol. He pointed it at Kate. Instead of speaking, he smiled. A very final smile.

Val made a stupid, empty, fish-out-of-water sound.

He could manipulate his environment. He could visualize Rich's heart. A fist-sized hunk of throbbing muscle… and the fat veins leading to it…

"You gone stupid, boy?" Rich crowed, leering at him over Kate's head.

Was there blood on her hairline? In her hair?

Val sucked in a great heap of air and squeezed.

Rich's eyes bulged. Now it was his turn to gasp. He struggled to disentangle his hand from his sister's hair, the side of his face twitching, the color leeched from his face. Once free, Kate bolted, and Rich clasped at his chest.

When Kate came to him he didn't move, he had to keep squeezing, keep the pressure on. How long could the brain go without blood? The blood carried the oxygen, so the real question was how long could he go without air?

The strength left him in a non-tangible *whoosh,* and he crumpled.

Through the hum and a high-pitched whine in his ears he could hear Kate's questions: *Where were you? How did you get here? What's wrong? Are you all right?* But he couldn't find words for them.

"Is he dead?" Val managed to ask, squeaking the words out, feeling like he'd run for ten miles.

"I don't know."

"See if he's dead."

"What if he is?"

"Good."

Val turned away from the look she gave him. She went to the body, touched the throat. His skin had to still be warm.

"He was my brother," she said.

Good. He was dead.

"He…wasn't a nice guy." Val could have said a mouthful on this topic, but Kate's sad eyes convinced him to leave it at that.

The hum backed off in his head to background levels, and Val wiped at his nose. His hand came away with a delicate ribbon of snotty blood. Moving things with his brain didn't feel like it was particularly good for him. A parlor trick for special occasions only.

"You used to like him," Kate said.

Why was she getting into this?

"We need to get out of here," Val said, struggling to stand.

Kate came back to him, offering her shoulder. Her

eyes were wet with tears. Blood matted her hair near one temple, a bruise marked the other. He'd hit her. Did she have a concussion? Her pupils looked okay. Val resisted the urge to spit on his corpse.

"Go where?"

"Anywhere. We need to run."

"There's no evidence you killed him," Kate said. "Did you do that?"

"I'm not worried about the cops."

"Then who?"

Val shook his head. "This is going to sound crazy. Like my mother." He paused, scanning the yard. "I have been abducted by aliens."

"Is that why you can..." she let her voice trail off and she pointed at her temple.

"Yeah. They'll be back for me. Felix is one of them."

"Are you all right?" she asked, she reached out and touched his forehead. "And what are you wearing?"

Val looked down at the khaki pants and white cotton shirt, a v-necked thing like an orderly would wear. Both were streaked with dirt.

"These are the kind of clothes aliens give you, I guess. When you and Rich came out, did you see anyone with me?"

"Anyone with you? No. You were standing there, looking out into the desert. How did you get here?"

"They brought me. We...never mind. Let's get some shit packed and hit the road."

"What about my car?"

"Shit." Val rubbed at his face. "I can't go to the mine. I really can't handle the thought of going there."

"What else are we going to do? I've been trying to figure how to burn the car up. What if we drop the whole car down the shaft?"

Val chewed at his lip until he tasted blood. Tasted his own contaminated blood. He sucked at it while he thought. "We don't know what's down there. It could blow some shit up. And if we did, then everyone would know it was us."

He glanced up and saw Kate was staring at him, her eyes locked with his.

"We can frame Rich."

"What?"

"Get his prints on the shovel, put him in the car. I can report it stolen, and they can find it."

"They'll know the body's been in there longer than the car's been stolen. They can do tests. With the maggots and shit. I don't even want to look in there to see what shape she's in."

"Can we burn it with both of them inside? A murder-suicide thing?"

They needed to decide, and they needed to decide now. The options flitted around his mind like crazed bats, if only one would settle long enough so he could get a good look at it. He rubbed at his eyes. Fuck all of this. When he was in jail, everything was simple. He didn't have to worry about a thing. Well, about some things. But he was nice, and people generally only tried to kick his ass (or worse) once, so it was mostly only the new guys he had to worry about.

Fucking Felix.

"Let's take it out to the woods, as deep in as we can get, douse it in gas, a lot on her in the back, so all the stained carpet burns up."

"Then I'll report it stolen. Spence knows we're out of here. I told him three days ago you and I were blowing town as soon as we could."

"It's been that long? Are you kidding?" They had him for three days. Amazing how time stretched and flexed. It didn't feel like that long, but it also felt like it had been much longer. Three days.

"I was worried sick about you. I was starting to think

about taking your truck and heading up to Santa Fe without you. Then Rich showed up."

"Are you all right?"

She started out nodding, but it turned into shaking her head no, then she started to cry, loud braying sobs. Val touched her hair, feeling the blood in it. He wanted to ask "what did he do to you," but he was afraid to. He didn't want to hear it, not again. They'd been through this before.

But this time, the bastard was dead.

Val glanced back and saw the body was gone.

No. That was horror movie stuff.

"Fuck."

Kate looked at him, hearing his tone.

"What?"

"He's not dead."

Her muscles went tight, all of them, all at once. She whipped her head around, flogging him with hair. He reached up and stroked it down, out of his face and mouth. Where was he?

"Rich?" Val called, leaving her. "Let's get this done." He turned back to Kate. "Get in the truck, let me handle this."

She looked at him, her face blank. Then she narrowed her eyes. "Fuck you. You wait in the truck. He's *my* brother."

"Or that."

The driveway was baked in afternoon sunlight, but it still left too many places to hide. Val shielded his eyes from the sun and scanned the brown earth. Where was the fucking Space Puma when he needed it? He could really use those claws right about now.

Rich could be anywhere. He could have circled around behind them by now. Who knows how long he'd been gone? Val turned three hundred and sixty degrees, looking for anything out of place. Crickets chirped, insects droned past his face, and a flock of swifts called from the trees. If only nature would shut up to let him listen. He remembered the quiet in his white cell and took it back.

Rich was a big guy, and wounded or at least confused. He wouldn't be terribly stealthy.

Kate took a few steps away from him. "Rich!" she called. He'd have to be an idiot to respond to something like that. She moved away, and Val gritted his teeth, he didn't want to see her grabbed, or shot, or anything. Maybe they should get in the truck and drive. He wondered if they could get across the border into Mexico, live out the rest of their days on the beach. Probably not. The cops were the least of his worries.

He moved up next to Kate. "Is the gun still in Mom's room?" he asked, his words a breath on her neck. She nodded. "I'm going to go get it." She nodded again, but he didn't move. Was he supposed to leave her here, exposed, and out in the open? "Come with me."

And they moved towards the trailer together. The shovel he'd used on Maria was with her in the trunk. It wasn't worth it to get it. He didn't want to see or smell that. He dismissed the idea of getting a kitchen knife, Rich had always been better than he was with knives. The gun was where it was at, either that or something big and blunt. He had an aluminum baseball bat in the cab of the truck.

Val went for it, leaving Kate's side, opening the door as quietly as he could, trying to quiet the grinding sound the truck's door made. It felt good and sturdy in his hands, and he couldn't wait to place it upside Rich's skull. Wanting it almost made him salivate, the fucker had made every day of his life miserable for the past six years.

He turned back to Kate, who stood in the middle of the driveway. She gestured towards the trailer with her head. He wasn't sure if it meant "let's go get the gun" or "Rich is over there." He went to her.

"I saw the curtain move."

"The AC is on."

"Or he's in there."

"Let's go find out." Val took the lead, hefting the bat in his hands. He threw open the door. It looked very dark in the trailer, in contrast with the sun. The curtains were all drawn to keep the heat out, and there were no lights on inside. Advantage there would go to Rich.

It was even darker than he feared. The familiar shapes of the sofa, the counter where the boy had died were hulking shadows, and the air smelled of bleach and blood. They were getting out of here as soon as this little problem was taken care of. Val hefted the bat in his hands, his grip firm but not too tight. Kate turned the light on. Everything looked normal, except the counter was too clean. As a pair they moved down the hall. The back door hung open, kicked in, the latch busted.

"That's how he got in," she whispered.

They checked the bathroom. Val's room, with the shower curtain on the floor? He looked at Kate, questioning. She looked away. He squeezed the aluminum, his knuckles going white. No more playing. This was it.

Only his mother's room was left. Was her ghost inside? That inspired a whole new level of paranoia, would her ghost help Rich, since he'd been such a shitty son?

Kate opened the door and clicked on the light while he brandished the bat. Nothing. Kate went for the gun while Val covered the door.

Rich wouldn't have gone away, would he?

As soon as Kate got her security blanket, they went back outside. The sunlight flared in their eyes, reflected from the truck's windshield.

Rich hadn't gone away.

Kate pointed the gun at him and fired, cringing as she did so. There was a miserable click, and Val knew it was because he'd left the stupid thing loaded all those years.

He'd kind of been amazed it fired the first time.

Val didn't get a chance to swing his bat before Rich was upon him. His head bounced off the trailer wall and he saw bright flashes of white. Rich punched at him, and he twisted his head to the side, but still caught a grazing from hairy knuckles. Val sucked in Rich's old-sweat smell, like rancid onions, with every inhale, could feel his heat through his thin shirt. Val was outweighed by at least a hundred pounds. But that was why he went to the gym. He shoved up and Rich shifted, enough so Val and his pounding skull could move away. He swung the bat and it glanced off Rich's shoulder. They looked at one another.

Rich's skin had a bluish tint to it, from lack of oxygen, maybe? Deep black circles lurked under his eyes. Sweat glossed his unshaven, flabby face, and his breath caught in his throat with a rattle every time he breathed. Should be easy to finish him off. If only he could get the weight off of him. Rich hit him in the side, and Val couldn't tell if that sound had been the snapping of his rib or not. He kneed at Rich, not able to get enough momentum to make his jabs hurt. After one more failed attempt, the aluminum bat rolled out of his fingers. Well, shit.

The next time Rich hit him, he was pretty sure his rib did break. Breathing was getting to be a challenge, and now it was accompanied by a sharp pain in his side.

Rich had time to get him once more, a left hook into his kidney, when all of his almost three hundred pounds dropped onto Val, dead weight. Rich's face landed on Val's, like they were kissing, and some of the salty mucus, sweat or spit dripped into Val's mouth. The weight on him twitched once before Val could shrug him off, almost in time to get Kate's baseball bat to the face.

He turned away, and it smashed the wood by his head.

Val spat and spat, trying to clear his mouth of salty slime. It made him think of prison. He pawed at his tongue with dirty hands, preferring the earthy grit to Rich's salty warmth. He pushed himself up, standing, using the trailer wall, siding warm in the sun, as a support.

Kate stood over Rich like a tyrant, dropping the bat on him over and over again, reducing the flabby face to a pulp. Tears streamed down her face and her shoulders shook. Now wasn't the time to comfort her. Val winced as she gave Rich's junk a soccer style kick, she threw the bloody bat down into the dirt so she could focus on kicking him, drilling her sneakers into him with all she had. Val watched; a hand on his ribcage. Almost a decade of hate for Rich bubbled inside him, and watching the bastard's poor sister get her revenge was the sweetest prize for Val.

They still needed to get out of here. He suspected if his little gray friends didn't come along, Felix would, and he still wasn't sure what that monster's agenda was.

He was about to clear his throat, not sure how to go about pulling Kate away from her grisly task when she stopped. She stood, looking down at her brother. Then she turned her watery, red-rimmed eyes to Val. Her hair was a tangle and she had blood on her shoes. She reached out her arms to him, and though he thought she might be turning on him now, he took her in his arms where she dissolved into sobs.

"I loved him," she cried. "And I hate myself for it. But he was there when they left, and he took care of me and made sure I went to school."

Now, Val thought, was not the time to point out the flip side of this coin. And although Rich's face was a compressed ruin, Val did feel the need to check for a pulse this time. Who knew how much of the blows had been deflected by all of Rich's padding?

"I shouldn't even care. I should be glad. He was your friend too, though."

She pulled back to look at Val, her eyes panicked and lost. She looked like a wild-child rescued from the desert.

"The Rich I knew and liked hasn't been around for a long time," Val said.

"You were best friends," she said, her voice soft.

Val nodded. "I still remember the good stuff," he told her, which wasn't entirely true because a lot of "the good stuff" involved an awful lot of booze and drugs. "Let's go inside. Get some cool water on your face."

"Will he be okay out here?" she asked.

Val smiled, unable to help himself. "He's with Maria now. They're together again."

And that seemed to help bring her out of it. Her eyes lost the far off look, and she wiped at them with her hand, leaving a dirt streak across her face. She took a deep unsteady breath, looked at Rich again, then back to Val. "What are we going to do?"

"Put him in the trunk, and we ditch the car. Then we head out of town."

"Okay," she said. "Let's do it."

34

The bags were packed. They were on their way out. A quick stop at the mine to send the Daytona into oblivion, and they were on their way to Santa Fe. Kate's heart plummeted when she saw the brown and white sheriff's department car. *No no no!* It was all her fault because she'd gotten Spence involved.

The Daytona stank, a rotten, sweet smell. Rich and Maria, together again. The realization her brother was dead hadn't quite sunk in yet. Her shoulders ached from wielding the bat, but a kind of disconnect snapped on in her brain. She wanted to leave Lott. When they were somewhere else, somewhere quiet and they were alone, then she could start to process. She'd drawn the line when it came to putting Rich in the trunk. She'd walked around to the other side of the burned-out shed and left Val to it. He'd offered to drive this car, give her the truck, but she said no. She was responsible for it, now.

Maybe Spence wouldn't notice.

The thought was stupid. It was a quiet dirt road, her car was obnoxious yellow, and Val's truck was pretty distinct. She couldn't think of any reason they'd be out here, other than to look for Val. She started to wish they wouldn't see her, but then her wish snowballed...how far back to wish? Wish she'd never called Spence, wish Val wasn't babbling about superpowers? Wish they hadn't had to kill Maria? Wish Rich had never been born? Wish she had never been born?

The car rolled past them and Kate kept her eyes straight ahead, focusing on the road ahead of her, not looking at the cop car. In her peripheral vision she could see Spence and his passenger turning to look at her.

Val followed her in the truck, their bags packed and resting in the bed. Val never intended to go back to the trailer, not ever. This was it, goodbye Lott. Val didn't slow down either, she noticed, stealing a glance in the rear-view mirror. Spence rolled his window down and waved a brown arm at them. When they didn't stop, he did a three- point-turn and put his lights on.

The turn off to the mine was ahead...but what good would it do? They wouldn't be hard to follow, and neither the Daytona nor the pickup could outrun the police cruiser. She pulled over. Maybe they wouldn't smell the rotting stink from her trunk.

She was going to jail.

Val pulled over behind her, and Kate jumped out of the Daytona and went to him, getting to the truck at the same time as Spence and Anderson, the FBI guy.

"Val, where the hell have you been?" Spence asked.

Val rolled down his window. What was he going to say?

"Are you all right? Who was that guy? The real Vargas is out on sick leave."

For a moment Val wore a desperate, hunted look on his face. He looked from Spence to Anderson and back again. Then he took a deep breath and smiled. "Vargas. From Immigration. That was actually my prison buddy

Felix. Playing a joke. Funny guy, Felix."

"That's part of what we wanted to talk to you about," said Anderson. "We ran a background check on Felix Nasiverra and I couldn't come up with anyone with that name in the New Mexico Penn. Does match a man who's been missing for six years."

"Odd," said Val.

Kate watched around his eyes. He kept them flat and expressionless.

"I'm going to ask you to come down to the station with us for questioning," said Anderson. He sniffed the air, but seemed to ignore whatever he smelled. The sun beat down, heating the inside of the trunk. It was like her very own slow cooker.

"Ask or tell?" asked Val.

"Tell. Please get in the car, Mr. Slade."

"I'm sorry Kate," said Spence. "The deeper we dug, the fishier it got. I figured we could kill some time by looking up this Felix guy, and we couldn't come up with anything." Spence looked to Val. "You missed your parole meeting, buddy."

Val glanced at Kate.

"Step out of the truck, man."

What was he going to do?

Val opened the door, keeping his hands plainly visible. Kate tried to keep her body between the Daytona and the cops. Sweat poured off her forehead, more than the day's temperatures warranted.

"What's going to happen?" she asked.

Her question was never answered. From a distance they heard the sound of a revved up engine, then a flash of red bulleted towards them.

The car was aimed straight at them.

Val shoved Spence out of the way and Anderson jumped free as a new red Monte Carlo slammed into the Otero County Sheriff's Office sedan.

The driver stepped out. Tall and thin, with a neat shock of dark hair, his features were almost feminine. Felix.

Val's eyes went wide and he looked around. He landed his gaze on the Daytona and bolted. He pushed past Kate, not even giving her a chance to head for the passenger seat. He slammed the driver's seat back, started the car, and with a loud backfire that sounded like a gunshot, he took off towards the mine, screeching around the corner and down the turn-off.

Felix looked from Anderson, to Spence, to Kate, and jumped back in the Monte Carlo. He spun dirt as he backed up, and took off after Val.

"That was Vargas," Spence said.

"We need to take the truck."

"I'll drive," said Kate.

They piled into the cab of Val's old pickup. *The Misfits* blasted from the radio, and Spence turned it off. "Same old Val," he said.

Kate slammed the truck into gear and followed after Val and Felix. The gate was pushed aside, zinc-yellow paint smeared across it. The truck was better suited for the rutted dirt road than either of the other two cars, and she pushed it towards them.

35

His head feeling like it was about to explode, Val pulled the emergency brake out in front of the mine. The Daytona slammed to a halt, carrying with it the sickening odor of death.

Now what? Why had he come here?

They said he could control his environment, surely that meant he could deal with this fucking hum, this pressure. He spent the moment before Felix was on him with his eyes closed, he could make a wall, construct a barrier, to keep it at bay.

It worked. The pressure on his sinuses relaxed, his ears, his brain, his eyes, all of them seemed to deflate. Just in time for Felix to pull the door open.

"You left without saying goodbye."

Val punched him in the nose, his knuckles howling in pain, and used Felix's distraction to get himself out of the car.

Now what?

Kate was fucked if the cops found the bodies in the car; he was fucked since Felix pretty much had him. They could have a nice long car chase with the shitty Daytona and the smashed up Monte Carlo, but what was the point? Felix would win. Val was one man; Felix had an army behind him.

Something tan, moving among the rocks caught Val's eye. He wasn't just one man. But even if the monster killed Felix, they'd send someone else, on and on until Val threw up his hands and sacrificed himself.

Felix, a hand at his nose, followed Val's gaze.

"I wondered when that thing would show up." He fired his funny little pistol at it, striking a rock, which glowed red for a moment after the blast. The creature tucked itself behind a rock, waiting.

"Your girlie and the cops will be here any minute. Come with me. We'll take your shitty car, take the bodies, she'll be in the clear, and you'll be gone. No one will look for corpses up there." Felix cast an eye to the sky.

Bodies in space. What the fuck.

But how did he know? Val rubbed at his temple…not the hum now, but the enormity of it all.

"You can save my entire race."

Val shook his head. "I—" he started. What was there to say?

The animal moved behind Felix, and this time Val didn't look. If it bought him some time…then what? He still had the cops and the FBI to deal with.

"Yeah, I'll go with you." He could get Felix's guard down; give the monster an easy in. He moved towards the Daytona. "Let's go."

Felix narrowed his eyes, turned around, but there was no sign of the creature.

It came from behind a rock, Felix squeezed off a laser blast but it went wide, off into the sky. It landed on him, all claws. It pinned Felix to the ground, but instead of julienning him, it looked to Val, as if for approval.

Val looked down at Felix, took a step in closer.

"You win. Just do it," Felix said, coughing under the weight of the animal.

"Aren't you stoic." Val thought back to the good times, all the fun they'd had. Could he order this man's death?

"If I let you go, will you leave me alone?" Val asked.

"Never."

Val looked up to see his own truck bouncing along the rutted road. The cavalry was here. Except if they saved him, they were then going to arrest him. The ground started to shake, and he almost lost his balance. Felix used the opportunity to shove off the animal. He leveled his pistol at the truck but the creature was on him again, slicing this time. It managed a cut down Felix's torso, but not deep enough. Felix fired point blank into its side and it dropped; a smoldering hole in its fur.

Val cried out, and stumbled across the shaking ground to it. The truck stopped, its inhabitants stepped out onto the quaking desert, but Kate, Anderson and Spence weren't looking at Felix, they were looking behind him, into the gaping mouth of the mine. Felix pulled out a strange phone and dialed a code into it, then tossed it back into his pocket.

The dark mine lit up, all at once, an explosion of white light. From that light, a ship emerged, a flat silver, shaped like a disc. *I wonder if we can communicate with music?* Normally Val would've had to bite the inside of his cheek to keep from laughing.

Not now.

"Come with me, now." Felix's voice was a command.

"Are you crazy?"

Felix turned, leveled the gun.

How many shots does that thing have? Val wondered.

Felix aimed at Kate.

And he fired.

No. No. No. Impossible. Val's knees couldn't support his weight, but he couldn't drop, he had to go to her. He crossed the rocky barrens to where Spence laid her down on the ground. His eyes said it all.

Val looked around. They told him he could manipulate his environment. He sucked in a deep breath. Val turned; saw the stinking yellow cur of a car. It reeked of death in the literal sense, but also years of bad memories. Now that he was a superhero, he could melt that fucking thing into a cadmium-yellow puddle. He sent his energy to it. The air smelled of barbecued flesh and gas, hot metal and burning foam. Flames engulfed the car. It looked the best it had since it rolled off the Detroit assembly line. He could feel the heat from where he stood, yards away. The center of the car burned hot—white-hot—and he gave it a push that sent the flames blue. How hot does a crematorium get? How hot does a sun get?

Then everything froze…the tendrils of flame, Spence doing CPR on Kate even though it was useless and she would never breathe again, Felix holding his shitty little pistol.

One of them stood behind him in the deafening quiet, eyes big and black, skin pale and ash colored. The earth no longer rumbled, and Spence, Anderson and Felix looked like statues in a wax museum.

Val turned to face them.

Come with us.

His mind was a tornado, swirling and exploding. He got Kate killed. His one, his only, his love was dead, and he'd done it.

Only we can keep you safe from them.

"Keep me safe? Like you did here? With that?" He pointed at the animal's corpse. If he'd told it to kill Felix when it had the chance, it would still be alive. And so would Kate. Each thought jabbed into him like an icy needle. He wasn't worth loving. Like Rich always said: loving him was the single worst decision Kate ever made. And now it killed her.

A weak little pathetic sound squeaked out of his lips. His mother, his girl...even the monster from space who was supposed to protect him. All dead.

We can help her. In exchange for you.

"Help her? How?"

Your biological systems are not so advanced.

Val's mind thundered. If they could do it, could he? He wasn't going to leave her. He wouldn't. How? He looked to Kate. Pictured her healthy, breathing. Pictured the blood off her shirt, the hole in her chest sealed.

You grow strong. The being sounded like he approved. *But they are stronger. Kill this one,* it gestured with a three-fingered hand to Felix, *and many more will come. They will hunt you always.*

"So what do I do?" Val asked. Kate lay under Spence's fists, looking like a woman taking a nap. The color was back in her cheeks. Val knew that when time resumed, her chest would rise and fall again.

Come with us. They will leave Kate alone. It is critically important that they do.

Why? Val thought; it seemed like an odd thing to say, but now wasn't the time.

"No," he said. "I stay with her."

You must come with us. The being was more insistent now.

Panic burned in Val's chest. I can control the environment. Each time it got a little easier. He looked at the beings, imagined its head. Exploding.

We helped you!

"I just want to be left alone!"

They started to scream in his mind as he increased the pressure. The black eyes went wide, just a little bit, the first semblance of emotion Val had seen from one of their kind. The shiny dome-like head exploded then, splattering the ground and Val with gray matter the same color as their skin. Time resumed. Sound whooshed in like air into a vacuum. Kate crawled away from Spence, wondering what he was doing.

"You were shot!"

Val sent the Sangauman ship pitching into the earth. It went up in a rumbling explosion, the shock wave dropping all of them. Anderson started to move towards him, and Val shoved him back with a blast of air.

Felix.

It all came so much easier now, like a gate in his head had popped open. Val felt strong like a god as he broke the bones in Felix's forearm. Felix gaped at him, and Val snapped the bones of his other arm.

"You fucked with me one too many times. Buddy."

Felix dropped as Val shattered his knee.

Val pictured Felix's heart, red throbbing muscle, and with a furrow of his brow, he crushed it. Felix dropped. This time Val looked for a pulse and found nothing. A kick to the ribs and he was satisfied.

The sight of Felix made him stop, and suddenly shame washed over him. He didn't want to be a killer. He wanted to turn over a new leaf. Be an upstanding citizen. There was a monster in him, though. He was no better than the Space Puma, worse even because it looked like a monster. He'd left Kate behind with Felix and he'd run. He rubbed at his temples. If only he could cry now…but that part of him felt numb and dead. He didn't want to turn around. He didn't want to see Kate dead, didn't want to face her.

"Val, stop!" It was her. Asking him to stop. All around him was destruction and burning. The Daytona, the ship. Fallen beings. None of them human, at least.

He turned to her, standing near Spence. Where was Anderson?

"Please!" Her face was wet with tears. Her hair a mess. What had he done? What was he doing?

"I can't stop." He'd run. He'd implode Spence's heart, Anderson's heart, take Kate and run. They could come at him forever, let them. He was infinite. He could destroy them. Look at how easy it was with Felix.

"Come on," Spence took a step towards him.

"Don't move."

"We can help you, man."

Val raised his hand.

"Don't move. Kate, get away from him."

She looked at Val. She looked scared. Scared of him. Why the fuck would she be scared of him?

Spence moved again, and Val pictured his heart. He started to squeeze, when from behind him, Anderson stepped up and handcuffed him in one slick, fluid motion. Val let Spence be, wheezing and clutching his chest.

The cuffs were a piece of cake to melt. His hands were free in no time, a jangly bracelet on each wrist, and he went after Anderson this time. Then Spence was on him—he couldn't do both at once. Spence pulled his nightstick, and for Val, everything went black.

36

Anderson stood talking to the new agent. They looked through two-way glass at the man, bound in a straitjacket. He stared at the white wall, once-piercing ice blue eyes dull and staring. His mouth hung open, slack.

"Tele-what?" the new agent said. The badge at his lapel identified him as Agent Johnson.

"Telekinesis. He can move things with his mind. Gotta keep him drugged to the teeth. It broke his mind, though. Poor sonofabitch babbles about aliens, non-stop. They got his mother, he says, and now they're after him."

"What'd you charge him with?" Johnson asked.

"Can't try him. He's crazy. Look at the guy. But he killed several people, including a state trooper and his wife. Killed another guy in front of me, using the mind thing. The man is a threat. Guys like him are why we ought to have kept the death penalty around."

Johnson went to the window.

"I'll take the case from here."

"With what the psychiatrists have him on, it's unlikely he'll ever really wake up. If he comes back, he can kill all of us, even from that jacket. They're putting a bed in at Juniper Hill for him, and they'll keep him on this dose forever. Would be kinder to put a bullet in him."

"Did you know him?" Johnson asked.

"Met him once. Near the end. Guy seemed terrified."

"I would be."

"His girlfriend, Kate Fulton—"

Johnson checked the file. "Sister of deceased trooper Rich Fulton?"

"Yeah. Reads like a soap opera. She loves him. So he must not have been a terrible guy. She visits him, holds his hand, talks to him. Stuck by him when he was in the penn, with him now. I'd watch her."

Johnson nodded, looking at the black and white photo of her, smiling at the camera. He looked at the next photo of one Valentine Slade. He looked a lot different in the candid black and white, eating an ice cream and grinning. Johnson bet that grin had knocked the ladies dead. The next page was Slade's mug shot. Even there he smirked at the camera, cocky and ready to take on the world.

Johnson looked up at the man in the straitjacket. No sign of that smile now. He closed the folder and shook Anderson's hand.

"So there are no aliens, right?" he asked.

Anderson gave a condescending chuckle. "Nope. No aliens. Some really weird shit, but no aliens."

Johnson smiled at him, and left the psychiatric facility for his car, a black Monte Carlo.

He started the engine and waited for a moment.

Sure, Val killed the body. But he didn't kill the Alpha inside. And now Val was out of reach, locked up again. No subtle way to get him out of the facility. And no promise the meds they kept him on hadn't destroyed his mind.

But it didn't matter.

Johnson opened the folder on the passenger seat and looked at Kate's photo. Someone had a baby bump. The

DNA he needed would be as strong in the child as it had been in the father.

He'd start slow. Be a friend. A sympathetic shoulder for her to cry on in her time of loss. Then they'd be more than that. She'd have the baby, and it would be his.

Johnson eased the Monte Carlo out of the parking spot, and headed it for Lott.

He had a meeting with Miss Fulton to attend to.

ABOUT THE AUTHOR

Kristin Dearborn has never been abducted by aliens (that she knows of). She has an MFA in Writing Popular Fiction from Seton Hill University, loves motorcycles, rock climbing and cheesy horror flicks (particularly creature features). She lives, and has always lived, in New England: fertile ground for horror writers.

CPSIA information can be obtained at www.ICGtesting.com
Printed in the USA
LVOW011852201212

312640LV00028B/1136/P